Capsule

A Search for Identity in Modern Japan

Capsule

A Search for Identity in Modern Japan

by

John K. Press

Social Books
New York, New York

"Capsules"

From : "john press" <pressjohn@hotmail.com>
To : pressjohn@hotmail.com
Subject : Re: capsule
Date : Sat, 23 Aug 1925 12:57:22 +0000

Thollem,

Thanks for the encouragement.

Right now I am high off my ass in Tokyo! I have decided to dedicate this night and high to trying to write the great G-d's-eye-view of an "American-in Japan" book. Right now I am writing you from a compartment in a 24-hour internet place. It is great. It has everything I could ever want. Good light, cheap food, and free drinks. It's like owning a 7-11. Slushies, coffee, tea, the works! It's JohnnyP heaven. Conceivably, there would never be a reason for me to leave this place.

I'm going to call the work "capsule." You'll see why later. Just sending you my love across the distant cyber divide.

Your pal, - JP - the goat.

NEW NUMBER: 646-522-4691
www.pressjohn.com

- Capsule One: Strangers -

This really happened. I say this while remembering that walls between fiction and fact are never as clear as we'd like them to be. In fact, more than most people, Adam (who is my co-star in this book) was fictional. He lived a life that he designed himself.

We were both facing big decisions when we met. Mine was whether or not to stick with my fiancé. His was whether or not to stick with the life he'd built for himself in Japan. Big decisions really require you to ask fundamental questions about yourself. Decisions that will define you for years are best made after scrupulously exploring who you are.

This book contains our wide - ranging scrutiny of identities. The final tally will hopefully reveal who we are and what we must do.

When you travel, everything is fiction. You can tell a stranger you work as a gardener or a gold broker. Your story is as convincing as you make it. Traveling is always as much about uncharted identity exploration as it is about uncharted terrain. Distance from home makes a free-zone possible, where you can try on different masks.

In reality one does have a life history. But that too is a montage. Which parts do you emphasize when introducing yourself? How deeply do you go into your secrets? Every time a traveler speaks, she or he is subtly conscious of the fact that they might not be believed.

Traveling also facilitates the most perfect honesty possible. Telling strangers of your deviancy and regrets is often easier than telling intimates (or those who might know your intimates).

That is why, Thollem, I can let you read this book and trust your feedback. It would be disastrous if my fiancé found out about the contents of this book - Drugs and worse! Similarly, Adam will only get an edited version in order to not hurt his feelings. [Note to self: Erase the previous line after finishing the Adam version].

Both Adam and I were painfully aware that deciding what type of life to have, and person to be, is fatal. Your tombstone refers to what you did do, not to what you didn't do. Very often life is strikingly either/or. The path not taken, isn't.

Japan is an amazing backdrop. Being in Japan allowed me to learn about being an American. It is a known irony that you cannot understand your culture until you leave it. One's own ways are "what people do." One's understandings of one's own culture seem to be common sense. From the outside, however, American idiosyncrasies become stark. To be in a country so alien, is to encounter parables concerning culture (and self) on nearly every street.

When people ask me where I'm from, for example, I usually avoid the word "America." The name "America" rightfully belongs to the whole western hemisphere, both North and South America. Those of us from the United States are rude and ignorant to usurp it. In Japan no one understands when you say, "The States." Despite the politically correct discomfort, you quickly learn to understand that here (more than at home), you are from "America."

Leftist geo-political hesitations about unfairly usurping names (like my using "America") have a generosity that is foreign here. The virtue of cultures as equals is a given in American minds. Fairness for all people is what we assume

----

all cultures want. The Japanese assume, rather, racial nationalist competitiveness. American notions of universalism don't translate. They aren't common sense here.

Gems of realization emanate when difference gets noticed.

Rappongi is the area in Tokyo where most of my story happened. Rappongi is well known as the section of Tokyo where foreigners party. The name Rappongi means "six," "oblong shaped objects," "wood." But translations cannot always be done with a dictionary. Like lives, words without context have no meaning. Without understanding the culture, there is no way for me to appreciate the physical and emotional resonance to "six," "oblong shaped objects," "wood."

The buildings of Rappongi sparkle and crowds upon crowds pack these streets. It sports an international bazaar. French, Nigerian, Israeli, Americans, Chinese. We are all united by the fact that we are strangers in a strange land. Debauchery and sleaze are the common currency on the surface of Rappongi. Marketing and anonymity enlarge the exploding crowd assembled for the illicit. But a need to understand each other and find community as foreigners really explains the congregation. Rappongi is very popular.

Only a minimal amount of talking is required for commerce. A lot more conversation permeates Rappongi than material needs dictate. Talking provides imagined connections. For the conversation to be comforting, people minimize the exploration of differences. Connection is also reinforced by the fact that people mainly speak with those who share their heritage. Being foreign is existentially terrifying.

Adam and I felt urgency in exploring the walls of misunderstanding and the ways in which they encircle all of us. Finding the bedrocks of our identities didn't only have

---

abstract relevance to our lives. This urgency was, again, born out of our both having important decisions to make.

On the night on which I met Adam, I was on a long and arduous search to find a bar where I might interact with some of Rappongi's international scene. When I met him I had already had a lonely drink at one promising bar (where I spoke with absolutely no one) and was heading to another.

My Lonely Planet guidebook said there was a bar nearby, called Bar None, where one could meet foreigners without being overwhelmed by techno music.

Having a guidebook named Lonely Planet is ingenious. The name keeps people dissatisfied and searching. Anyhow, I needed a goal. Being lost, I could ask strangers if they knew where the bar I sought was located. This opening provided a slight hope of companionship.

As I turned right to go up a hill, I had the marvelous fortune of encountering my future friend, Adam. Adam said he had no idea where Bar None was, but wanted to know what I sought there. What could be discovered?

The description appealed to him. He could go for a place where he could hear himself think. And he was gratified to find someone of his age out and about in this Tokyo party district. Most travelers tended to be younger.

Adam is half a foot taller than I and looks like a school marm. Thin as a rail, his round wire-rimmed spectacles make his shaven face look intelligent and upper - crusty. He would not be out of place on a yacht.

Though we are both in our late thirties, my years wear more obviously on me. Usually adorned with a moustache and goatee, my bulk is Russian peasant with early teen years spent working out. He's Where's Waldo. I am aging ultimate cage fighter.

How oddly our descriptions clash with our characters (at least in my mind). He looks suave and refined and I look like a football player. Yet, despite his image, Adam prefers sex to books. Meanwhile I received the nomination for the, "academic most likely to be confused with a truck driver" award. My too big belted blue jeans and generic white, collared, short sleeve shirt, with feint vertical stripes of blue and yellow, tagged me as just another dude.

Even our knowledge bases are backwards. I've spent years in academia, love the study of language, and yet am nearly monolingual. Adam can speak five languages fluently. He has the background to have all kinds of academic insights, but he's never sought them.

Originally I suspected that Adam was gay. This suspicion came partly from his tall thin frame, worn light blue polo shirt, and glasses. Then there were his mannerisms. He had a comfort in his own skin that was very feminine.

I realize now that I was falling into the trap of confusing the femininity/masculinity scale with the gay/straight scale. But as far as first impressions go, his body type, cleanliness, and high-pitched raspy voice seemed convincing.

It didn't take ten minutes to know that this man would be an interesting person to spend time with. He had been in Japan for seven years and was rather excited. He had just landed two really good jobs.

Tomorrow he was to sign a contract to work in a university. It was a teaching job that would get him maximum pay for minimum hours. Both that he had gotten this position, and that he valued it for the freedom it would provide, impressed me.

Adam shone as he told me that he was also going to go from being hourly to salaried in his weekend gig as a minister in wedding ceremonies. A priest! My gay suspicion grew.

"The ceremonies are only twenty minutes, and then I can go. I do this about eight times a weekend and get paid a tremendous amount. It's too easy," He beamed.

"Are you ordained?" I asked, suspecting that he was.

"Oh, no! I found a Web site that said that anybody should be able to be ordained. I just printed a certificate from their web site and no one has ever questioned the legitimacy of my credentials! It's amazing. But I really put a lot of love and good intentions into every ceremony. I don't take it lightly."

"Are you supposed to stay after the ceremony, to meet the bride or groom, though?" I asked, journalistically, but actually interested.

"No."

"It sounds like in India where you'll see groups of wandering transvestites. They survive by attending weddings. It's considered good luck to have a transvestite at your wedding." I wondered if my India reference would impress him.

"Exactly. Here, it's considered up-scale to have a White guy take part in the ceremony. I just say some memorized words in Japanese. After that I'm not expected to hang out at all." He surreptitiously trumped my attempt to impress. His not even mentioning my having been to India, as being special, impressed me.

"Wow! That is great. I used to live with a gay priest. He did gay wedding ceremonies. And since not a lot of people do those weddings, he got a lot of business." My statement served the double purpose of conveying that I had worthwhile conversation to share and implying that I was gay. If flirting was what it took to get a friend, I wasn't entirely above the idea.

But when he asked what I was doing in Asia, I had to burst the bubble on the gay ambiguity. I told him I was visiting my fiancée in Korea.

He, like everybody else, was amazed that I could have a relationship at such a long distance. And, happily, his voice conveyed no hint of diminished enthusiasm now that my sexual orientation was apparent.

"I just got married," Adam volunteered.

"Congratulations." I said with an enthusiasm that was partially about my realization that he wasn't gay.

"Well, it was just for visa purposes. I was going to have to leave the country and a girl friend of mine helped me out. Now I can stay regardless of whether we continue to live together or not. And in four years I'll have permanent status. I'll be able to do everything but vote and never have to worry about my visa again."

"Wow. That is great. You'll be like a citizen."

"I'm not Japanese though." His face conveyed disappointment with an upside down smile that cringed at the edges.

"But legally, for all practical purposes you'd be married." I confirmed.

"Yeah, you're right, In terms of legal working and paperwork status . . ."

"That's great." My tentative enthusiasm reflected his dimmed tone.

"It's great and it's scary. These positions are too perfect . . . this situation, citizenship and easy money. It feels like it may trap me. It may have already trapped me. I don't know if this is where I want to end up or invest more years."

Without hesitation, I commiserated, "I can totally relate to the question of whether or not you should continue to be wed to a cushy job. I teach history, psychology, and philosophy in a high school in L.A. It is a great job, but I'm in my seventh year and I think that life should repeat as little as possible."

"Teaching high school is a great job?" Adam shrieked a bit incredulously.

"Totally! Our kids are great. We're the fifth best high school in L.A. That's why it is so hard to leave. I don't know that I'll ever find another school this good that lets me teach what I want."

"Traps." Adam summarized.

"Gilded." I punctuated.

And with those two words we had found a connection. It was a friendship bonded by a similarity of linguistic styles. We had similar backgrounds. We understood each other. Adam agreed to search for Bar None with me. If it wasn't loud he said he would come in and have a drink with me.

When Adam described himself as being American he didn't mention the fact that he hadn't been there since he was seventeen. Using early memories and location to describe oneself -- when one is older and hasn't been home in so long -- seems illogical at first. But travelers know the depth to which their country of origin defines them.

Reiterating our earliest times makes us a known commodity (to ourselves as well as others). At any rate, it was too early in our relationship for Adam to delve into his convoluted history with me. I still got the standard "American" answer.

When I am asked where I am from, specifically, I must say, "Los Angeles." This never seems to sit well with me. Am I really, once more, of that city that I had left for so long? Perhaps being in Los Angeles for years, and it being the city my family is in, gives me the mental luxury of being able to question my loyalty to that place – I am not a real stranger.

Adam needed the connection more than I. He asserted American affiliation without question. There is a certain intimacy with which early memories, that ground us, are held.

While we talked, we walked, and asked for directions. In Rappongi, when someone gives you directions they are based on the fact that behind every certainty is a hunch backed by some vague beer-drowned memory. Fantastically, random people -- with their more often right than wrong guesses about where they think your destination is -- can eventually get you to your destination.

Bar None was perfectly to our liking. No one was there. At first we thought a comedy show was about to start, but it turned out that it had just finished. The only entertainment left were two comedians getting their publicity stills taken on stage.

"The photo they are taking," Adam informed me, "comes from a common comedy formula here in Japan. There is one straight guy and one slap sticker." (All being metaphor, I'm not sure which I am in this tale.)

Adam's comment made me feel like I had just received a gift. Though not very important, you can only get that kind of insight from a local person. Learning the nuances of cultures and mindscapes constitutes the very delicacy for which I travel. Learning culture is why I cross oceans.

Speaking of straight and comedic men, when we got drinks Adam wanted water and I had a beer. They were 500 yen each. Japan is expensive. Four-dollar water! Adam paid for both without comment. I said I'd get the next round. I will never be even with him.

Without my asking, he reassured me that although he didn't drink he didn't mind at all if I did. He was in Alcoholics Anonymous, but just for alcohol and smoking. He still smoked pot occasionally.

Adam lived the life of a nomad. That resonated with me. Californians in my generation connect with the romantic nomad tradition. We were raised in the post-sixties dream of endless choices. We anticipated the post-modern, in that there were no limits of class or culture or obligation that applied. This lack of limits was made extra romantic by the fact that, one so free was so excruciatingly alone. In our nomad ways we forsook the normal affirming, comfortable social identities. That's what we told ourselves.

Morally stringent, the true nomad traveled with nearly no possessions to embody the possible utopia where St. Frances Assisi style poverty would save the world. Yet, "utopia" literally means "no place." Nomad's not having a commitment or tie to something larger than one's day-to-day existence means you cannot accumulate.

You don't reap what you sow, you reap what you sow and tend. Cultivation of structures (be they religion, culture, country, history or relationships) pays dividends. And, I knew that someone had to cultivate society for us to have our "freedoms." Jack Kerouac, the iconic head of the Beat Poet Movement, found jobs, cars, and money for drinks waiting wherever he went. His freedom depended on America's economy.

He who would give up his liberty for security deserves neither. Golden cages are still cages. Damn the scaffolding that supports us, Californians dream of endless varieties of freedoms never lost. We sparkle.

I have known many people who live a faith-based life. They care not for tomorrow and have many great todays. They are comforted by Jesus saying that the lord will take care of us - each and all. Less theologically, they believe that the "universe will provide" for them. And, as often as not, greater things happen in their lives than they could have consciously planned. For example, fate (accepting such a concept for now) led me to Adam.

You yourself, Thollem, are a great example of this. You probably don't have two cents to rub together. But you are living your dreams. You're really brave.

My friend, Friar Moose, would be another example. He taught me the difference between a friar and a monk. Friars are homeless. Monks take shelter in monasteries, like a pope faithlessly cowering in the "Pope-mobile." California dreams are born of the deeper Friar-like spiritual faith.

Again, after having worked for seven years, doing nine months a year of full-time teaching, I was at a pivotal moment. At thirty-eight, youthful dreams of cutting loose called me. They would call me one last time or never again. I trembled at the destruction of the rocky crash that might greet me were I to cut loose. And a sense of duty to country, history, culture, and community also impelled me to stay. Yet teaching the same courses year after year is like having a book with just one repeating chapter. Working a repetitive job is the ultimate existential death for Californians of my bent. Old habits die hard.

Would Adam push me towards destruction? Perhaps, by bad example, he would scare me back into the cage. At any rate, the musings of one who has unequivocally chosen freedom are always more interesting than one who has accepted (not chosen) the straight and narrow. I was on board for this adventure!

Capsule Two: Intelligence

Adam and I sat at two of the many empty Bar None bar stools surrounding many small tables that were scattered (in order to make as many islands as possible) around the vast wood floor.

We did what most men who don't know each other do: we spoke of our work. Work is a safe source of connection and identity. In courtship one first talks of one's glories, not one's issues. In our case, we both had creative extracurricular projects to disclose. I think we impressed each other. I know we enjoyed talking with each other.

Adam was working on something I was not to appreciate the genius of until later, until I actually heard it. That was probably because he discussed it in terms of business and not in terms of art.

"I have a fully produced langauge CD that kids can learn English with," Adam said with an intense squinting that made him look slightly unstable. "It has songs and dialogues, and I'm working on the work book. It alternates. First a song, then a dialogue, then a song ... Each dialogue and song combination covers particular areas of language.

"The theory is that singing is speaking. It's all making sound. The Japanese really have trouble with this. They learn the words and grammar and then don't take that final step and speak."

"It's the same in Korea." I added. "I taught there for nine months."

"Really? Neat. When?"

"Seven years ago. And I remember how hard it was to get them to speak. Because of constant testing, for them, answers were either wrong or right. And the students were afraid of making mistakes."

"Exactly the same thing happens here." He affirmed, "With my songs they will hopefully enjoy the singing and characters and will disassociate the whole class with schoolwork.

"All the characters in the language CD are kids going to a high school.

"Textbooks have that school feeling to them. Plus they are never looked at once they are finished. This CD is something they will use it at home long after I'm gone; its good music. My CD and book can get the Japanese to speak.

"Actually the entire thing should teach itself without me. That's the goal." Adam concluded.

"Wouldn't it kind of put you out of business -- not needing a teacher?"

"Well that hasn't happened yet!" Adam laughed, "In the past I've played the songs and worked hard for the students. But this year at university, I'm going to make the students almost exclusively use my CD and workbook.

"I've been told I can be really lazy with the kids, but I'm going to be really strict. These tapes aren't just for fun. The students will have to work the system. There will be practice sheets and they will have to memorize passages for each class."

"So is this totally made?" I poked my enthusiastic friend.

"The CD is recorded and packaged. But I'm still working on the workbook. That is what I have to do as we're working through the CD this semester. I really want this workbook to be spectacular with amazing art. It will take some time to compile."

"Is it just you on guitar?" Why do I have the sadistic tendency to destroy and belittle other's accomplishments? I hope he didn't pick up on my nasty undercurrent.

"No. I have a whole band. There is a female vocalist, a bassist a cellist and a drummer. There are actors. I hired them and rented the studio time and made this product. I'm really proud of it."

"Wow. What a lot of effort. I'd love to hear it." I said somewhat relieved that my spiteful condescension hadn't sabotaged our newly born friendship.

"Sure! Except for the workbook, the product is done. It's in several bookstores, but it isn't selling. Not yet. The stores aren't pushing it. I'm sure it would do better if only they would market it for me. I went to one store and it was on the bottom shelf and almost hidden. But if I *can* get it selling, it could be really popular, because you don't need to be enrolled in a school or arrange for a teacher to use it."

"It's the old catch-twenty two -- it has to be popular to sell a lot, but you have to sell a lot before it'll be popular." I offered. "It sounds like, if you don't need an institution to use it, a lot of people could potentially buy it independently. And if it worked, it could spread by word of mouth." People like people who concur with them and I was concurring.

"That's the idea. I've put the product out there, and the Japanese need it. They are a rich country and study a lot, but they *cannot speak English.*" Adam emphasized the last three words. "Unless they find a different way than what they've been doing, they'll never learn English as a country."

"Your CD could foster international understanding. If it is self-teaching, it could be a real Rosetta Stone." Adam's face seemed to indicate that he knew about the ancient translating stone that serves as the key to deciphering Egyptian text by placing it next to Greek. His looking over his glasses seemed more to indicate incredulity over the coming concept.

"The world is supposedly moving towards English. And to the extent that people want to be linked, your CD could make it so that we could all understand each other. Who knows, if it fostered enough global communication, your language program could help stop the Japanese from bombing us again!" I smiled.

"Well, that's a little lofty. Anyhow, their culture is their culture and talking at each other wouldn't stop them from attacking us again. That's my thought." Adam honestly assessed the situation and astonishingly implied that the Japanese may well attack us again. Wow!

I confessed my nationalistic bias, "Yeah, when I taught in Korea I always felt like I was aiding the enemy because Korea is our economic competitor and I was helping their kids get better instead of helping ours." Eesh. I hoped I hadn't just degraded his profession. Adam looked down reflectively for a moment, heightening my anxiety.

Dejectedly, Adam mumbled, "I've never thought of that, thanks for being honest about how you see it."

"I try to push things into lofty geo-political categories." I said defensively. "That's just my tendency." Without some larger purpose the language CD is just another language CD. Why bother? I completed this thought internally.

"But whether it unites the world or just teaches English, it's impressive." I continued the thread aloud. "It's conceptual. I like it."

"My real goal," Adam continued unabated, "is just to get my product out there and then be able to live off of it. If people were teaching themselves and these things were selling themselves I could be free and financially independent."

"Right now it's not selling at all?" My motives for asking this were tawdry.

"It's selling okay in a couple of cities. Best in Nagasaki and Kobe."

"Nagasaki. That's shows cosmic significance. More than others, they know the value of discussion . . . or negotiations . . . or mutual understanding. You know what I mean?" Then I swooped back down from my lofty perch. "How many do you sell a year there?"

"Only about twenty a year. I need to sell about 2,000 a year to be self – sufficient. That would get me about twenty thousand dollars a year. At retail I make about ten dollars a sale."

I was honestly encouraging. "Two thousand is nothing when you think of the millions of school kids in this country. You'd just need to get about . . . thirty schools a year to adopt it at about eighty per school. Traveling could be a part of your work, as you'd sell them in different cities. Then you could fly as you re-did the CDs for other countries and languages."

"And translate the workbook." He added to remind me of the workload. "And rerecord songs to address the particular needs of the different countries' problems."

But Adam wasn't just mechanically refuting all the possibilities I brought up. He mused, "If it took off I would consider making versions for other countries. Now I'm just trying to get it bought here now. I've thought about it though. I purposely made the vocal tracks different from the other tracks so I could rerecord in other languages."

"An idea without marketing is like a tree in the woods. It barely exists. I guess that's how ideas are just like people. Marketing, marketing, marketing." That was my attempt at a joke, maybe not the best joke, but a joke nonetheless.

Nearly instantaneously, I was thinking about the purpose of this conversation. Getting to know each other excluded more information than it generated. Had we reached our peak of intimacy?

"You're totally right about the importance of marketing." Adam said in apparent agreement that showed he didn't fully get my sense of humor yet. "This product is self-teaching and sorely needed. But I don't know anything about marketing. That is the thing stopping my sales . . . and, " Adam paused and looked at me, "stopping your world-wide revolution of peace and understanding via Adam's Language Songs." I enjoyed this gentle jab at my overblown meta-goals.

In the name of full disclosure, I revealed, "I've written a book too." I slyly mentioned, and moved on quickly enough for it to be ignored. "But you're right. The marketing and publishing thing is really hard."

"So you've got a product too, eh? What's it about?" Adam fished.

"I kind of hesitate to say. My book is really controversial." I really didn't want to alienate my new friend by getting into this topic. But it was too late now; the cat was out of the bag. I was going for broke.

"My book is an environmental manifesto. But you really need a lot of background before you jump to conclusions about the conclusion, though."

"Oh, I won't. I almost promise." He said coyly, flirtingly, and humorously. "You can tell *meeeee* what it's about."

"Well, in the preface I start by saying it is like an inoculation against the main idea it presents. It is a poor argument for an evil idea. That way when someone who is eloquent comes along with the same evil idea, society will already have practice at fighting against these sorts of arguments."

Nervousness always made me extend the telling about the preliminary parts of my book until I couldn't stall any more and had to announce what the end was about.

"A good disclaimer is always important before you make an argument." Adam remarked, revealing some droll humor skills.

"Yeah. Thanks." My flat reply acknowledged his humor. We were building some rapport. It felt good.

"After the disclaimer, the book goes on to talk about the origin of consciousness. Ooohhhh. Heady topic! It traces the long, tortuous process of how our modern mind came about. Most folks don't know that our Western way of thinking is earned and cultivated, not automatic."

Adam concurred, "Most people haven't spent years in other countries. It's beyond a gap in thinking. At some point, it's a gap in feeling, seeing, in…everything. I cannot -- no foreigner cannot -- be friends with the Japanese. All my friends are ganjis."

"Ganjis?" I asked, really curious in addition to my being relieved to be off the topic of my book.

"'People from another land.' Is what the term means. After being told you're not part of the Japanese people many times, that you're Ganji, you realize that your community must come from outsiders." Adam offered.

"Wow! That's totally fascinating to me. I normally just talk about the distance between modern minds and ancient minds. I think -- maybe I'm wrong -- that the gap between us and the ancients is an even huger one."

"Cool." Adam agreed, in order to shut me up. "So what is the shocker in your book that you're so cautious about?"

"Well, once I establish intelligence as special, I show that we are not the last stop in intelligence's development. Computers and machines are getting this special characteristic of intelligence and consciousness too."

"I don't know about that. But…?" Then Adam got direct again, "Long story short, hit me with it!"

"Hold on! We also need an ethic that will guide us as neuroscience re-engineers man and destroys his sacredness. That ethic is based on intelligence as the ultimate value -- be it computer intelligence, human or whatever."

"Intelligence?" Adam checked.

"Yeah, intelligence." I paused as he pondered. I wanted him to get that intelligence was the highest value. "You as your thoughts." Then after one last breath. I launched into it as to not build more resentment through continuing excessive stalling.

"Okay. I conclude that in order to protect man and intelligence, both, from getting destroyed by the coming environmental ruin - my book is, again, an environmental manifesto – we need to use intelligence to protect the intelligence we've cultivated, we need to implement a selective mass sterilization policy worldwide to allow mankind and intelligence to survive."

"That's what your book argues for – sterilizing people? Mass sterilization?"

"Yeah, for the environment, it's environmental."

I nervously checked his expression for some kind of shock. But he just seemed to continue nonchalantly looking at me.

"And of course I deal with Hitler because any book like this has to. But you have to read my whole argument before you can judge it." I added in defensive haste.

"Well, I can see why people would be shocked. Genocide is wrong. Isn't that obvious?" Adam queried with what I imagined was a little rise in ire.

"No . . ." I started.

"No. It's not wrong?!" Adam shrieked a little when he was upset. I hoped our friendship would survive this disagreement.

"Of course genocide is wrong! But no, it's not genocide. With selective mass sterilization no one would be killed – no one. People just wouldn't be able to have kids.

"And it isn't genocide, 'cause I'd count on it not being perfectly efficient or used everywhere. Some people would continue to reproduce. Obviously we need people.

"But, no one would be killed at all. Killing is wrong, if for no other reason than the fact that panic and death aren't conducive to intelligence. They make people hide."

"OK, sorry I got tense, John." Wow. He knew he had a tendency to shriek and lose his cool, self-awareness.

"That's okay. But statements out of context can be radically misinterpreted. That's why I like to tell everything about this book slowly. Genocide is not only wrong, it's," I paused and gave the knowing tilt of a head of an ironic provocateur, "it's inefficient."

"Inefficient?" Adam checked with a big grin that acknowledged my enjoyment. I was relieved, as he seemed to have gotten over the hump to where he could calmly understand my thesis and forget about it. And, I enjoyed playing with the fact that he didn't seem to know if I was joking or serious. Half of both.

"Still," He continued on the topic of sterilization, "I believe in Mother Nature and I think that eventually water and stuff will get scarce, and disease and the greenhouse effect will cause the population levels drop. We should let nature take care of herself."

"We can do it that way." I reassured him, "But it'll be really messy and we'll have wars from drought refugees going into other nations and no intelligent selection about who survives.

"And ask yourself who would survive the famines from letting Mother Nature take her course -- doctors or warriors? Do you want to live in a world where there is famine and war and tough guys rule? Intelligence can do better."

"No. I guess maybe it is better that we interfere in potential disasters rather than just let nature go." Adam admitted.

"The only question is who to choose." I continued, throwing hesitancy away. Feeling quite professorial and confident on my own turf, I continued my rant. "It isn't feasible to do sterilization person by person. So we can just blanket all the earth with sterilizing chemicals equally, be random about it, or we can choose where to do it. And, as you probably figured out, I'm pro-choice."

I paused as we both smiled. He was getting my humor.

"We don't want to diminish diversity. There is information, wisdom, stored in cultures. But we need to privilege cultures that foster intelligence best."

Here Adam pushed back, "You sure do put a high premium on intelligence! What about art and music and heart and soul?"

"Prior to civilization, to the Western explosion of science, life was nasty, brutal, and short. We can enjoy tribal music, but you wouldn't want to go back to that sort of thing.

"And if you look at the direction of the world, progress, the creation of apes, then humans, then the creation of computers, it moves towards more and more intelligence. Humans are not the goal, we are a transition to higher computerized life forms."

Adam charged, "That is freaky. The whole premise is absurd – intelligence worship." I held back from defensiveness. "So is sterilization the best humans can do?" He asked.

"The book is an environmental manifesto. It assumes the coming ecological collapse. If you believe in the Global Warming or Climate Change or whatever, it may be the best thing humans can do.

"But, don't worry Adam. As I said, it is just fiction, social science fiction."

"Who is your target audience for the book?" Adam asked, realizing that we had a common obstacle: marketing our ideas and making them more than just private musings.

"Everyone. If I really believed in sterilization, everyone would need to hear it. Ultimately, a rogue scientist or group would have to take on sterilization and do it without government support. But to consider guerilla sterilization, the must be on the list of popularly discussed topics. If something isn't in the public discourse, it isn't an option. It won't be considered. If an idea is not thought about, it doesn't exist."

"But seeing as how the book is just for fun, I just want people that enjoy shocking non-fiction to read it. The real point of the book is that we can muster evidence to support nearly any policy position. So I guess it is aimed at radical post – modern philosophy students."

"Yep," Adam mocked, "its aimed at them and everyone."

Our projects had a commonality in that they created absolute self-contained worlds that were potentially transformative. His work could make students self-sufficient learners. It could work without help from outside itself.

Mine includes a system of morals based on making intelligence man's most valuable attribute. From that premise, when you considered the environment and Global Warming, you could not logically escape the sterilization conclusion. Intelligence, being intelligence, must intelligently defend itself intelligently.

The logic was self-contained in both projects.

Meeting Adam was a really neat happenstance. People that have the ability to create thought constructs are rare. When worlds collide, new ones are formed. We could have fun and insights exploring worldviews together.

We decided to get falafels.

Capsule Three: Traps

Everyone should walk in Rappongi once in his or her lives. It gives you the opportunity to explore your limits.

Rappongi offers the delicious but mundane attractions that have always tempted man. Every ten feet there are Nigerians trying to strong-arm you into a bar or Chinese girls trying to sweet-talk you into their full-body massage parlor.

"Hey. What you looking for?" "Come in. Cheap beer." "Come look. Girls. Why not?" "Massaggeee?" "Where you from?" Now their arms interlock with yours. "You want messaggeee?"

Extricating yourself takes effort, and the pitch doesn't lessen as you become a recognized refuser, it just gets more friendly or whiny or somehow nuanced. The constant effort to entrap you by means of your physical needs is bothersome in proportion to its being tempting and insulting. You want it. But you're not proud that you do.

Adam said he had a way to get rid of them, but he'd never tried it. So when the next girl approached him, he uttered the magic words and gestured. She fled as though propelled.

"What did you say to her?" I asked in amazement.

"I told her that my penis is spent. I had been taken care of."

"And the hand movement?" I prodded.

"The hand movement backs up what the Japanese words mean: literally, the words mean 'the towel has been rung out.'"

"So romantic!" I laughed.

Apart from the ubiquitous tragic consumers, a great variety of worldly characters to can be encountered in this district. Asians, Europeans, Africans, Americans, rich and poor, from whore-wear to casual, circulating together. They are all going somewhere.

Some are with friends, some headed to meet friends. Some were doing what Adam and I had been doing: just wandering lost and waiting to get hooked in.

Individually these were neat folk. They engaged in their world like refugees or explorers. As we walked I thought about the various combinations of thoughts passing us; I was fascinated.

The masses come to reap the promise of Rappongi's million lighted signs. When people go out they want stimulation. This happens in art houses as well as whorehouses. Something exciting, different, and random would make the evening memorable.

People's inability to deal with life on its own terms, their seeking of something more, is laudable. Doing it in the most predictable of ways is pathetic. Because the area is so tawdry, part of me doubted that we'd learn anything from the international adventurers in this district of spectacle.

But Rappongi didn't disappoint. Just nodding at the black men with that combination of "Hey we're tight cause we're Americans in Japan," and "I'm down with American black folks" and "sorry about slavery" looks was interesting.

It was interesting because you realized right away that these men had never been to America. They were Nigerian and had no idea about the cultural background your look entailed. In Rappongi, just nodding brought insights.

What would you, dear reader, do in Rappongi's streets of red-light promises? If you have morals you are limited in what you can do. There are many varieties of wickedness to be avoided or explored here. Sensual variation without end is available.

If you have no prejudices, then you do not have the "you" – the moral compass - to control the situation. You will get lured by whatever stimulating situations come at "you." They will consume you.

Then again, if you want to look at it differently, you can either experience Rappongi's joys and be alive or your can be moral and right and dead. Choose.

These are the streets that try men's souls.

We found the street falafel stand Adam had been leading us to, and I got a beer. As he didn't drink, self-consciously, I sort of apologized for having another beer. Adam reassured me that he had no attitude at all about my getting tipsy. We shared histories of addiction. His was with alcohol and all kinds of smoke. Mine was with marijuana.

"Beer doesn't imprison me." I stated. "Every person has their drug that they cannot do in moderation. Mine is marijuana. It controlled me for much of my young life. Then I went nine years without smoking it.

"I knew that if we wrestled, pot won. My actions became all about getting smoke. It was like it colonized my brain and turned me into one of its minions. I had to go cold turkey to get free again."

"So either Mary Jane had to go, or you had to go. I understand that. Wow. Nine years. That is an accomplishment." Adam relayed soberly.

"Was." I corrected him, "I recently broke my sobriety streak. I am in the danger-lands again."

Happy to have a story to relay, I launched. "Some friends and I went to Mammoth Mountain to snowboard. And one of them, Leo, was being so selfish and inconsiderate that I was really pissed at him. For days he had been making impulsive whimsical demands on us. 'Go left! We're leaving! Go right!'"

"I was pissed and trapped in this pissy mood when a hand came out of our van right before we were to snowboard. 'Johnny P. You wanna hit on some of this?'" I imitated Leo speaking and holding in a hit simultaneously.

"I did it. And as soon as I hit it my mood inverted. I was happy. The mountain was glistening white and amazing. I couldn't wait to get at the mountain."

"How about your attitude towards your friend you were angry at?" Adam led me.

"He squinted up at me as he was putting on his boots and just a little after we smoked and he said, 'Johnny P., you know I love you.' And all bad feelings between us melted instantaneously.

"So I successfully got myself back to happiness and had a fabulous time."

"One little hit can definitely invert the way you see things." Adam concurred.

"It is amazing." We both shook our heads in wonderment.

"And how has your control been since?" Adam pursued.

"I've been near perfect at keeping that stuff away from me. Only once in Brazil. . . no, twice in Brazil. Those were contained under the rule, 'no smoking except on foreign land.' Then I did smoke once at my ex-Principal's house too. That was another exception to the rule."

"Watch out for those multiplying exceptions eating at the rule."

"It hasn't been a problem, even without constructing elaborate rules. And anyhow, Adam, I'm glad that you don't mind that I drink beer."

"Not at all. Alcohol and smoking are all I stay away from. I smoke pot sometimes. But cigarettes, never again."

Wow. It seems that most AA people are allergic to all things that control their minds except for AA itself. I was really impressed that someone could go to AA and not become one of their black-and-white, God-versus-the-Devil, types. He was committed to AA but not entrapped by their dogma.

Adam picked and chose what he wished to accept from AA. To the extent that one is aware of traps, they are immune to indoctrination. Adam knew how to create his own realities on his own terms.

Later, as we walked back from the falafel stand in Rappongi, Adam stopped to talk with one of the street vendors. And to my surprise, he went into a fluent Hebraic conversation with him. I knew he spoke several languages, but it was still sort of jarring to see Adam just open up in a foreign tongue.

Whereas Adam was clean cut, his vendor friend was a dirty hippy and had the long curly hair and prominent lip and nose that many Israelis have. He was selling what looked to be North African jewelry. He also had some Indian looking statues.

In the middle of the conversation, Adam turned to me and asked, "Are you Jewish?" I nodded with an affirmative mumble. Then, before I could explain that I didn't speak any Hebrew, they went back into speaking that incomprehensible language.

Right after we left that guy Adam said rather enthusiastically, "I thought you were Jewish! But you didn't respond when I said 'Le Chiam' to you."

"I didn't hear you. You said that in the bar?"

"Yep." Adam nodded confidently with taught lips and a quick nod.

"Isn't that interesting how you only hear what you expect to hear?" I added.

"I thought you might be Jewish when we first met. But then when you didn't respond to 'Le Chaim', I figured you weren't." He repeated this as if he didn't think I'd heard him the first time.

"Adam, how many languages do you speak?" I was uncomfortable with the topic of Judaism and wanted to steer away.

"I speak five."

"Jeez!"

"That is how I have survived." My new friend explained, "When I was 14 my mother died. That fractured my family. I got sent to Israel at sixteen and stayed seven years. I studied and studied before leaving to Israel. I began to think of language as my ticket and passport and I have been moving with it ever since. I've hardly been back to the United States."

"Where have you been?" I probed.

"I spent seven years in Israel and then went back to America for school. And I decided to study languages. And since America is such a monolingual country I got scholarships to go abroad and study languages there. At one point I had two simultaneous scholarships. I went to France. I was there 5 years. Then I went to Germany for a couple of years. I spent a little over a year in Russia. But I never got good at Russian. I was four years in Spain…"

"Wow! You stay a long time in each place you visit."

"To really learn a culture and a language you have to stay in a place a while. Like in Israel, I went knowing some Hebrew. When people asked me where I was from I told them France. That way people wouldn't bother speaking to me in English, and only spoke to me in Hebrew. I got good pretty quickly."

"I've been," I said, throwing down the gauntlet of competition (or at least trying to qualify to talk with such a worldly person as Adam), "to West Africa, North Africa, South America, Central America, Europe and lots of other places. But the place I like best is India. I stayed there three and a half months."

Then I added with deference, "Other than that I haven't stayed in any one place for a long time. Well.... I guess I was in London for six months and Korea for nine months."

"I came here because of the language," Adam said, resuming his train of thought. "The grammar is pretty much the same as ours. I was going to go to China, but I figured the economy was stronger here. I don't know if I made a mistake or not. The grammar of Chinese is supposed to be really simple. But the sounds are intimidating."

"Yeah. China is taking off. But they're very cloistered. There is more opportunity here." I guessed. "Things seem freer. Like, I don't think your Jewish friend could just set up on the sidewalk and start selling in China."

"Oh, it looks like that, huh? That guy's been here for about fifteen years."

"Fifteen years!" I said, astonished.

"Oh, yeah. It isn't at all what it seems like. That guy's actually a wealthy businessman."

"A wealthy business man?" I asked with fresh astonishment.

"Yeah. He has a Lexus and a really nice home. It's a costume. He sells way more if he looks like a sort of nomadic gypsy type. People buy more from him."

"Huh." I said absorbing the reasonableness of the situation and only half believing it.

"It's funny. People buy from him, in a way 'cause they feel sorry for him. But he's way richer than the folks that buy from him." Adam confided.

"Damn." That one took time to flush all the way down. "But, still, that proves my point. There's opportunity here. In China the sidewalk is not free for the taking."

"That's another thing. There's more control here than you think. He has to pay off the mafia to have that space."

"The mafia!" I exclaimed too loudly.

"Yeah. The Japanese mafia controls a lot of things. If you set up a street stand without permission they find you immediately. And, you have to pay for protection or split."

"Wow really!? A mafia. A real working mafia?" I nearly stammered in disbelief.

"Oh, really real. They don't fuck around. If you don't pay, if you try to defy them, you will die. It is their way or no way. Anyhow, my friend has long-standing relations with them. There are others, but no one but him will sell goods like his in this prime part of Rappongi."

"Wow!" I looked at the three or four vendors up the street. All of these vendors were part of a brutal hit-squad mafia organization. And I confirmed that the others didn't have stuff like Adam's hippy-looking friend.

"Have you been to Israel?" Adam asked.

"Yeah, but I didn't like it. The kibbutz seemed like a cross between an old folk's home and an insane asylum to me. Along with China and Cuba, it is the third Communist place I've been.

"Folks were so beaten down, that they couldn't conceive of leaving the kibbutz. I remember folks who were eating the always-white food saying too adamantly that they were going to escape. But I knew they weren't. If you're in your thirties and you haven't escaped, you won't." I enjoyed sharing this well-worn story and garnered wisdom of mine.

"So I filled up the floor of my kibbutz cabin six inches deep with plastic beads that came from the plastic factory I worked in, as an expression of madness. I threw eggs at the cabin wall and split from the Kibbutz in the middle of the night.

"The first thing I did, when I got to a town, was get a falafel and a Coke. That was significant because these foods were my choice; no one bought them for me. My choosing Coke was a celebration of capitalism and freedom. I was glad to be in the real world again."

"Why do you think they couldn't leave?" Adam asked.

"When you are used to others making your decisions and designing your life for you, you lose the ability to walk on your own. Your independence muscles atrophy. These people couldn't conceive of finding a job and a place to stay, and getting their phone hooked up and all you need to do to get set up in the real world.

"You must exercise your freedoms or lose them. And those kibbutz people had been sucked down into a system that smothered them like an over-bearing mother. Their ability to be self-reliant and apart was gone. They were encased like a mummy. Kibbutzes kill people." I concluded.

These statements accurately reflected my memories of the kibbutz. But only stressing the horrors also kind of helped release my tension around this topic. To me, Judaism is like a big monster that wants to consume me. It comes like a zombie repeating, "Make Jewish babies, you are a Jew, Make Jewish babies." Judaism has always made me feel claustrophobic.

In what must have seemed like a non sequitur to Adam, I continued my personal thoughts. "My family was atheist and, as such, not traditional. My secular acceptance of the Enlightenment stresses individual conscience over the group. I don't like the thought of being part of a group or controlled by a religion."

But, I admitted, "But I guess that if Judaism was not a temptation, it wouldn't bother me to talk about it."

"I guess it's like my sterilization project or Judaism itself. You have to beware of people and systems that have thought of everything for you. If you get raised in a Kibbutz you can get trapped. Then you're living another person's dream, not your own world construct."

"Well," Adam finally interrupted me, "I really loved my years on the kibbutz." He then paused and assumed a more thoughtful and introspective looking expression than I had seen on him - a new facet to Adam.

"I had the power to leave.... I was in the Israeli military, ya' know." Adam continued after thoughtful silence in which he seemed to be deciding whether or not to open up this still raw subject. "I probably spent too much time in Lebanon. I left when they wanted me to kill. I just couldn't hate other people. It's like you said. You can get trapped by these systems. Thank God I was strong enough to just refuse to shoot."

"Maybe it was your world travels that gave you the perspective to see how parochial – 'er -- local the war concerns were." I feared being considered condescending, but didn't want to use words that were not in Adam's vocabulary. It is a teacher problem.

"Maybe. But I remember one moment in particular that really made me decide to leave the Israeli army.

"This man came at me and really wanted to hurt me. He was a Palestinian who had had his son killed and his home destroyed by the Israelis. I have never seen or felt such rage. I sure he was going to kill me.

"Luckily, the man's friends held him back and explained that this particular young Jew -- me -- had nothing to do with it. I wasn't in uniform at the time.

"I realized then that killing wasn't going to work. I couldn't hate this man. I cried a lot afterwards from just absorbing some of his rage. God, I hope I never know pain and anger like that.

"After that I quit the military. I left Israel and never went back." Adam ending the story.

As we sat on the sidewalk and ate the last of our falafels, Adam made a stunning suggestion. "Hey. How'd you like to do some psychedelics with me tomorrow night?"

"Wow!!! Yeah, cool! Would I?!?! That would be too much and great. Is that possible here in Japan?" Oh, my God, I thought, wait until the fellas back home hear about this.

"Oh, yeah. There are places where they sell them on the street. They made mushrooms illegal, but there are other things. I think it is time for me to do this sort of thing right now. You'd make a good partner in the experience. We'll stay up all night and explore and be free and wild."

His invitation flattered and enthused me. Adam said he'd take me to a capsule hotel that I could book for the next night. My mission to find a place to stay close to the center of Rappongi and make connections to people had succeeded beyond my expectations.

Underground, on the subway ride to the hotel I hoped to stay in the next night, two hot looking Asian girls moving through the car passed us. One of them, the taller one, I thought, sort of turned and looked back at us with a slowness that conveyed interest.

At that moment I made a resolution. I was going to be bold with them and thereby cement the deal with Adam. Hanging out with me would be more enticing if I was someone I totally wasn't: a sexual predator. With all of my nerve I transcended myself.

"Hey! How are you? You're dressed beautifully, and it's early. Why are you going home?" I spontaneously blurted, my nervousness showing.

To my total astonishment, they were receptive. Perhaps transcending my limits would lead to a new me. It seemed, momentarily, as if I were no longer there. I wasn't sure who the hustler that had replaced me was.

The requisite 'where are you from,' 'why are you here,' and 'how do you like Japan' were quickly supplanted by more immediate concerns as our stops were coming soon. Nothing cuts small talk like the knowledge of the scarcity of time. I asked them to come out with us.

"We cannot go out. My friend is student. She must to go home and to study." It seemed almost as if the shorter one couldn't speak English as her friend spoke for her.

"But even if she must stay home, you can go out." I pressed, knowing she'd refuse, and so risking nothing while appearing daring.

"No. I tonight start new job and I tired."

"What is your new job?" Adam asked, taking over and asking the obvious but potentially inappropriate question.

"I am dancer."

"I thought you might be. You have such a hot little body." Adam uttered, going way past anything I could ever imagine myself saying to a woman. I thought it might infuriate her, but…

"Where do you dance?" I asked.

"The club name 'Climax.' Did you go there?" She offered, seemingly oblivious to the sexual nature of the name, though she was wearing five-inch heels and a short dress.

"No. We were asked by many people, but we didn't go into any of those types of clubs." My subtext was that I wasn't like the other johns. I was a good and respectable guy. My upbringing dictates that I think that women respect feminist values and wouldn't have sex for fun or profit. I'm also programmed to believe that women will get angry if you are crude.

"We'd love to come see you dance, though. You are so hot." Adam said, returning to the obvious and uncomfortable subject of their being very, very attractive. I agreed with the sentiment, but prudishly.

"Thank you." Her appreciative response did damage to my categories of decorum and propriety. I am a sheltered nerd.

"Do you like stripping?" While I had neurotic conversations with myself about pangs of conscience and morals, Adam verbalized the obvious connotation that dancing meant stripping.

"I like dance." She replied while demonstrating some serious gyrating. "The mens look at me is strange." The vindication of my feminist upbringing was undercut by her too-sensual-for-public grinding while she made this statement.

"I think that it should be an Olympic sport. In Mexico," I told her, "I saw girls hold themselves on the top of the pole with their ankles and slide down in really beautiful and graceful ways." I tried to demonstrate my complicity in seediness and transcend my nerd image. And though all enjoyed the idea of stripping as an Olympic sport, my elevating the art form still somehow aimed at cleaning up my image.

We found out when she was doing her thing before she got off the subway, and said we'd try to catch her show and maybe go out afterwards. I think she was attracted to Adam's directness.

Adam seemed really hyped by the prospect of a guy's night out with a hunter like myself. I had pulled it off my image manipulation. What a man won't do for company. In faking I had confused myself – I had felt the exhilaration of growth and the fear of the unknown. How divergent can your self-image be from your actions before that self-image must bend? Who would I be if I ceased to be me? Did I want to find out?

Values tell us who we are. Borders and boundaries make a conscience. We are as defined by what we wouldn't do as we are by what we do. In the military, for example, Adam wouldn't kill.

I have often been adversarial to those who are proud of their having an "open mind." Study and reason developed my well-considered opinions and decisions. I have made my mind up; it is not simply "open" for any crap to be put in. To not be "prejudiced" can be interpreted as not having previously judged anything. Would one be proud of never having decided anything?

"If one doesn't stand for something, one may fall for anything," goes the trope.

Of course we get our values from our surroundings. In this way we all share something with the stuck kibbutzim. We largely cannot escape our beliefs. Some people transform their fear of temptation into virtues. The extent of their moral resoluteness is a measure of their fear. Still, they too reinforce the limits of the culture they grew up in.

Perhaps the liberation that comes from the anonymity of travel will help me cocoon into a new person. Would I pervert my beliefs or actions to be an entertaining friend? Did I speak to the stripper chicks to have Adam's company or was I actually aiming to be free from my own moral restrictions?

Maybe an experiment of how far I could push myself into being that party-animal we all dream of would be an interesting check-up in identity land. I suppose one must occasionally leave their comfort zone in order to say that they are really choosing what they usually do.

Capsule four: Borders

The capsule hotel was in the ROI building.

Upon entry to the capsule hotel, you have to take off your shoes. You put your shoes in a locker and insert two quarter-sized coins. This allows the key to be released. Key in hand, you then put on a pair of the numerous blue hotel sandals waiting in the shoe rack. You can then proceed into the reception area. When you give the front desk the key from your shoe locker, they give you the key to the locker you can put your clothes in.

The entire time you are in the capsule hotel you wear their blue sandals and a robe. When leaving, you change into your street clothes, but keep your hotel sandals on. At reception, when you return the key to your clothes locker they give you back the key to your shoe locker. When you use that key to get your outside shoes back, you get your two quarter-sized coins back.

Thus, is the capsule hotel hermetically sealed.

Adam had dropped me off at this hotel last night. He wanted to show me a great place to stay. The hotel also served as a rendezvous spot. But after seeing it, I had gone back to my original hotel to spend the night. I returned to the capsule hotel, hoping to check in, a little before 11 A.M.

I arrived at the capsule hotel really needing to go to the bathroom. Fortunately, I was able to sneak behind a big plant pot, street shoes undetected, as I entered the reception restroom. And, thankfully, I made it to the bathroom on time. But as I crossed through the reception office space to get back to the shoe storage lockers, a considerable clucking was made. They had seen my street shoes. Sometimes such strict codes and lines must give into nature's demands.

I will probably never understand the significance of shoes in the Asian world. A fair amount of protocol surrounds them; protocol verging on ritual. Hygiene cannot suffice to explain this obsession. The enforcement of boundaries over which the Japanese cannot cross seems superstitious. And the enforcement and emotional impact of transgression are too strong for it to be rational.

Every traveler, perhaps most tourists too, have as an unstated goal the understanding just these sorts of cultural rules and their underlying perceptions. Shoes crossing lines could represent disrespect to the establishment or the established social order. Pondering the significance of the shoe ritual amused me.

My problem in analyzing possible reasons for Japanese shoe rules stems from the fact that neither respect nor class nor aesthetics carry the same nuances in Japanese as they do for the American mind in English. Manners are just another synonym for lack of authenticity for us. We do not have the patience for such beautiful signs of cultivation.

Class and poverty are also terms that carry assumptions concerning the meaning of life, dignity, and shame. Assumptions about their significance would not be similar across cultures.

America assumes the romantic ideal of freedom. Conformity to rebellion's dictates is our version of cultivation. Kicking a librarian in the butt makes more sense to us than elaborate shoe protocols.

Once I'd negotiated myself back over to the hotel reservation counter, properly sandaled and keyed, I ran into three harsh rules. A sign in English said that no one would be admitted to the facilities who did not speak Japanese. The woman and two men behind the counter pointed to this rule to let me know that they didn't want to let me in.

Having already checked out of my affordable and often sold-out hotel an hour plus away, this was an emergency. Somehow, I conveyed to them that my Japanese-speaking friend, with whom I had been there with the night before, was going to be joining me at 5 p.m. They remembered Adam and that he spoke Japanese. With the language hurdle of rule number one overcome, they let me in.

The capsule hotel's sleeping compartments are amazing. I simultaneously shudder at their implications as I am impressed by their efficiency. They are approximately 3X3X7-foot boxes with beds in them. If you are lacking for a visual, think of square shower stalls lying down and stacked or look at the cover of this book. Creepier yet, remember the mausoleums in which undertakers put bodies in filing-cabinet-style drawers.

Outfitted with TVs, lights, radios, air conditioning units, and smooth walls that paradoxically suggest an absence of limits, capsules are self-enclosed worlds you could live in without lack. Everything a human being needs is there. Except for food and waste-elimination, they are self-contained and you need not ever leave them.

Just think – between showers, toilets, and food, humans are only three tubes away from being totally storable. And if these capsules had those car washes brushes that go back and forth over your car installed in lieu of showers, we'd be two easy-to-set-up tubes away from being ready to be sealed.

To be in a capsule is to experience a return-to-the-womb lack of differentiation that defies conveyance. One difference being that the capsule experience isn't warm and fuzzy or biological. As the walls and dials and all you see is plastic, you feel as though you might be plastic. Biology ceases there. It is very clean inside.

The capsule is an impossible space. It has no cultural or ideological references. It is life sheered down to what would be required in outer space. As one of many identical bodies stored in identical rows and columns, you cease to be individual or human. Life support without reference to real lives. My capsule is '44c,' five boxes in from the left side of the wall, third row from the floor.

Unfortunately, I have a tattoo on my left shoulder. It is the logo of the band "Black Flag." If you didn't know, the Black Flag logo consists of four staggered vertical rectangles that look something like a bar code. The reason I called the fact of my tattoo unfortunate is that rule number two at the capsule hotel is, "No Tattoos."

"The bars," as this tattoo is often called, represent prisons and limits, either mental or physical. The bars are an attempt to subvert the good that the capsule hotel and society represent via a muckraking exposé based on primitive emotion. Rage exists in the clean little capsule boxes.

My rebellion is not for this place. Tattoos mess with the hotel's placid image. I must join them in the stifling conspiracy of silence, and deny my tattoo, if I am to fit in here. And, with nowhere else that I could afford having vacancies, I was trapped.

The night before, Adam had told me not to worry about having a tattoo, that this rule is just to protect against mafia types. They are the only tattooed people in Japan. But I worried about it. Not only was the 'no tattoo' sign in English, but it had pictures of tattoos encircled with red lines through them. There was no pleading ignorance. I did not want to get kicked out of my hotel and rendezvous site.

Second to getting a capsule, my goal was to take a shower. The guy that handed out towels could easily see the locker they had assigned me. Changing without revealing my tattoo to him would be difficult.

Strategically, I started a pattern of pacing as I readied my possessions for storage. One time when I paced back towards the locker, I quickly took off my shirt and put a towel over my left shoulder. Done.

Suddenly, a woman walked past me! How could she not know to stay out of the men's dressing area? What was a woman doing in the men's locker room? I asked myself these questions with an indignity fueled by my nervousness over having just broken a rule and gotten away with it.

My shower came straight out of a Hitchcock film. Right across from the shower stalls, the woman who had passed me as I dressed, and another one, started to give natural mud massages to two men on tables. The massage room was across the walkway from the room with all the showers. I would have to hide my tattoo from this massage lady.

The women's intrusion into our sanctum of nudity was justified by their jobs. Apparently, these women touching naked men was not seen as sexual or sensual. For this reason their entrance into our private world of male nudity was not provocative. Nevertheless, having women in our locker room made me uncomfortable.

As this was a space for men, there was no curtain across the shower room entrance. As strange as it was to shower in front of strange women, hiding my tattoo while I showered was stranger yet. I showered with my left shoulder to the wall and wrapped the towel around my tattoo when I emerged.

I wanted to have one of these mud massages. But there was no way of knowing if the women would have turned me in for my tattoo violation. When I went into the saunas I didn't remove my towel. As nonchalantly as possible I kept the towel draped over my left shoulder. This gesture was designed to look casual, but I'm sure it looked suspicious.

So this was what it was like to be hiding and afraid of expulsion. I felt like a cross between a clandestine World War II Jew and an illegal alien. I avoided detection.

The influence of their system on my internal state was profound. My actions and public identity concentrated on concealing my body. I would conform for the sake of housing. Was this deal with the devil too big? No. I didn't plan on spending much time in their capsule anyway.

The third capsule hotel rule was that you could not be under the influence of any intoxicating substance. Thank God that only showed on the inside. I could do all the psychedelics I wanted to and still conceal my insides. I could surrender without giving myself away. Appearances and reality could coincide in harmony.

Later in the afternoon, I waited for Adam in one of the overly cushioned recliners that faced the giant TV in the lower-level hotel lounge. Unlike the other people reclining, I was in street clothes rather than a bathrobe. I was waiting to go out.

I hoped that I didn't detract from the hotel's perfectly reassuring environment. My suggestion of non-sterility and the need for movement didn't seem to annoy anyone. They were oblivious. Serene in the assurance that their walls, rules, and recliners, would stave away the terror, they relaxed.

Adam sent me several apologetic texts with estimated arrival time updates. At heart I still wondered if Adam would come. He showed! This was actually going to happen!

He had changed into a worn red t-shirt, with no logo on the pocket, and tan corduroy shorts. He had hairy long legs. And despite the casualness and age of what he wore, his wire-frame glasses, perfect part and demeanor still gave him the upper crusty feel his polo had earlier. His preppy white ankle socks might have helped with this too.

Upon arrival he apologized again for how long the signing of his university contract took.

"But all went well?" I queried, with any potential annoyance I might have felt otherwise completely overwhelmed with enthusiasm.

"Yeah. Really well. I negotiated and got the salary and bonus structure I wanted. Negotiating isn't part of their culture, but the bonus structure they offered didn't make any sense. I explained why it didn't. I stuck to my guns and got what I wanted."

When I mentioned my tattoo-based ordeal, Adam said he hadn't realized that I had a tattoo. This lapse made me wonder if he had a hole in his memory or had more serious mental problems. We had discussed the tattoo rule only being for mafia types and my concern about my tattoo the night before.

"They might have kicked you out. It's not just mafia that they are excluding, but a feeling of elegance that they are protecting. They are drawing class lines." This also contradicted what he had told me earlier about their only aiming to exclude mafia. Wanting this adventure to come off, I didn't challenge him on his inconsistency.

He told me that capsule hotels aimed to create relaxing country-club style gentility. Tattoos weren't part of the sensibility they sought to cultivate. Good thing I went with my instincts about hiding.

Adam also said he really worried about his smell. I suggested he use my deodorant. He must have asked five times if that wasn't going to violate my standards of hygiene. It sort of did, but I wanted to flow with this experience.

When he finished using my roll-on, he gingerly wiped the deodorant with tissue paper to remove the top layer of deodorant. The mixing had been avoided. The potential for unpleasant contamination had been sufficiently covered.

In order that we could get to know one another better prior to our excursion (and to get the nutrition required before lift-off), we went to a Denny's restaurant.

Denny's as you might know, is an American coffee shop chain. Adam chose Denny's so that I might experience their version of our vision. He was into cultural exposé. Our encounter was a blessing.

We sat down in the cushy puke colored booths that Denny has. Adam's casual outfit seemed agreeable to the comfort level that this home grown chain brought out in me.

The décor was a perfect replica of any Denny's in the U.S. The Japanese are noted for the ability to emulate. When Admiral Perry, the first Western invader of Japan, came to their shores, they begged to be left alone for 50 years in order that they might give consideration to allowing trade with us. In the interim the Japanese mastered our technologies and created a bit of a balance of power.

I had originally planned to go to the Tokyo Disneyland. That is, until I heard that it was an inch-for-inch duplicate of the one in Los Angeles. I wanted to see the copy of my old stomping grounds. But the exact copy idea also made me feel creepy and disappointed. My funds and time could not justify my visiting a place I had been before.

In Asian art generally, innovation is not as valued as perfectly replicating the classic style. To perfect a form that has already been repeated repeatedly is excellence. This view contrasts sharply with the constant revolution and rebellion against last year's style in Western art history. This Denny's served their need for replication as it served my need for the novel.

In this Denny's replica, it soon became apparent that books often vary from their covers. The first hint of difference was apparent when I looked at the menu. Apart from the salads, I had never heard of anything that they were serving. No "grand slam" omelet breakfasts here. The resemblance was purely superficial.

Adam started the conversation. "So, you teach history, eh?"

"Hm-hm."

"My girl and I, we talked about history and I found out that she had never seen the 'American Century' video series. Do you know that one? With Peter Jennings."

"Yep. I sure do. It's a staple of all American High Schools." I explained.

"That's why I think she should see it. She'd get me more if she understood the past of my country I think."

"That's a good idea. I should get Soo Hee, my fiancé, too watch it too. It's hard when neither spouse knows the background to the story of the other one's history or culture. So you liked that series, eh?"

"It was okay." At that Adam made an upside down smirk and tilted his head. "Well Peter Jennings is a Cannuc."

"A Canadian!" I laughed in sympathy. "Really."

"Yeah. Couldn't you hear his 'Aboots' and 'Found Oots?'" Adam could still conjure up a little America-centered chauvinism. After decades away, it amazed me that he still identified so strongly as a citizen of the United States. I guess his time away made him more aware of just how American he was.

Just before our smiles wore off he continued. "But I always found that series a bit strange for other reasons too."

"Really? Why?"

"Because it seems to short change life. All those people had lived and died - so many lives. A whole damn decade and they turn it into an hour. Was that all the decade was worth? Was that all that happened that might even have mattered?" He pleaded with some intensity.

I humbly and gratefully accepted Adam's historiography concepts, "I guess you're right. And I guess it doesn't bother me because I do assume that the real stuff of history, of life, is the broad ideas that carry through in time. But that's a great observation."

The waitress came totally clad in authentic Denny's wear, gave us menus, poured us some water, spoke to us in Japanese and bowed away.

"I'm glad you're here to translate." I said with earnest appreciation.

"Do you know what she is doing?" Adam asked with a somewhat insane glint in his eye. "When she pours us water, she apologizes for it. She is saying that she is sorry for disturbing us. Can you imagine that? We should be thanking her, but Japanese do not take credit. They apologize for everything and are sure to always make everyone feel like… like they are not responsible, or, how can I say it?"

He paused and really thought, rolling his eyes up a little to the right and pursing his lips. "They apologize for themselves instead of taking credit and make you feel like you shouldn't blame them."

"Its like super defensiveness in advance." I checked.

"Exactly." Adam enthused. "It's so weird. But they mean it. And this defensiveness is in all spheres of life."

"But when a teacher teaches, he doesn't apologize. Does he?" I queried.

"No, then the student does. It rides on the back of a constant hierarchy in which all relationships are boss-to-worker. There is no human warmth of equality. There is always this apologizing, groveling, servant thing going on."

It crossed my mind that Adam had possibly been in Japan too long. He was fond of pointing out the ludicrousness of their habits. Perhaps his interest level had dropped because he pretty much knew everything about Japan. I thought if he really didn't like Japan he shouldn't be living here.

"Adam, are you just amazed by the Japanese culture or do you not like it? Is it interesting to you or do you hate it?"

"There are good parts, but I've got to tell you, the Japanese are the meanest people I have ever known. "

"Oh!" I spontaneously protested. "But whenever I've been lost they have gone really far out their way to help me."

"Yes. But that is superficial. When it gets down to it, you are always Ganji."

"You mentioned that before. That's the word that means 'foreigner' right?"

"It literally means, 'foreign land.' But what it really means is you don't belong here."

"Yeah, the Koreans are racist like that," I conveyed from brutal experiences. "They won't let half-breeds into their public schools. They are nice, but wouldn't let you marry their daughter."

"Or even be friends with you." Adam supplemented, "I worked at this one school for nearly two years. I worked my brains out playing music and singing with the kids. You know what they told me?"

Normally I would have put in the rhetorical 'what?' here, but Adam was starting to get into one of his hurt and angry wind-up-to-a-diatribe moods. I didn't want to interrupt.

"They told me to stop wasting time with the kids. After years of passionately teaching there, no one had ever taken the time to see what I was doing. Furthermore, they never asked me why I did what I did." His look of anguished self-pity was so over the top now that it created a little spontaneous revulsion reaction in me.

"Students, teachers, parents -- anyone that had been in my classes -- never talked about what I had been doing with other staff members. No communication happened. Nor did they care to listen. When I tried to explain what I had been working on and what I was so passionate about, do you know what their response was?"

I shook my head.

"They said, "You are Ganji. Do your job. You are here to work. That is all.

"That was with people that I had worked with for years. I had gone on canoeing trips with them. There was no interest in my thoughts or care about me as a person. There was no communication."

Adam looked so seriously hurt that I had to stay serious. "It sounds like being Ganji puts you in the servant part of the hierarchy." I offered.

"Its worse than that. It means that you are put in another separated category from "us Japanese." And for them, Japanese equals human. I don't really mean human. I don't know how to put it, but you are put into a separate category from them.

"No sentiment or human kindness or sympathy crosses that gap. Not only are you not a priority, but you are totally unimportant to the mission of the group. Owed no sentiment."

He capped it off, "You can ask any Ganji, if they have Japanese friends. They will all say no. You can go on boat trips and out drinking with them and think you're friends. But there will never be any love there. They consider us inferior, tools. They can be so cold it's monstrous. "

"That would fit in with these nice helpful folk's behavior in World War II! They were insanely cruel." I added.

Right then the waitress came back. She took our orders and bowed at us as she walked away backwards.

Adam repeated, with fresh amazement, "She apologized again in Japanese for taking our order and the time it took!" Then with a radical shift in posture and voice he said, as though he was revealing some really juicy hot gossip, "Hey she's pretty hot, isn't she? She has hot tits."

Inside I was shocked. I don't talk to or about women that way. I had made a step in that direction on the subway the night before. But, it remained uncomfortable to me.

I mean, she was an attractive young girl. But talk of asses and tits just always struck me as indecent and gross.

Besides, sex is messy and a confusing topic for me. I'd rather not discuss it. I had been never comfortable joining in women-ogling discussions.

I could feel a rift opening up between Adam and I. But I followed the thread of the conversation without acceding to its content, "Yeah she is something. I think she is half-black. She has nappy hair."

Adam said that he didn't think so and that it hadn't even occurred to him. I was sure that it was because he hadn't looked above her neck!

When she came back, Adam addressed her in English. She smiled one of those enchanting, blushing, beaming smiles that only Asian societies' sense of shame puts on women's faces.

She immediately broke into black-accented English. "Ma daddy was in the service. Ma momma is from here."

"But you grew up in the States?" I asked, taking a clue from her accent.

"Yeah. I only been here 'bout three years."

"How's your Japanese?" Adam probed in his area of expertise.

"Not good. It's comin' along though."

"Your mother didn't teach you Japanese?" I asked.

"She always spoke to us in English. Its funny 'cause her English ain't that good."

"What a shame. What a missed opportunity." Adam said shaking his head and looking downward.

"Yeah. It's alright. I'm getting' it. You want anymore water or anything? I gotta keep working."

"No, we're cool thanks." I offered.

She bowed as she walked away backwards!

Adam thereafter glared at her with a nearly slobbering enthusiasm. "Asian eyes always predominate in interracial offspring. It makes the women so beautiful. I just want to eat them out. Ummn."

Wow. Eesh. Adam was a quality person, but he was great at giving me that feeling of alienation that people who aren't me often evoke; the feeling that either I'm an alien or they are, but we're not from the same world.

Deep down I know that I'm the alien.

The problem isn't feeling self-conscious or less than proud about my prudish nature. I accept that that is who I am and its okay. And, it ties in well with my values system. Rather, I worry that others will not accept me for being the way I am. They might shun me because I make them feel self - conscious. I usually try to reassure them with a little inauthentic, leering-body-part ogling of my own.

Later, as our comfort grew, we discussed such issues. But for the time being I just changed the subject.

"In my classes I used to use an article about the L.A. Riots. You heard about those, right?"

"Yep."

"Many of the hostilities were between blacks and the Koreans who had liquor stores in the black neighborhoods. The article went over how the tensions were largely over differences in cultural expression.

"Black culture is really expressive. You come into a store with your hands held high for a high-five and you yell, 'Whassup homie?' In Korean society you always keep your hands at your sides. I demonstrated both options.

"Due to body language, the Korean sees the black as out of control and animal-like. And the black sees the Korean as totally cold and inhuman. Communication is really important. It must be a trip for our waitress. She came from a boisterous culture to one of the most polite societies on earth."

Even after we spoke in English, the waitress continued to bow before walking away from our table backwards.

"I wonder how long it took before the whole bowing thing was just second nature to her?" I asked myself out loud. "She knows she needn't bow to us. We're westerners. But it's second nature to her now."

"I don't know." Adam replied. "Culture is really physical. Language and bowing and all that stuff goes down to your bones. She seems to have it in hers now."

Despite our differences Adam and I could connect. We enjoyed talking about some of the same topics.

What about the greetings of the black, the Korean, and the white person? Words were not the only things that separated our languages. Emotion separates cultures at an experiential level. I have never truly felt the deferential meaning of a bow. These differences in aesthetics meant that we inhabited different worlds at the same time that we inhabited the same world.

Contemplating the world of the Japanese's hierarchal categories also fascinated me. The categories of higher and lower person themselves don't exist in our culture. Adam and I, for example, are equals.

What were the nuances in interaction? All white Americans wonder what it's like to have that authentic exuberance of the black man. It is a national white obsession. What would it mean to have soul?

American whites never ask what it would be like to be totally formal, to be Asian. Perhaps the attraction to black culture wasn't so foreign after all.

Hurt feelings, riots, wars, and even slavery could be justified on such vacuum-sealed cultural chasms, on the idea that people inhabit different worlds, that they don't have any commonality. These were dangerous thoughts.

Perhaps the answer to the problem of cultural distance lies in people like our waitress who straddles both sides. Maybe, with explanation, the people in my capsule hotel could accept and appreciate my tattoo's significance, or at least its lack of mafia overtones or anarchistic tendencies.

Then again, my tattoo aims at blowing up the calm of their antiseptic world.

--Capsule five: Surface—

On the subway over to psychedelics I noticed nearly everyone was on cell phones. As a traveler, I did not have a working cell phone. I felt so isolated that if saw someone without a cell phone I imagined we were secretly conspiring. Japanese girls are particularly obsessed with cell phones. They always seem to be checking messages or looking at pictures on them. They rarely talk.

The men look at softcore porn on their phone displays. Aren't they aware that people were watching them look at these pictures? These business types don't look particularly macho. Yet, in our culture, only macho men have pin-ups visibly hanging around their environment.

But the Japanese men had pin-ups is on a phone in public. I guess the Asian notion of looking at such images is different than ours. These men are probably married too. Does lust for a hot pixel image, cyber cheating, constitute cheating in this culture? Men looking at pin-up women might be akin to females leering at a Vogue magazine spread in America.

I would be embarrassed to be seen looking with such serious, sensuous intent on my face in public. To me, leering at an image of a woman is more embarrassing than leering at a real one. Technology is tricking you by mimicking that which biology programs you to be interested in – female shapes.

I wanted to talk to Adam about the cell phone phenomenon, but the elevator phenomenon kicked in. It is rude to talk about your co-passengers while riding on a subway. It is pretty much rude to talk too much on a subway, period.

As we got off the subway, there was a couple with a stroller standing on the platform.

"What a cute monkey." Adam lilted to the baby in a baby-talk voice. It was an exceptionally cute child. Pangs of sentiment for the beauty of family momentarily stirred in me. "So sad that I didn't have one." Tears threatened at the words.

As usual, my feelings quickly went to the geopolitical. The baby's Mom was Asian and Dad was white. I fleetingly considered the political and logistical difficulties of that.

"What a gorgeous baby you have." Adam said, directing his statement at the Dad while looking at the child.

"Yeah. Shay ez (she is)," Dad replied receptively with a strong English accent and tilting his head as the English do when they wink.

"How old is she?" Adam queried.

"She'll be two in four monfs." Dad voiced, looking down in the cradle as if he was considering whether or not to keep her.

We asked for directions and he nearly leaped as he exclaimed, "You're going to be going… and den you're going to be going…" The way he delivered directions conveyed for excitement for our apparent mission. At the same time, his emphasis on the "you're" conveyed sadness over not being able to join us.

Adam thanked and congratulated him, and my spirits soared as we nearly jogged off in excitement. As I looked back I saw the family stalled and not sure which exit to use. For that moment I was glad I didn't have a family. Baby was nice to see. But running with the boys was more fun for now. No stroller. No old lady.

Nothing too important. All was a game.

It was finally fully Friday night, I silently exclaimed as we emerged from the subway and into the evening. I was nearly overwhelmed. Thousands of young partygoers were crossing an intersection that went to a plaza in front of a super-mall building. Never in all my life had I seen such a concentration of people walking. It was more of a swarm than a crowd.

When the light signaled pedestrians to walk, it looked like dams cracking and spilling their water in slow motion. In the background, on the sides of buildings, I could see masses of peoples walking through glass tubes. It really is remarkable, without GPS, how easily we distinguish ourselves from all of the people that surround us.

I turned to see that the real action lay behind us. Wall-to-wall night-clubbers filled these sign-blanketed sci-fi streets. The streets had the feel of hipsterism of bohemian artistic poverty. They were streets with the feel of alleys. But I could not figure out what gave me that impression. The streets were immaculately paved and all was bright.

We had arrived in Tokyo's party region, Shinjuki. Not only were the buildings sci-fi, the people wore costumes. We weren't in California anymore. Had the down-to-earth hippy thing ever existed here? If so, it had been skittlized (become as manufactured as the Skittles candy) and forgotten. Artificial colors and flavors abounded.

What did these modern-day vampires want? Was this a psychedelic freak scene or an orgy waiting to happen, a protest or just good clean fun? It was a spectacle! As part of the crowd we could just as well ask ourselves the vampire question. We were of, as well as in, the churning mass.

Adam moved us towards the belly of the beast, the direction of the most lights and the giant TVs. I noticed that one of the several enormous television screens mounted on the side of a building fully reached two stories high. The screen played advertisements that featured bands.

The commercialization of culture spreads. Still, the fantasy element of the local's clothes didn't express lifestyle as much as style life – life dominated by style. Starkly, the medium was the message.

The TV commercials wouldn't have flown in the youth scenes of my day. "Sell-out," meaning one who traded their artistic values for money, is an old concept. I don't think it's been relevant in America for decades. Observing that the music industry is an effective "ministry of consumer programming," no longer counts as news. Buying the look of a lifestyle conveys all the energy of that lifestyle or style of life, without living it. Store bought identity.

It was almost hard to follow Adam through the rapids of the crowd. But a bit upstream he paused at a street vendor. Oh my Gawd! The street vendor had an open suitcase – the type of set - up apple sellers had during America's Great Depression. The difference here being that the sign on the inside of this open suitcase read, "Legal Drug. Psychedelic Love Happy. Kaos International."

Adam decisively decided, "Let's go to the next one. I know the other guy. I'm comfortable with him." As far as I could tell the assortment was the same. The case had many organized baggies. The display included vials called "Pinky," black bags that said "DMT," bags of pure crushed herbs of some sort, baggies of black powder, and one bag held a capsule called "Trip Thunder."

The proprietor of this small enterprise looked like an L.A. skater stoner. He had black hair with dyed brown highlights that intimated that he'd spent a lot of his time in the sun, surfing. Authentically, he also had the requisite Levi's and quasi-military light jacket over his blue tee shirt. No, rather than a surfer, this guy looked he lived in one of the many vans that lined some of California's beaches.

His was the only retro-style outfit on the street that wasn't totally iconoclastic. It seemed to fit him.

Adam and the vendor spoke in Japanese for a while. It was the only time I saw Adam ask for information without confidence. Not demanding, he was a petitioner. My friend appeared to be trying to get a personal selection recommendation from a guy who had good things to say about each product. I wondered how deep his relationship with this guy went. It seemed like a standard salesman-customer relationship to me.

Finally we decided to go ahead exactly as had been planned. He got two vials each of the clear "Pinky" liquid. He had cautioned that I might only want to get one due to their strength, but I went for the whole shebang.

Thirty bucks per vial. Ouch. But this was for a once-in-a-lifetime ticket. Mostly I was just wowed at my fortune, being in this unreal situation in Japan, with such a cool guide, and about to take psychedelics.

"Okay!" I exclaimed as we were now facing each other with two baggies each. "Which way and where?"

Needing a liquid to pour Pinky in, we went to a fast food joint. We got cheap burgers to make us look like legitimate customers, drinks for consumption, and went upstairs.

The décor was cool. The world wide-diffusion of icons in our age is amazing. Newspapers' front pages each with headlines describing a Beatle adorned the walls. "John. The literary Beatle," "George. The quiet Beatle." The relation of these sound bytes to the Beatles as we know them was interesting. Each Beatle pretty much stayed true to their packaging.

Also posterized and shrunken to cuteness in an antiseptic future, a cartoon caricature of Jimi Hendrix hung on the wall, upside down and bent backwards into a ball, most definitely riding in a whirlwind of drugs and sound. The marketers had gone to lengths to portray this American icon as anything but dangerous. But Jimi's lifestyle and energy were not things passively consumed.

I smirked at the Beatles and said a little prayer to Jimi.

Nearly talking to myself, I told Adam, "I like the decorations. John really was the 'Literary' Beatle."

"We are the only ones here that have ever heard their songs. No one here knows what any of their English lyrics mean. They are just images of famous Americans."

We both smiled knowingly at the "Americans" part.

Sharing an insight, I plumbed deeper, "Even in the States, they only play certain ditties over and over. The heavy stuff doesn't get on the radio. The musical memory of the 1960s has been controlled and made into just another easily consumed pop era. The bands didn't sell out; they got sold out.

"Anyhow, I'm not sure what the Beatles mean to our culture anymore."

"Well they're not just another pop band." Adam declared confidently, letting me know that he was a fan who had a personal stake in their authenticity.

"No. I'm not sure anymore. They just give smiles as people enjoy their ditties. Don't they?" I pushed.

"Look at that Jimi. He wasn't into ditties. What a maniac. Too bad he died from drugs." Adam sidestepped.

"Nah." I chimed in agreement, "He had to sacrifice himself to take us on the journey he wanted to take us on. There is no way he could have gotten to where he got to -- into that little ball playing backwards -- without going all the way."

"You can't fake that level of intensity, huh." Adam agreed with my agreement.

"No way. Jim Morrison didn't write "There's a killer on the road" without knowing about it. He took himself on a real adventure. Boyce and Hart, the song writers for the Monkeys, could never have conceived of those lyrics." Boyce and Hart! I know too much about rock history

"I guess its only a shame that they died young, embarrassing us lingering half-assed, slow-livin', old farts." Adam relayed with a self-satisfied sarcastic smirk.

"Now I know the purpose of these safe little icons behind glass. They are our connection with an adventure we never meant to have. Rock provides the illusion of adventure for the dead."

"Well, Jimi will live again in us tonight!" Adam cheered.

"Righteous. My dose will be done with a toast to his burning chaos. But first though, though I know it's only a superstition...I feel like taking a drug and then going to the bathroom is a waste. So I'm going to try. I'll be right back."

Adam waved me off with a pontiff like movement of two fingers and an expression that indicated that vomit was on its way. I think he had taken his as I got up.

I smiled and winked as I turned to walk away. Or maybe Adam's expression came from my talking to him about going to the bathroom just as he was to eat drugs.

The toilets talked in this establishment. When you entered the stall a message was spoken in Japanese. And then the sound of a small waterfall played as you sat 'n' shat. Another fine cover up on our way to a clean antiseptic world.

No one, not even you, need ever hear or know what transpired in the stall. When you emerged and your friend saw you, you could pretend that you'd just been for a leisurely swim. Maybe the water was to spare the listener from the sound. Who knows? Either way, it showed a schizophrenic approach to defecation.

The hot-air hand dryer was folded over on itself so as to create a two-sided slot for your hands. Air that blew from both sides, why hadn't Americans thought of and adopted that? Ours just have circular vents that blow air out.

Author's note: You may now have seen double-sided hand dryers in America. Please excuse the out-of-date discovery. Since quite a bit of time elapsed between the writing and the publishing of this book, the text itself as become a bit of a time capsule.

Drugs existed in Japan. This clean-cut, antiseptic culture included psychedelic visions. The Japanese had made everything safe and consumable. Clean and total, this realization made me both comfortable and paranoid. Everything on this trip would be safe. I had nothing to fear but fear itself.

When I came out of the bathroom Adam was ready to go in. When he left I sucked out the last drops of his Pinky vials and poured all of mine into my drink.

How is it that the Japanese allow drugs to be sold on their clean streets? I wondered.

I read my "Kaos International" baggie that the vials had come in. It featured a declaration explaining how much their business was opposed to drugs. Subtle. Warnings can make one sense limits and then lunge desperately, desirous of that which as been forbidden. A battle between the cultural desire to control everything from shits to zits, and a tendency to entropy and the ugly truths about life and death, existed in tension in this Kaos baggie.

I took my Pinky vials with as sacramental an attitude as my atheist spirituality could muster. I invited this substance into the holies of holies, across the blood-brain barrier. The liquid was going into my personal thought machine. Grateful for all I had enjoyed in the region where imagination reigns supreme, I reverently welcomed the stranger in.

Adam stayed in the toilet so long I started to worry about him. Had he been hypnotized by the waterfall sound? All I could do was wait.

The booths Jimi and the lads from Liverpool hung over were completely occupied by girls with notebooks full of photograph stickers that they manically showed each other. Some were dressed in public school uniforms, some were not.

I had been in a five-story entertainment complex earlier. There I saw a floor of girls using photo booths. Always in costume, they would pretend to be other people and pose as if having the time of their lives. Earlier I had since seen the girls silently sending each other photos on the subway, I now had the rest of the story.

The photos came out as stickers. The girls were sticking the photo booth pictures into photo albums. Then they took photos of each other sharing photos, and sent them to each other on their phones. How fractal like, how circular; photos of photos of photos being taken; how bizarre.

The posed photos of the girls sharing photos served as the documented memories that cemented their relationships. Their social life was an elongated, "smile for the camera" moment. They were smiling because they were supposed to be smiling. They weren't doing anything that was fun except taking pictures of them looking like they were having fun. The image sufficed.

All models' smiles are forced. Weren't these poses for the camera somehow false? When one pretends to be happy, are they? The capturing of the moments of fun was the fun. Perhaps this was a new form of happiness; a greater happiness, happiness without reasons.

Pausing for a moment I thought I'd better make up a name for these photos-turned-into-stickers-for-trade and collector's albums. After a quick attempt at word manipulation, the words just came together: "Purest happy-feeling stickers." I liked it. It had a Japanese ring.

Fortunately, two-dimensional images don't talk and move yet. That could have forced them to include content with their pictures. I don't think I'm being a curmudgeon here. I don't see that pictures taken in costume, when received by the intended target, convey any substantive message.

Another reason we're fortunate that two-dimensional images don't talk and move yet is that if they did, unfrozen chards of glass would fly out of Jimi's chaos-moment poster and cut the cute "purest happy - feeling sticker" girls. Perhaps they'd smile, wave, and pose in front of the blood and chaos.

Will stickers of people you've never met suffice for a circle of friends? Facebook is anonymous. How about sending the photos to a random computer photo exchanger. The computer photoshops together years of pictures of us -- and wa-la! We are instantly really good happy friends with long shared memories. Petting your composite friend's image on a screen demonstrates the depth of our nostalgia. Surface as tear-jerker.

Americans are big into knowing, and somehow relating to, our celebrities. Are these relationships any more real than the sticker relationships? Isn't celebrity-following just a lame relation to mass-produced consumer items? The purest happy-feeling stickers girls were Andy Warhols.

Many of these outlaw rockers in the posters tie us into a set of memories and attitudes that we, as audience members, take pride in, but never really lived.

There is only one person that should ever hang a Jim Morrison poster: Jim Morrison. Perhaps you could existentially justify his band mates and his parents, if they're still alive, possessing such posters. Also people on enough drugs to be open to these icon's musical experiences can have pictures of celebrities like Jim Morrison. I'd like to think my adventures make Morrison's songs more than just jingles to me.

Sticking stickers and sending costume pictures is a celebration of the surface beyond what an American could stomach. I've seen the purest happy-feeling sticker booths in the States. But they've never caught on. At best they are glorified passport photo booths, even with the sticker functions. People don't realize how important the booths are supposed to be. Americans are too hung up on the real for photos to be so important in a relationship.

Japanese pop runs deep. It is a reassurance. It is a digital way of feeling connected in the Tokyo matrix. Perhaps in this increasingly digital world, the future as intimacy by quantity of stickers and photos shared is America's future too. My loved ones are mostly remembered through images.

Still, the mature me prefers real things to pop. How would I define real things? That is a good question. Is there a reason that having read a book is seen to be a legitimate learning activity and seeing a movie isn't?

Here's a stab. Reality is something that is heavily nuanced. It is better than stickers because it stimulates thinking and involves a variety of emotions. Celebrities don't have in depth interactions with us. Movie experiences fail to reach the profundity of life over time. Happy sticker photos cover more than they reveal.

When will America learn the lessons of Andy Warhol? When will I be able to enjoy my pop icons with no intimations of "real experience"? The stars of my generation worked to communicate meaning. American Idol's corporate pop bands let us know that the medium is the message.

Who am I kidding? MTV jingles also sold my generation it's bands, brands, outfits, and outlooks on life. Christ, I have a logo of a band tattooed on my arm! That was marketing.

Yes, strife and confusion are signs of a life well lived. As much as I enjoy the pure superficial rapture of pop art – the rat-a-tat-tat of a Roy Lichtenstein war image for example – I understand that these plastic icons make a point. I cannot and I will not give affection to "Hello Kitty." It scares me. My resistant 1960s American upbringing endures.

About an hour later Adam emerged from the bathroom! I asked no questions. We went downstairs and decided to walk to the park. I hadn't entered a park in Tokyo, but Asia is known for having fantastic parks in the middle of their cities.

The parks aim at a size large enough that within them you cannot see anything of the surrounding city. These natured cloisters evoke the quiet space of nature as the necessary corollary to the urban jungle. I've always believed that if gang kids could see stars and nature they would lose their animosity and stop fighting due to that paradigm shift.

The Japanese likely connect to nature in a way that Americans do not. In contrast to our abstracted playground parks, theirs attempt to completely remove you from the city's frequency and take away from the urban story of your life. Asian parks connect you to the context of nature.

How does this nature-centered perspective coincide with Japanese pop glorification of all things artificial? Perhaps our investment in the importance of the unique individual means we do not need to immerse ourselves in the natural world. Angst and the very individual striving for epoch self-actualization and glory take you away from the natural order. Asians don't feel they've lost themselves in nature; perhaps they don't feel they have an important individual self that the pop world of mass commerce misses.

But as with the accent that the black-American waitress used at Denny's, a subtle wall distinguishes my interaction from the world from those from other cultures. I will never understand what photo stickers, pin-ups phone porn on subways, "Hello Kitty," or parks mean to the Japanese.

"Elvis impersonators congregate here during the day." Adam informed me, breaking my interior chain of thought. Snapped from my interior monologue, I noticed how many fewer people surrounded since after walking just a few blocks away from Shinjuki.

Amazed, I exclaimed, "Wow! How can they conceive of the cultural roots of Elvis? That is why I love the Japanese, I exclaimed. They are pure post-modern pop. They are unconcerned about the real. There is no center. They seem to stop at the surface. No other culture could have invented 'Hello Kitty.' She is a dissociative testament to vacuity. 'The Kitty' has no story. Pure image. Pure pop."

Then I revisited my interior conversation with Adam, "I don't know how a people that are so dedicated to parks that integrate you into nature can seem to be so very astronaut at other times."

As we entered the park, nature started to sway in spirals. The silhouettes of large bonsai-like trees violently danced in the wind. Shiva the destroyer, represented in a force field of physics blowing the branches, disturbed the seemingly real veil framing our reality. Shiva was attempting to have us see the patterns beneath the surface of our consciously concerned lives.

Adam had to keep reminding me to slow down. The persistence of my feet's ambition often outstrips my mind's ability to rein them in. My feet have their own agenda. Walking slightly behind Adam was the only way I could to go at the slower pace the two of us had decided upon.

"Do you see the wind?" I asked.

"No. But I see the trees moving. Is that seeing the wind?" Adam either mocked or hinted at deeper meaning.

"They are connected." I offered with trust.

"We are engulfed in the same wind." Adam uttered without humor, as though talking to himself. "It's nice to see wind. It's like breathing. I remember breathing. The shit is starting to kick in."

"No doubt. I'm not only seeing things differently, I am starting to have insights. Like, that buildings deceive us into thinking that everything isn't moving." I mused with a strange new roaming quality to my speech.

"Right. Nothing is still. All things are being affected and worn by time in a dance of life and death at all times." Adam affirmed

"Scary. And, yet, it's nice to be connected at another level." I uttered this, partially out of the fear of knowing that I was going off on a trip with someone I barely knew.

"Dark cues you into the larger contexts of our existence. The cycles of night and day are important reminders. Night is especially important."

When Adam said this, the Dark Ages came to my mind. "I often wonder how we are different from the people that had to endure the long night, without the option of artificial light."

"The nights put us in a context of the infinite and the finite. People without lights probably had less hope." Adam realized.

"And less illusions about safety." I guessed.

"Right on!" Adam exclaimed in a way that countered our move towards the interior and contemplative, "We are groovin' together. Two minds chewing on the same awarenesses and thoughts."

"Nice to be hanging with you, bro." I offered.

"Ditto. I'm glad we got hooked up."

Just then, while looking over a small lake with the moonlight in it, Adam's cell phone rang.

As he spoke to his friend about some business or other, I drummed on the bridge railing. The bridge was made of brown wood and went over a small stream. My drumming was patterned on the spirals of the dancing, breathing trees on both sides of the stream.

He made a second call to his wife Aya to tell her he'd be back in the middle of the night or later and to not wait up for him.

Drums, and the ability to conjure fractals through them, are dividends from my long - term investment in rhythm. I've played drums so long that pattern weaving is burned into my essence. I can easily lose myself in the trances of the beats my hands conjure.

Perhaps my drumming calms me because it reassures me of my having some special skill to call my own or it is evidence of my past. Perhaps it is calming because it ties me in with tribes of old and the rhythmic roots of the universe.

Beyond the concerns about pop art and thoughts about Jesus and words and noise, lives a heartbeat of existence. Every day we all subtly and slowly burn and die like Jim Morrison did, only it goes so slowly that we don't see it. My beat was the hypnotic flame that drew the moths in to their end. Rather than a trap, the beats seduce to enlightenment, based on an acceptance of death.

For brief moments I disappeared into the beat. My hands worked the rhythm themselves. I was just immersed in listening to the beat. Then I would realize that I was playing and my thoughts about playing would obscure the sound of the beats. Then I'd dive back into the beats. Then, a thought; going in and out of consciousness of drumming itself created a rhythm.

At one point I realized that the word surface, like the one that I was drumming on, was a combination of two words. "Surf" and "face." Waves crashed on rocks with faces in them, wearing them smooth. In my imagination, waves landed on rocks made of faces, slowly eroding them. Then a little surfer came through the wave! I laughed out loud. It took a while for that image to subside, but eventually I subsided back into the rhythm.

I came out of a nice drumming session with my eyes closed to see Adam standing in front of me.

He apologized for being away on the phone. He was ready to submerge with me.

-----Capsule six: Intimacy----

As we walked deeper into the park I asked if it would be okay if I took a seat. "I want to get grounded. Feel the earth."

"Cool." After much silence Adam asked, "What are you looking at?"

"The stick figures on that walk sign have been moving. It's not that they are moving much, but this stuff is great. Can we walk?"

"Like the people in the sign?" Adam asked with a broad smile.

"Yeah." We began walking again and then he turned to me and brought our meandering to a halt.

"John?" Adam asked too earnestly.

"Yes." I replied, afraid of what was going to come next.

"What do you think of me?"

Wow. What a direct question. I was uncomfortable. No one had asked me that question so directly in a long time, if ever. We instantly froze and faced each other.

"You're a really admirable person." I offered vaguely.

"No, really. Do you think my life is on an okay path?"

"I don't think you know how spectacular you are or your life has been. It is amazing that you are able to ask yourself if what you are doing is the greatest thing. It means you're in the not far from doing the greatest thing. That is something that you've earned by seeing possibilities and going for it. Not everyone considers international options as real possibilities.

"Adam, you are brave to be living without a built-in identity made out of a culture. Most people, they do what their society expects. They are comfortable and watch football and go to work and don't question what they could be doing. You have definitely not gotten to where you are by blind accident."

At that point, my confrontation with this too direct topic somewhat disposed of, I restarted our walking down the dark trail in the park.

There were so few lights that we could see a couple of stars in the dark of the sky. They seemed to be following me.

"I don't know." Adam continued his questioning, "I think that I am getting too comfortable. I used to be that adventurous person you described, but now I am doing what I am doing because it is convenient. I'm not sure it's the greatest thing I could be doing with my life.

"The new job will be great. My house is really in a nice neighborhood. But is this where I want to make my stand and home?

"After three more years I'll have all the rights of a full citizen. Except voting…which I've never done anyways."

"You've never voted anywhere?" I asked incredulously. This act being so tied into my identity, Adam's lack of tie-in to politics shocked, momentarily disgusted, and confused me.

"No. I left the States when I was 16 and haven't really been back since. Foreigners can't vote anywhere. I've lived in so many places that I can't make up my mind about staying here. So maybe I shouldn't be allowed to vote here.

"I'm not really friendly with the Japanese, but this is a nice place and it would give me a pension, and, health care. And that is really important when you get older. I just don't know what I'm doing with my life. It feels like I'm not doing anything but getting by for no real reason.

"One of the other professors that I work with actually told me that I don't have to teach anything. You can have the students sit and read the textbook and then give them oral exams. If you give them a lot of A's you won't hear anything from them.

"But that would be boring. So I'll work on my workbook and program really hard. But after a few years, it'll be no sweat, no challenge, uninteresting."

"That sounds like a great plan, perfecting your art, your teaching." I countered, aware that my compulsive sugarcoating mechanic had kicked in.

"Yeah," Adam agreed, "Maybe my life is settling down and I don't know what that feels like. I am afraid of it. Where do you get your passion when you just have a safe routine?"

"I don't know. That's a hard one. I guess one benefit of staying on this path is that, if you stay in this place long enough, you'll eventually feel a part of it. Even if you can't, you might actually want to vote. You might care about the community and think about its long-term health, as an extension of your life, and not just a place you hit, like a tourist, consume and leave. I've put a lot of blood, sweat and tears into America. I don't think I've ever missed an election. In fact, I usually work on them."

And for the first time I had the realization that I was much more conservative than Adam, much more concerned with place, economics, and the geo-political. Adam was nearly entirely consumed with what was good for Adam than geo-politics. That sort of thing did not enter into his decision making.

"I've thought about going over to China. That is where I was thinking of going when I came to Japan seven years ago." He announced, jarring my vague memory of his having said it before.

"If you keep teaching here you'll probably get summers off. You could go to South America during the summers." I offered.

"Yep. That's true. But I told you, just touching a culture isn't enough for me; to really understand it you have to live the language. The Japanese aren't my favorites. I don't think that I could ever feel settled living amongst the Japanese. They'll never let me be a part of their community."

"And, as a foreigner in Japan, I guess you couldn't really ever experience the joy of voting." I tried to joke. But Adam was deep in thought over this issue.

"Yeah, voting." Adam mustered with only half of his attention. In the back of my mind I was still thinking about my connection to America. I think that Adam had hit upon the very importance of place. The Japanese had it in spades.

The Japanese people belonged here. They were not alienated strangers in a strange land. Adam and I truly couldn't belong outside of America. At least I couldn't.

Out of fear of seeming too patriotic, too parochial, I kept my feelings about his being in the wrong nation to myself. And checked what I thought might be another important variable.

"How about the woman you're married to. You live together, right?" I queried.

"We're married and live together. But I didn't ask her to marry me. When I told her about my visa problem, she just offered to marry me. I told her that we can do it in ceremony, and that'd be good enough for me.

"Anyhow, she's not, the one. She isn't the one I want to spend the rest of my life with. She is not someone I can naturally call pet names. She said she understood my feelings and that we could just be lovers. That was enough for her.

"So we got married and moved in together. Only now I'm sure that she's starting to get more and more emotionally attached. She started to ask me where I was going at night and stuff. We had an argument and now she doesn't usually ask, but I call her when I go out and... but she's getting more attached.

"She is a resting place. Maybe I need to break free and look for that real one. I mean, I mean, it's the same thing as my job. I'm pretty much just having sex with her because she's convenient."

"How long have you known each other and lived together?" I inquired.

"We've lived together for two years and known each other for six. We've been good friends for most of those six."

"Why don't you stay and try to see if you could make your relationship with her work? You guys have a lot of history. She sounds like a good person who really cares about you. And you must know each other well. Maybe that's enough. Perhaps a heavier love will develop as you get older."

"When I wake up I'm not excited to see her. She knows it. I could never be in love with her."

Adam started speaking to himself a bit maniacally, "Such a fine line separates loving someone and being 'in love' with someone, especially unrequited love. Our relationship is one-sided and so very sharp.

"I feel terrible when I tell her, 'I love you but I'm not in love with you.' She always reassures me that, 'It's not your fault you're not in love with me.'

"The devil must be happy." Adam concluded.

I gave him the advice I give myself. "I don't remember much from high school, but I remember one teacher that said 'love is a choice.' He said that every morning when he woke up he made a conscious decision to love the woman he had woken up next to for so many years. He'd just say, 'I love her,' to himself.

"Don't you think you could decide to love her? I mean, I mean, you'll never find that perfect One. Maybe that is a myth. Maybe you should love the one you're with. If you wake up and tell yourself that she isn't the one you love, you won't love her, et cetera, then you won't ever love her. But if you try . . ."

"I've told her repeatedly that I don't love her and I could never love her. I mean, I love her as a friend. A lot. But, no..." Adam explained.

"Ouch!" I thought. He tells her that he could never love her. What a weird relationship. This man is awesome. He may be crippled emotionally or whatever, but he has the capacity to be brutally honest. If I could do that, I wouldn't linger in the permanent quandary about my relationship status, that I'm always in.

I've never been able to be totally honest with any of my girlfriends for fear of hurting them. The closest I ever come to honesty is being passive aggressive; trying to bust up the relationship by being a jerk. Adam told her he could never love her directly! Ouch! Wow! I am impressed.

Adam continued right over my thoughts. "I mean, I tell her why I go to Thailand, that I go for sex. She knows. But after the last time I went, she asked me she asked me to stop telling her that I could never love her. So I don't say it anymore. But I don't want to lead her into hoping for something that isn't coming.

"And worrying about her falling in love has mess up my sex with her. I mean, we have good sex. But, I am always asking if it is right? For her? For me?"

"Maybe you can't love her because you can't love a woman that takes that much shit from you!" I blurted out. "I'm sorry . . . I didn't mean to say that. But, it sounds like you're really brutal to her."

"No. I'm just honest. I mean, my father -- he's been married six times and now travels around with his wife in a mobile home -- he tells me that the problem is me. He says that I'm fucked up. That I can't love. He says the problem is not with the girls, but with me. But he's one to talk. All of his many marriages were serious, right? He tells me he's really loved each one and the current one is the real one.

"Maybe he's right. But the way I see it, either you entirely love them or you don't. Aya isn't the one. And maybe I'll never find the one. I'm getting older so I worry that it will never happen. And, the more time I spend with Aya, the older I get."

I tried to fix my new friend by making him see the folly of romanticism, "I just think that that concept of 'The One' is a destructive concept. Love goes through phases. There is that early lusty love phase. But that gives way to bills and the mundane. Then there is that deeper love of sharing a life."

"She knows, and I know, that it isn't going to work out, John. Didn't I tell you? I DON'T LOVE HER THAT WAY. God, you're like a fuckin' machine. 'Couldn't you just lie to yourself? Just pretend and it'll be true.' Eegads, what an attitude you have.

"There is a One out there!" Adam pleaded. "I had one and lost her. Now she's married and I'll never get her back. But I still know that Aya could never equal or be the love of my life."

Adam was so hot under the collar that I just fell into silence. After a bit, he turned to me with calm and compassion.

"So should I leave Aya? I don't want her to feel bad. I do care about her. But being romantic with her is hard. And if she had a baby! That would be the end of my life."

"Have you discussed what you'd do?" I re-engaged.

"Yeah. I told her I'd want an abortion. A baby would be a terrible thing, it would land-lock me. I wouldn't have any more choices. It would be a disaster. She says she agrees and would do it. But I'm not so sure she would."

"If not, you and Aya would be stuck together for at least eighteen years. And there is always a risk. I really believe that if you take that risk and she gets pregnant and she decides to have the baby, you should stay together till it's grown. The baby's life is your responsibility. I'm conservative that way."

"No. I've decided," I declared. "I think the two of you shouldn't be together. Not if you're not willing to raise a baby with her and see no hope of staying with her. I mean, you wouldn't work at making this relationship last because you don't love her. So there's no long-term hope there. Every day invested in the relationship is a day wasted if you're not going to stay." I was trying to understand him from his point of view and without judgment.

"But, we do like each other's company, and we live together and…"

"It's convenient." I finished his thought. "I'd just feel sorry for a child that came out of such an arrangement. Every time you have sex with her you are betting against a twenty year commitment and the misery of the child."

Rather than make a choice, Adam was just repeating himself, "I don't know if what I'm doing with my life is meaningful right now. I mean, am I just hanging out? My new job is going to give me more free time. Is there something else that I'm supposed to do?

"I've thought about working on playing guitar with all my free time. I mean, really dedicating myself to learning how to read and write and play properly. I made the CD. But my songwriting gets stuck in the same patterns because I don't read music. Right now I just diddle on the guitar. If I learn to read music with my free time, I could write some worthwhile music."

I could barely keep from laughing at the idea that playing guitar could give someone entering their late thirtees meaning in life. This was a child's thinking. Real men don't consider guitar lessons wrestling with destiny. Adam epitomized the waywardness of today's males for me. Feeling cautious, I bit my tongue and approved of what he said.

"Working seriously on your guitar is probably a good idea. You need to invest in something. Just diddling, as you said, doesn't get you anywhere. My drumming doesn't improve because for years I've just putzed around.

Adding dignity to my approval, I continued, "There is something beautiful about an old person who has really refined their craft. Someone who's put a lifetime into that one craft and is able to make exceptional music or art or whatever. It is a pure refined beauty."

"Maybe you're right." Adam said with a small lift in pep. "Maybe I'll just take this year to enjoy the comfort and the time my new job allows me. I'll dedicate myself to classical guitar, which is something I've been meaning to do forever. And I can work on getting my workbook done."

No matter how silly I considering his messing around on guitar as a meaning of life, the questions Adam asked hit home.

I shared my thoughts, "I am often filled with despair over the wasting of my life. I don't know if life is supposed to have a meaning, but it lays heavily on me too.

"My book and the books I'm working on are meaningful to me. Most people find meaning in their relationships, but I'm not taking care of anyone. Like, if you were taking care of your kids you'd feel needed. You'd have a purpose. But Soo Hee, my fiancée, is always far away and independent. She doesn't need me.

"And, beyond not finding meaning through it," I continued, "my relationship is one of turmoil and anguish and just generally not very good. I have been with Soo Hee for seven years, but we're separated by a lot of water. Literally. She lives in Korea and I live in Los Angeles."

These days when I tell strangers, I hedge. I say we've been together for six years. It sounds less ridiculous that I've been waiting for her for six years rather than seven. In fact it's coming up on eight years that I've been waiting for Soo Hee. It has been really painful.

Oh, my Gawd, Tommers, I have lasted typing for sooooo long. But now it is time to pee. It was a really commendable stretch of effort. It looks like mixing drugs and typing was a good gamble. I'm able to type under the influence after all. And the story has barely begun – this will be fun!

Okay. Returned from the head with a slurpy drink and coffee! I love this place!

John

"Why doesn't sooni... What is her name?"

"Soo Hee. S-o-o space H-e-e." I always hated spelling out her name. It made me feel the futility of my relationship with her and the distance between us. The spelling was always done with a burning rage and indignity.

"Why hasn't Soo Hee come to America yet?"

"Well the snare is that there is always one more thing before she's coming. There was the rice farm lawsuit, and her restaurant, and waiting for her sister to get married, and selling properties.

"And it seems that it just goes on and on and it seems that you can't get off. And the whole thing seems like an obvious parable in that the more time you sink into a bad arrangement the more time of your life is spent alone and wasted. Except it's not a parable, its my life that I feel is wasted.

"About two weeks ago, at night, we were driving through a part of Seoul together called Itaewon. It's where the military and other sordid people go for nightlife. I mentioned stopping and walking. The traffic was making our progress nearly non-existent anyhow.

"She said 'No. Why? So I can go chasing the cheap girl again? What was the Canadian girl's name?' She asked.'

"This was a reference to the last woman I went out with before Soo Hee. This has become the only thing that she ever mentions to me with a feeling of spite. When she and I were just friends, Soo Hee had once driven me from club to club to find a Canadian girl I had gone out with.

"I didn't even remember the Canadian girl's name anymore. And Soo Hee rarely mentions her. But the thing that disgusted me is the way that Soo Hee called her 'The cheap girl.' At that moment I had to ask myself, what do I have in common with someone who uses the phrase 'the cheap girl?' What have I done with my life? Who have I thrown it away on?

"The night she cursed the Canadian, I nearly cried out loud in our shared bed. Actually, Soo Hee laid in the other room. She likes to sleep on the floor with the air conditioning on when it's hot. All of my thirties wasted and gone. Wasted on such a stupid dream.

"The last time I was free was the night I first met my Soo Hee in Itaewon. That was it. I have been on a shelf ever since.

"Oh, the shame the indignity." I concluded melodramatically imitating Lee Marvin in the film, the Wild Ones.

Then I thought about how, if I had had kids when I first met Soo Hee, my kids could be six to seven years old by now. Instead, if I have kids, they're going to have an old Dad.

Adam asked the obvious questions, "You wouldn't consider living in Korea?"

"No. Her English is better than my Korean could ever be. And, anyhow, I'm not interested in Korea. There's nothing there for me. They are very racist when it comes to mixed couples and it'd just be way easier for us to blend into America."

"So what're you going to do?" Adam asked.

"Actually, I planned this trip after she, for the first time ever, said that she didn't think we were as close anymore and suggested we break up. It had been ten months since she'd come to see me. And I am damn sick of it. But then we decided that a phone break up was too weak. We decided to see each other one last time and break up in person.

"We planned this trip to Japan together, but her passport had expired. That's why I'm out here with you alone in Japan.

"So, anyhow, this is a break-up tour. But I can guarantee you we won't break up. We've been through so many confirmed break-ups. I won't be able to, like you, tell her that I can't love her and that it's over. And, so I'll plead for it not to end and we'll stay together. That's how this movie ends."

Adam just stayed silent.

"To top things off," I continued, "these days I keep thinking I want a family. And I am so out of touch that I can't even tell anymore if I really want a family or if I just want a way out of my relationship with Soo Hee that doesn't involve hurting her or confronting her.

"If I stay with her, I can't have kids. She has known that she was sterile since she was old enough to know what sterile means."

"Oh, cool." Adam finally interjected. "So you can do it to her and never have to wear a condom or worry about her getting pregnant." It was a revolting statement.

"God, Adam! Soo Hee is a remarkably strong and wonderful woman." I shot out, angry and defensive for that last slight to her honor. "She knew that she was sterile from an early age and so had to think up how to survive in a world where women are only prized for their male offspring.

"Sexism is outrageous in Korea. Women without babies don't have identities. Women friends in Korea don't refer to each other by their first names or last names. They call each other 'Mother of so and so.'

"If a woman doesn't produce a male, the husband is allowed to get a second wife. Then he can send her back, the first wife, and not return the dowry.

"Soo Hee had to 'de-breast' herself like Lady Macbeth and find a way to fit into the male world. She has used her brain to amass a fortune and position in a world with no place for her.

"'Doing it to her without a condom has nothing to do with anything!' I said with obvious outrage.

"Sorry." Adam said, with a look of true contrition.

I only barely acknowledged this apology with a hint of a facial expression of disappointment. To get things back to the appropriate level of sensitivity, I made a heartfelt statement.

"I think she might love me because I am the only person who she can be totally feminine with. She has had to do battle in the male world for a long time. With me she doesn't have to battle for position."

I decided to take a leap. "To be brutally honest, my thinking goes partially like this. She has money . . ." My discomfort with discussing this matter was evident by my momentarily positioning my pointed horizontal index finger along my closed lips. But I continued, "Our plan has always been for us to quit work and just travel together. That has been our ultimate plan for years now.

"But since I met her I have traveled less than ever and do nothing but work and remain alone. Well, if I'm going to be working every year for the rest of my life anyhow, I might as well have a family.

"The fantasy of endless travel and freedom is a big pull for someone that has so little use for the mundane work world as I do. But, maybe I'm getting older and it's time for that childish fantasy of never having to work or grow up to end. Maybe part of a full adult life is taking on responsibilities."

My outwardly expressed inner dialogue continued, "But then I think about working and struggling through twenty-five years of hard labor to have kids. And when they're grown they'll move to a different city and I won't even see them again anyhow. That is a bad investment."

On safer ground than talking about the importance of Soo Hee's finances to my staying with her I took refuge in a commonplace.

"Families used to be a much better deal. My family isn't close. I don't even speak to my sister. I have issues with family generally."

Then I exploded the commonplace, "My family was torn apart by my mother's death. I haven't felt at home on the planet since."

"Wow. That's heavy." Adam said giving me his full attention.

Wow! I lied about my mother being dead and just let it sit there and milked that for all of the huge sentiment it entails. Where did that come from? It seemed to arise out of a part of myself I didn't know about.

"Okay?" Adam asked pleadingly to ask if he might let the funeral mood pass.

Perhaps I mentioned my mother being dead because I always felt like people would accuse me of being a whore when I mentioned that Soo Hee had money and I put that into my equation of waiting for her. No one would press you on an issue like that if the topic were changed to the death of your mother.

I didn't stop with claiming my mother was dead. In a preemptive defense, I further justified abstract and rational considerations when choosing a mate.

"By the way, it may not seem romantic, but I totally feel that geo-political historical thinking should enter into your life choices. And that includes who you choose as a mate.

"To live you must have a nation that facilitates economic strength. Your decisions, even love decisions, should consider their impact on the economic well-being of your nation.

"Remember, without an infrastructure and a dependable system of law, utilities, and economics, our secure and blissful lives would fall into an abyss. Without this stuff you wouldn't have time to ponder questions of identity.

"Even our emblematic beat hippy archetype Jack Kerouac," I flinched thinking he wouldn't know who that was, but saw his attention was still focused on me as we paced down the park trail. "Even romantic Jack Kerouac depended on an economy where he could always find a job in the next town to support his vagabond lifestyle."

"With Soo Hee's money, I am not a burden to society. We'd import money into the States. I would not think of importing an impoverished person to our nation. And we could not be as happy without money as we could be loaded. Love should consider economics."

Knowing that this might seem like an overly wrought justification for my including money in my considerations of choosing Soo Hee, I asserted, "And I'm not just avoiding my feelings by putting love in its economic context or some such Freudian crap. The economics of your relationship are important."

"Feelings are not the center of the universe. Our civilization didn't advance on the basis of feelings. That's a 1960s romantic thought. Politics and economics always pervade the decision-making processes of conscious thinkers.

"I also wouldn't bring someone into our nation from a hostile culture. As alien as the Korean culture is, it does not have a historic grudge to settle against America. Korea has no sense of Jihad. Choosing Korean spouses does not weaken America or our civilization.

"Values exist in the context of a working civilization. They rise and fall with civilizations. I love my values. To not consider the economic and political bases of your thoughts is to not have your thoughts grounded, to not be conscious of the deep and social roots of your thoughts."

"I guess that makes me unconscious." Adam grumbled. That short reply to my long defensive rant, didn't convince me that he was listening, understood me, agreed, or had found the argument as distasteful as I assumed he might. It certainly ran counter to his search for 'The One."

Adam broke the silence, "Even with all of that going, I say if you really loved Soo Hee, it's a done deal. All that economic and cultural support with economy shit just doesn't wash for me. I don't trust your logical love or any of that stuff you're talking about. Relationships run deeper into you than any of that stuff."

We disagreed. And, I knew that my position of considering geo-political and economic factors when choosing a mate were strange to most people.

"I do love her tremendously." I insisted.

"You're full of shit." Adam cut me no slack at all.

"We've been together for seven years. What the hell? You don't know how I feel or what I feel." I argued.

"Staying together doesn't mean you love her. It doesn't mean that you even ever loved her."

"Well I do! She is a great woman." I said raising my voice.

"Fine." He was going to stop pressing me, but we both knew that my proofs of my romantic love were a ways off from proving that I was 'in love.'

"I just also love other things too, like my civilization." I defended myself, "I just think about the economic and geo-political consequences of relationships. I don't just make decisions based on emotion alone."

"That's passion for ya." Adam cut with ironic nasty biting sarcasm.

"Well, and it sounds to me like you could never love your woman or any woman but the One." We were having our real first fight. It was getting brutal.

Adam looked down like he was taking his chastening to heart. I was just hurt and needed to turn the tide from the defensive to the offensive. I hoped I hadn't wounded him or our friendship too much. I wondered what he would say next.

"Yeah." He said chillingly and then looked up and straight into my eyes as he continued, "And I'm starting to have to drink to have sex with Aya."

And for the second time in the last fifteen minutes I sort of felt pity for poor Adam. Then he mumbled in a melancholy and deflated tone that scared me, "We've been going I circles in the park for a long time."

"Well, we're both going in circles and stuck at a fork in the road at the same time." And with a soft tone of sympathy, I continued, "But it sounds to me like you and Aya may have hit a brick wall."

He didn't respond.

I told him that the way out of the park's loop was to just take a straight line in any direction, cut across paths, and walk until we found the way out, "Of course that's easier done in parks than in real life."

"But which way do we want to go to get back to Shinjuki?" My host wondered.

"When we get outside these woods, we'll be able to orient ourselves, to see where we are and where to go." I said as though departing some double entendre concerning our life choices.

"You know, I thought that we'd get higher." Adam said with an air of disappointment. He was reflective and down.

I told him that I thought it was a great trip. I wasn't that high, but I definitely had a keen awareness of my thoughts, if no visuals. It was about as much of a high as I had imagined.

And though we'd reached no conclusion, we had really spoken of some issues that were important to us. We'd discussed our relationship issues and rehearsed our existential fears. And I reassured him that I still considered our friendship solid even though we had had somewhat heated exchanges and slightly disrespected each other's reasons for saying in our relationships.

Adam temporarily raised his head in the middle of his funk over our weak high and looked me in the eyes. "No doubt. We have to disagree. I really like to see what other people think. It's cool. And I appreciate your honesty."

"And I yours."

"And anyhow," Adam continued as his head slunk back down, "I'm not saying it wasn't a good experience. Its just that the last time I got much higher."

I took his disappointment at our evening personally. He suggested that maybe we should go back and get some more drugs of a different type. His debating whether or not this was wise reassured me that his disappointment was strictly disappointed with the high. He wasn't sick of me or us.

I agreed to do more psychedelics with him if he wanted to. If you agree to a night out on the town with someone -- doing this kind of thing -- you do not bail out on them. Some relationship rules are simple.

Besides, regardless of rules, I was stoked to have a new plan, goal, and destination.

"Remember, though," I offered, "you shouldn't compare this moment to what you expected or got last time. Appreciate now for what it is. It's like comparing our relationships with fantasies of what else might exist out there for us and be preferable. It drives us crazy."

"Okay, but what I took last time got me way, way higher and tripped out. Believe me! Let's go back to Shinjuki and try to reach a new level of high."

In terms of highs, what we've done was about all I could imagine. While I was reassuring Adam that our high was great, and my expectations had been met, he knew we had barely lifted off.

Capsule Seven: Silence

As we walked back to get round two of psychedelics, Adam told me more about Aya.

Tragically, Aya was raped by her father from the age of seven on. It continued till she was fourteen. Her father used to come into her bedroom in the middle of the night and force himself upon her. When she slept with her father and mother, he would finger her in the same bed as her mother. Her father was bathing her in the bathtub and washing out her vagina until she was thirteen.

"She isn't sure if her mother knew." Adam conveyed matter-of-factly.

"How on earth could the mother not have known? If she didn't know, it was because she didn't want to know. Even then, it would be impossible." I enjoyed my indignation.

"That's what I've told her." Adam replied meekly.

"It isn't normal for a father to be in the bathroom when his fourteen-year-old daughter is bathing."

"Thirteen. The bathing stopped at thirteen."

This correction let me know that Adam had heard about this often enough to have it incorporated into his life knowledge base. Aya's story had become a part of his story.

"Either way. Dad, Mom, Aya. They all knew, and knew that the others knew." I, again, seemed to take some delight in my high horse of righteousness.

Adam pushed the story forward, "The bummer is that Aya's father had had a stroke at an early age. He was fifty-two. It was related to his heavy smoking. He became a partially paralyzed invalid. He needed to be fed and wiped, but didn't say much anymore. He lived for five years in that reduced state of independence. Four years and seven months and thirteen days to be exact." This was rattled off as automatically as a slogan.

"And," I guessed the horrible conclusion. "Aya took care of him after his stroke, didn't she?"

"It's the Japanese way." Adam said by way of confirmation. "If you don't take care of your parents... Well, it is darn near unthinkable. There were no other children."

"God. Jesus, what an unadulterated nightmare." The horror began to set in.

"That's what I figure too. Aya said it was bitter-sweet as she somehow still loved him."

"Oh, my God. Give me a break. Loved a man that raped her for years as a child?" My indignity was perhaps getting in the way of my listening.

"The family bond is strong." Adam offered by way of explanation.

"Not in my family." I rattled off. But upon even a slight amount of reflection, I had to back out of my statement.

"But there is an incipient connection that keeps us uniquely tied to each other. My sister has run away, she lives in France and never calls my father or me. But I'm sure her absentee family's existence still eats at her. I hope so. I would say I don't care, but it would be a lie.

"As horrible as it is, I guess I could see how Aya could still love her father."

"Its unfortunate that it wasn't all hate. It probably would have been easier if she only hated him." Adam lamented.

"That's true." I said trying to listen.

"When her father finally died Aya and her mother lived together, but they never spoke. They lived in a small apartment. The mother usually sat in a chair near the entrance. At least, that's where she was always sitting when Aya came home from her work as a librarian."

"God what a perfect job for Aya." I thought. Enforcing silence amidst all of those words, the job of a librarian, fit perfectly with the deafening silence that must have pervaded her home.

"Aya cooked her mother's food and did her laundry. But in all the years that they lived together they never spoke."

I intuitively understood why Aya had never spoken to her mother again; there would have just been never-ending glass-shattering screaming that would have deafened both of them: incredible unimaginable painful screaming. Why bother?

"Ours is the first place Aya has lived without a parent. She didn't tell her mother she was getting married or that she was moving before it was done. She didn't consult her mother about the marriage. She just finally told her that she was moving out and getting married. Resigned, her mother made no objection to her moving out."

"So her getting you a visa by marrying you wasn't all about her rescuing you." I uttered softly, confirming the obvious.

"It wasn't. But it's hard to live with her. Sometimes she just withdrawals into herself and won't communicate. I can't reach her when she's in that place. That is a space that I can't enter. I can't. Even if she would talk with me about it, I could never understand the depth of her horror."

"I guess weak empathy is as close as we can ever come to feeling another's pain," I realized out loud. "Too lonely. I couldn't know, but I do know that her silence is profound."

"You can almost feel it. When she's in that place, it's a thick invisible wall. One of those total 'don't talk about the elephant in the living room' things." Adam confirmed.

"Does she spend a lot of time in that space?"

"She's there pretty often." He nodded.

"Does it happen when you are affectionate?"

"No our sex life is pretty good!" Adam enthused.

Wow! I said affection and he heard sex. I finally understood why Aya was with Adam. There is safety in silence. Adam provided sex without any emotional content.

Adam said that Aya never liked it when he told her bluntly that he could never love her. But he had told her enough that she knew. On some level, that whole dynamic must have been very comforting to her. If I associated love with child rape, I would be skittish too.

Now the only missing piece of the puzzle was what happened to Adam that he was drawn to such a relationship - one that precluded intimacy.

After a long silence, I blurted, "What an horrific story."

"I only wish it was just a story." He instinctually replied.

"I sure am glad it's just a story for me. It gives new meaning to the phrase 'History is a nightmare from which I am trying to awake.' Jesus."

The silence that followed made the last one look like nothin'. Finally, I found a way out.

"An appreciation of silence is one of the main reasons that I am such a fan of India." As I said that I almost blushed with the realization of the irony that I was going to run away from the elephantine silence by eulogizing silence.

"Yeah? How so?" Adam followed, cementing the decision to move off of the all-to-heavy topic of Aya's silence.

"India has a cosmological sense of time. We worry about the minutes, the seconds; geologists, the tens of thousands of years. But the Indians measure time in kulpas.

"A kulpa," I passionately conveyed, "is like the time between a big bang, the expansion of the universe, its contraction, and the next big bang. In the Indian mind, this cycle of hundreds of billion of years has happened hundreds of billions of times.

"In fact, the head God, Brahma, floats down the river, and every time he sleeps a lotus flower grows out of his belly button. Vishnu is always in the flower when it opens. And every time that Vishnu blinks, a new kulpa, a new big bang, happens. That's every time he blinks!" I had conveyed this information as though I were a preacher telling the minions of a new truth.

"And, from that perspective of time, to care about the immediate problems you happen to have in one particular life in this one-of-many kulpas kulpa, doesn't make sense.

"Indians don't take themselves as the starting point of their reality; they are fully aware of the unimaginable magnitude of the universe. The awareness of the largeness of it all and their own smallness makes them tuned into existence in a way we aren't.

"This makes them able to deal with silence between sentences in a way that we cannot." I concluded.

"I've had the feeling of being overwhelmed by the size of it all." Adam said in agreement. "The Grand Canyon was one huuuuge place. It's too awesome. It overwhelms you for sure. It's indescribable."

"Exactly. The sensible reaction to the Grand Canyon is the same as that to kulpas; silent awe." And I did the little bobbing head gesture, with the warm smile, that the Indians do.

Adam caught my gesture and we both laughed. The heaviness of Aya's story had been displaced.

"Yes!" Adam tagged on, not pausing too long to appreciate the type of silence my story praised.

And just like every other person who ever hears about India he asked the mandatory question, "But don't they have a lot of poverty in India?"

"If you've never been in a home, it is normal not to be in one. The streets are lined with homeless people. As the sun comes up, they shake their families up and walk off to their respective jobs, just like everyone else. It is normal, just like what all other families do.

"Life happens framed by limits of what we know. People do not know that their situation is horrible don't know it is horrible. Even within that society, if you have more blankets or a new shirt, people might consider you rich!"

"With India you must lose your categories. Banares is the city of death. People run through the streets with covered dead bodies on gurneys, singing songs; hospices are full of people waiting to die.

"When they burn bodies, the smoke invades your nose. The heat from the fires is scorching hot. You baste along with the dead."

Taking a funny sidebar, I mentioned that, "In a city with this kind of consciousness, your dreams of living longer through clean air and jogging have no relevance. Have you ever seen an Indian muscle man?" I knew the answer.

Adam communicated his "no" through a broad smile.

"People are interested in being spiritually pure in order to get out of this cycle of birth and rebirth. In being buff . . . not so much.

"The silent assumptions, the very outlook on life even before they use words, resonates differently there. And then once they start speaking their themes are all foreign 'n' shit."

At that, we both pondered the truism that cultures have different suppositions and so cannot communicate, at some level. But, we ourselves couldn't really understand that the cultural assumptions we couldn't understand. Faced with this limit, my mind boggled like a computer that could not compute a line of code.

Then Adam brought the internal dialogues to a close with a conclusion, "Every land definitely has a different feel to their people for sure. That sounds like an interesting place to visit."

At that I bit off a bite of pride in having some real travel experience and insight.

"But it is a dangerous place too." I added, setting up Adam in a way that would further my ability to show I had some cultural insight.

"Crime?" Adam bit on my lure.

"No. When in India, if you don't remember your life back home and that you should take it seriously, you could end up dropping out and becoming part of the Indian world of kulpas forever. While there I often thought staying and becoming a wondering saint, praying, and eating rice.

"But," I said repeating a turn of phrase I made up, "duty screams. And so I returned to my homeland, to my world."

And at that my attention away from this conversation and onto the night streets we were walking through.

Lights were gaining in frequency. We had to be getting nearer to the youth party area, Shinjuki, and our next round of drugs. But, the blackness of the night skies still took up more of the sky than the artificial lights did.

As we walked I made my feet the most important topic in my life. I meditated on them. I tried to lose myself in their beat.

Then I wondered about the possibility of Aya just subsuming her fury into the foam of multiple Kukpas. I thought to tell Adam that she should just let go of the story of her abuse and experience the magnitude of the universe.

But, my gauge of Adam's temperament so far, and the seriousness with which he now seemed attached to Aya's story of pain, silence, abuse, and a terrible past, convinced me to stay away from confronting her story as just being a story.

Just when I decided that it would be better to keep mum on that line of thought, Adam interrupted me,

"Japan is sort of a culture of silence too. In the workplace here they pretty much have no ways to communicate dissent. Everyone must agree with the person above them.

"Tempered disagreement must be really hidden. If you disagree you have to apologize and pretend that your statement is a question that someone might ask. And you have to be on a near equal power footing to even go there. Mostly you just cannot disagree with others."

"But," I exaggerated to get to the heart at the matter, "If there is no room for dissent and you must always go with the group, then there aren't any individuals."

"I've met some cool Japanese overseas." Adam qualified, "But while they are here, yeah, the system is them. And they take on its values and are really defensive about it. They are unified -- like we were after 9-11. But they are that way normally."

"Does that even happen to the brash, loud, strident-looking wild punk dressers?" I gestured to one walking past us on the other side of the street. "Does the system grind them down?"

"Yep. They get ground down in the office. At first you're silent to afford your nightlife; you don't want to be fired. After marriage kills your nightlife, you silence your opinion to provide for your family. Then over time you forget that you might have ever had divergent thoughts. It's easiest. It's polite."

As we walked the number of brash strident punky and day-glo youths was slowly increasing. These were folks going home. Their dress was so outrageous – color wigs, leopard skin-tight pants, gaudy jewelry, and such - it was hard to believe that they could be silenced so competely and efficiently. Enough social pressure to silence God!

A couple of blocks later, Adam announced out of nowhere, "I hate to look at my face. When I look in there I see an old man. Being 39 is hard. Women who I want to pick up call me 'Sir.' My students call me 'Sir.' And when I think about it, I am old enough to be their father."

"Yeah, I know what you mean. Looking in the mirror sometimes gives me the creeps too." I agreed.

"I read a good essay in an anthology book about this, sort of. It pointed out that we normally never see our face, we only see a little fuzzy dot representing our nose and our hands and legs. We rarely get visual confirmation that we have heads. Our vision seems to jut out of nowhere."

"Its kind of a sad image for me. Two lonely eyes never able to see the head that supports them." Adam observed, either making an analogy to culture or not.

"But for me," I continued, "my thoughts about my aging face are not so much the fading ability to pick up girls. They are about the silent shroud of death slowly making me disappear, slowly silencing me." I dramatically paused between the final three words. "Silently," "Silencing," "Me." This greatly increased their profundity and sense of suspense.

"You sometimes speak like a poet Mr. John Press." Adam complimented me. "Maybe you should be one."

"Thanks." I said with a smile and small blush.

"But slowness of death really is silencing me. As I don't have any kids, there is no sound of life rejuvenating itself in my house. And, as I grow older and my grandparents and parents die, the sounds of life entering my home will diminish. Ultimately, there will be more talking, no more sounds of life, only silence – morose silence."

"That is pretty damn depressing." Adam commiserated staring intently at the sidewalk.

"Yes, but I think I have a way out," I chirped up, "Not having kids gives me more time to write. And by means of my writing I can add to the conversation that society has with itself. I mean I hope to add to the dialogue academics and politicians and pundits have. If I contribute to the lexicon, the vocabulary of society, memories of me will continue after I am dead. That will be my community, I'll belong to the ages."

Then I made a bold declarative statement I'd heard on TV. "You know Adam, that only ideas and art last in the long run. That is all that will remain of our civilization in 200 years."

"Is that right?" I gave him time as it was obvious he was thinking about this. "The people and the politicians die." He queried, "But what about the buildings? They last."

"Well, I'm counting those as art. And, from the ancient world we have buildings, art, philosophy, and literature left. Everything else has vanished."

"What about the technology?" Adam asked.

"Yeah. I guess I gotta say that is part of ideas, evolving ideas, that get carried forward. Those are ideas."

"Yeah. And the language of ancient times continues in many of the words we use." Adam added.

"Language, continues, though it mutates. But language isn't something we could exist without. That's just part of the assumption of life, like hair. Its like saying hair lasts throughout time. But, I guess we do pass down different versions of our language." I hadn't really made my observation to start a conversation, I just wanted to say something to show we had something to talk about. It was annoying that he really thought about it.

And then as quickly as it popped into my mind, I blurted, "What an amazing act of national character that was."

"What was that?" Adam asked.

"That the people of Israel decided as a nation to revise and use a dead language, Hebrew. Because of this collective decision, millions now speak a language that had been silent for over a thousand years."

"It had been totally dead?" Adam asked incredulously. I wasn't sure if he was saying he didn't know or was subtly insinuating that I was missing some crucial piece of information.

"Yes" I assured him. "It was dead." Then realizing I wasn't as sure as I thought, I hedged. "I mean, I mean, they brought back from being a language that only scholars and rabbis used and to being the street language of a nation.

"They brought the language back from the dead." I affirmed.

"I am pretty sure they did." I hedged.

"I guess I don't know." I concluded.

When people question your statements, it really is annoying. After my monopoly on India information, this was a bit deflating.

"I suppose that's just one of the many things I only halfway know a little bit about. Speaking of silence, I guess the ignorance surrounding the tiny fragments of things I think that I think that I know is enormous."

"I guess that in this vast world of kulpas, to tie one's identity to the small amount of knowledge we think we have is to tie oneself to a small leaky boat in a vast ocean.

"You know Adam," It occurs to me that nearly all the topics we're discussing have to do with silences."

"Really?" He asked.

"Yeah. In a sea of nothingness, our thoughts seem to be starkly about that. Our projects, our relationships, our quest for meaning, are all about shouting down the silence that surrounds them."

"Interesting." Adam said with an unconscious nodding that perfectly conveyed his thought process.

"I guess Aya is the opposite though." Adam chimed in, "She controls the world through her silence." Wow. Adam had been keeping his mind on her below the surface for a while.

I turned to the last thought I had had about her, "maybe her story and the silence it necessitates keeps her from just being the new being that she may be able to be. Perhaps, since she moved in with you, it is time for her to leave that story behind."

"It isn't just a story to her, it isn't just an intellectual exercise in meaning, this happened to her, in this lifetime!" Adam was fiercely clinging to his wife's justification for intimacy issues. And, when I say fiercely, I mean with emotion.

I almost asked if her past then needed to define her whole life going forward. But Adam's agitation, his meanness in discounting our discussions as 'intellectual exercises" took the air out of my security and charge.

"Anyhow," I added, finding a comfortable way to progress, "speaking of our connection to the past, I often wonder whether or not the word 'Judaism' has any meaning. Does the sound of that word correspond to any reality or is just a meaningless word. Is there really such a thing as this quality "Jewishness"?

With no answer I continued, "You and me, Adam, resonate as individuals. But I think just as individuals. I don't think I have more in common with most Jews than with other people. In fact, I don't even like most Israelis. They seem really gruff to me. Really macho Middle Eastern types."

"Hey, those are my friends you're talking about." Adam said with a mock censorious tone. His protest had more than a hint of silly to it; we were out of the Aya woods.

"Sorry. But I don't feel the connection. One of the only times that I felt connection to Judaism as something real was when I was in a synagogue in India that was build in 500 B.C."

"Wow. They have a synagogue from 500 B.C. there?" Adam queried.

"Yeah, it's supposed to be from that Babylonian exile of 500 B.C. or whatever." I was still a bit bitter from meditating on how limited my solid knowledge is.

"And just when I was meditating on what ties Jews together, I saw a little Jewish boy stumble up the aisle to a podium-like thing in the middle of the room and kind of drop himself into a big open book. 'Wow, I thought then, study. That's the trait that connects all Jews.' But, then I remembered that many Jews don't study at all."

"I never do." Adam said, blithely agreeing to the smaller point.

"Adam, did I tell you that I am the only full Jew, with my family name, left in my whole family? If I don't have a boy the Jewishness of the Press family dies."

"To make things worse, I'm a part of the priestly Cohen tribe too."

"So I get it," Adam smiled, "Within the theme of this discussion, not having kids silences your family line and your religion." He put air quotation marks around the word 'silences' and proclaimed, "I like this looking for the thematic in our conversation."

Then, toning down his happiness to the level to the conversation's proper tone, he shared, "I'm not the end of my line. My brother has lots of kids."

"See Adam, the question about the Jewish story sits close to my heart. Should I end the story? The story of my family line? Judaism? The Cohen tribe?

"But, I am, unfortunately, not convinced that the story of Judaism has anything to do with me, with my story. Does the tale speak to me? Or is it only a tale told by an idiot. Full of sound and fury...."

I paused to see if Adam would get the Shakespeare reference and finish my quote, but he didn't indicate it in any way. ". . . signifying nothing." I concluded.

"By what authority is it my burden to carry this supposed legacy of family and Judaism forward? I really don't believe in God. I'm what I call a pain-in-the-ass atheist."

Then I exclaimed, "Okay Adam I've got it."

Adam seemed amused by my rambling and the energy of this eureka moment. He smiled and asked, "Got what?"

"If our conversation has been about identity, identity in the face of silence. I think I can synthesize the whole thing into a formula from big to little."

"Okay, go!" Adam encouraged me.

"Those who don't feel the universe, get their identity from affiliation with God. Those without God can have a family. Those without a family, have their work to convince themselves that they matter. Those with don't find meaning in their work have stories from their past, and desperate hopes of significance to cling to for identity.

"Wow. I like that." Adam earnestly responded, "That's quotable."

"Thanks." I blushed.

And regaining myself, I continued, "Yep, you know. To make sense out of our lives, we can use God, history or our supposed cultural connections to give our lives context or meaning. But in the end it just comes down to a desperate hope of significance, an attempt to give an anchor to our lives in the great engulfing meaninglessness of it all. I mean I think we've both been talking about a desperate need to belong somewhere to have some reason to exist, to have some justification . . ."

"Yeah, I got it." Adam clarified, sounding irritated at a perceived assumption that the discussion might be over his head. "But family can give you more than meaning too. Its not just what they stand for or a family line or something, but their actual existence by your side that matters."

"Okay then. Family can also blot out the dark silence of the night, by dealing with you personally. But your life can still be meaningless."

I thought herein about how Aya's story about incest and silence in her family gave her a story to know herself with. I thought about how families too just shield us from thoughts of the grave. Then I remembered that I have to listen to people to have a conversation with them.

And replied, "But right, yes. Thanks for pointing that out."

"Sure. I mean, you have Soo Hee in your life." She isn't just an economic geo-politics concept.

"And," I added covering over my instant complaint concerning her absent, "Soo Hee is more real to me than Judaism or even a family name. She is more than those word constructs. What's in a name? A rose by any other name would smell as sweet."

"Shakespeare!" Adam uttered excitedly, proud to have recognized a literary allusion.

"That's for sure. My grandparents and history are real to me too. But my grandfather will be dead soon, and then that source of pressure to have a connection to Judaism will be dead and buried; completely gone."

I announced my well-worn conclusion on this topic, which perhaps had become well-worn in my effort to justify Soo Hee, "I don't believe in identities without cultures. But I don't need Judaism for my identity personally. I'm an American. I'm Western. And that is more real to me than any supposed connection to a religion."

"And in terms of having a legacy of ideas in the national discourse, Jews have kicked a lot of ass on that front. As such, my contributing to the national or national discourse, with a book would lift the profile of Jews, indirectly.

"But more than that, more than contributing to the knowledge base of your nation or civilization," I paused to let Adam know that a comic bomb was coming, "contributing to the knowledge base fulfills the evolutionary mandate of the universe's expansion towards intelligence."

Then I went into mock ghetto slang for fun, "Talk about your large contexts to fit into. I be a part of the mandated evolution of universal intelligence and shit. Motherfucker, you best believe that that is some large universal meaning an shit!"

"Oh, you're a weird one, John Press."

"Thanks!" I beamed. "But in all seriousness, all this is like the problem that Hamlet had. Do you know the story of Hamlet?"

"No." Adam admitted.

"Amongst other things, Hamlet's uncle kills his father and marries his mother. Can you dig it? His father's murdered marries his mother. And the meats not barely cold from the funeral were used to furnish the wedding." Adam smiled at Shakespeare's wicked humor.

"And the ghost of Hamlet's father is telling him to avenge his murder and kill his new stepfather. And if that weren't enough, there is an army marching against the kingdom. And he's in charge of seeing that the kingdom gets defended."

"Hamlet's whole question is, "How seriously do I take this play, this story, in which I am impressed?" That's what he means when he asks the famous, 'To be or not to be' in this play. Does all of this stuff matter to him? Does he really need to avenge his dead father's murder? Can he just walk away from this silly story he's been born into?"

"Well, what does he do? Does he do his duty?"

"In the very end he does avenge his father, he kills his uncle. But in the process his mother is also killed, his friend is killed too, and he is killed. It's a big Shakespearian blood bath that results directly from Hamlet's engaging with this world's drama.

"His last words are so beautiful. Nearly dead from doing his duty, he murmurs something to the effect of: "If I have meant anything to you, once in a while as you go romping through your merry day, remember me. The rest is silence."

"Sooo beautiful." I don't know why, but I said the last two words in the voice of Soo Hee. She loves deep poetics.

With her on my mind, I asked if I should I be responsible and suffer the slings and arrows of outrageous fortune by having a family and shit or melt into the world of travel and hedonism with Soo Hee?

Then Adam made a great Shakespeare joke! "To Soo Hee or not Soo Hee. That is the question!"
We both laughed a lot at that one. It was perfect.

"Hey John," Adam said gently and tentatively. "Would you come over to our house for dinner sometime? I'd like you to meet Aya. You could tell me what you think of her, our home, my situation."

"I'd love to." I replied grinning broadly in appreciation of my luck. But simultaneously, I had a spasm of my characteristic worry about time and productivity. These conversations had been interesting and I had an itch to go write some of them down. I wanted the evening to matter.

"Maybe tomorrow night?" Adam asked.

"Sounds good." I said, seeing no other response that would be acceptable.

"Yeah. It'll be neat for you. It's rare that a Japanese person invites a Ganji into their home. Plus she's a really good cook."

CAPSULE EIGHT: Memory

After some searching, we wound our way back to our dealer's stand and purchased another choice product from Kaos International's fine line of neuronal enhancers. After repeating the consultation ritual, rather than another round of Pinky, Adam's 'friend' sold us some capsules in a baggie labeled 'Trip Thunder.'

This stuff was said to take about an hour to infiltrate your system, make you a little nauseous, and then fly you far and high for about ten hours. Daunting.

After downing the capsules with water, we meandered into a fun little situation. Long story short, we went a-Karaoke-ing with three women!

We'd actually thought we'd be going out with just two girls. But, the wife of the owner of the bar where we met these women came along to chaperone.

Auspiciously, it was the grand opening of her husband's British style bar. So you'd think that she'd stay at the opening.

Unfortunately, however, her husband had passed out from drinking. And so, perhaps with an eye towards revenge, she came along for the fun.

"Country" was the translation of my companion's name. She spoke no English. This has happened to me before. It is awkward and draining to try to communicate with someone that knows absolutely none of your language. Talk about your walls! The only tidbits of English she spoke were tiny snippets sewn into the Japanese pop songs she sang.

Because Adam was able to communicate in Japanese and I couldn't, I occupied myself in a bookstore across the street while he convinced them to go with us. The Japanese bookstore only carried anime books. And since I could read any of them and they all looked the same to me, I quickly returned to the bar. By the time I did, the deal was sealed. We were going to serenade one other.

Neither of our ladies were hot items on the open market. Age had diminished their competitive edge. Being divorced in Japan creates a huge disgrace that also lowers your relationship market value. Besides that, Adam's companion had a tooth that looked like it had been replaced.

My associate had a nice roundness to her body. But was nearly too old to get married in Japan any longer. She'd, from the looks of it, spent as much time in bars as Adam's friend, but she hadn't met anyone to marry there. Exuding the freedom that giving up on your goals provides, she only seemed intent on innocent fun.

But, despite their market value or personal situations, all three women came off as nice, welcoming, and warm - hearted. They had nice souls and sang with spirit.

As was to be expected, Adam was too aggressive with his potential partner for my comfort. He told me that she smelled so good and it was driving him mad. Demonology.

When I put my hand on the back of my charge a couple of times without a reciprocal touch, I took it as a green light to ignore her.

The cultural oddity of the songs and the singing were more interesting to me than the thought of bedding my partner. And, oddly enough, she also seemed to consider singing the main attraction in the Karaoke room. In terms of the number of songs sung, we dominated.

Adam's big number song was "Alone Again, Naturally" by Gilbert O Sullivan. The lyrics paralleled the list of failed sources of identity I had made up. The vocalist sang up a list of support systems that had failed him. The last one to fail him is God. After that falls through, he is alone again, naturally. Cool song.

The girls only sang bad generic Japanese rock songs that were imitations of imitations of bad products of the American pop music industry. They didn't seem to understand these musak renditions of their own raunchy songs.

Perhaps there will be freer communication and total cross-cultural understanding when American industries have standardized all musical expression across the globe. Anyhow, I'm sure that's the plan.

The cultural power of the Karaoke maker awed me. Songs he deemed worthy of putting in the Karaoke catalogue would be preserved and continue to be sung. The excluded songs would be forgotten. Generations were culled into approximately 100 tracks by 30 bands.

I have always been a "shit disturber." As such, I took great delight in finding culturally inappropriate songs for Japan, and then singing them.

I knew 'White Riot' by the Clash would be totally incomprehensible to the Japanese, so I sang it. "Young Americans" by David Bowie got double points on the cultural alienation hits chart. It was a British person's imitation of the cultural stereotypes of America being sung in Japan. And my personal favorite for the "most-odd-here" song award was "Pink Pussycat" by Devo.

The singing scoring system reported me as the least faithful imitator of the original in our group. I was proud as this made me feel like my singing of these pop hits was somewhat original. My low score registered my resistance to the whole mass marketed jingles industry. I liked my own reality.

What an amazing juxtaposition. As a youth listening to these songs on my way to underground clubs full of proudly unpopular music, I could have never imagined I'd end up singing my rebellion anthems in a Japanese bar. These songs had represented radical rebellions based on fresh insights that the bourgeois were too lame to appreciate. Now they were mainstream enough to entertain Japanese housewives.

The songs also made me think of how I had changed over the years. I still had 'White Riot' levels of punk rock in me. It was not a coincidence that my book on sterilization and the new project I was considering starting, culturism, both defied and shocked common sense. I hated the idea of belonging and comfort.

The meaning of Bowie's "Young Americans" had faded with my sexual ambiguity. My forays into sexual exploration had given way to disgust with the whole bodily enterprise. Devo's "Pink Pussycat" had been an anthem of that disgust. But, in listening to it now, I realized that the song didn't denounce our body's sending us on strange missions to poke women; it actually celebrated the hunt!

All totaled, these songs convinced me that, rather than Bowie, I am the real alien. I had become less sexual. And, I no longer saw the random violent rebellion of White Riot as productive. Yet, there was continuity between the newer version me and the older one. A sense of strangeness, of alienation, still sat at the center of my identity.

Anyhow, I enjoyed the fact that I still knew the words to all of these songs. Life had somehow both stagnated and changed radically, while the songs remained the same.

Unexpectedly, when we parted, the girl who seemed obviously uncomfortable with having to constantly push away Adam's uninvited advances, gave him her phone number. My girl, whose autonomy I respected, just exchanged waves with me at a distance. That women want men who are forceful is an obvious a holdover from tribal times. Aggression is a sign of the virility of the ancient hunter.

When I told Adam about my observation, he disagreed. People in Japan always part with, "Lets have coffee." But when you call, you discover it was just a formality verging on a lie. He doesn't call them back anymore and tries not to resent their need to lie.

Anyhow, long live memory lane. May songs of our youth always invite us back. *Long live rock!*

Emerging from the Karaoke, the emptiness of the streets surprised us. We didn't realize how much time had passed – it was already after midnight. People had rushed to make the last subway just as we had gone in. There was a great early morning feel to the night. Late night taxis scavenged, driving near us slowly. And a few recalcitrant people lingered, refusing to acknowledge the end.

After Adam puked, we looked for a taxi to Rappongi. Watching him gave me an empathetic sickness. I walked away to protect my own stomach and then felt a slight sense of relief when we got in the taxi and sped away from his puke.

Driving on the wrong side of the road was fun. The whole evening had been fun and interesting. Our talks about identity and the decisions we had to make in our lives hadn't resolved anything. But, their poetic and exploratory nature inspired me. I wanted to write about them.

I had given up on the new batch of drugs having an effect. And I was glad to be moving in the direction of my capsule hotel in Rappongi. I felt very blessed for having had a chance to hang out with Adam. And the coming doze would be as welcome as it was well deserved.

Rappongi was still crowded. My first reaction to the realization that the party showed no signs of stopping was claustrophobia. Now I would never get an opportunity to write or to bed. I had to consciously hide my angry resentment as I agreed to walk around for a while and maybe get a drink.

It lifted me with a jerk. My feet seemed to rise off the sidewalk as both a heat wave and visual echo washed over me as then ran through me. After finding the ground and recovering myself, I uttered with needed deliberation and forethought, "I just got hit by a wave of high. It's starting!"

"I think I feel something too." Adam confirmed.

"I don't think, I know! Wow! This Trip Thunder capsule stuff is strong. Adam, we've got a long night ahead of us." Though thoughts of bed and writing lingered, I felt a newfound awareness that an adventure approached. The possibilities excited me!

As the buildings took on an air of bending, it got harder to walk. Well, it wasn't so much that it was hard to walk, but it was hard to concentrate on my feet. Trip Thunder was visually stunning. People became blurred obstacles we needed to avoid, as the buildings took more and more of my attention. Foreground became the background and background the foreground. I played with this switching.

Then, the entire skyline bellowed as if it were one big flag blowing in the wind. Everything was moving together and nothing was differentiated, as if all had been projected onto a single tapestry. Then with the visual change, the meaning of the buildings started to change.

I realized that these buildings were a decision. None of this needed to exist. None had been here long. It was as if man had conjured them, as a social structure, out of the wind. Our collective assent had created the skyline and allowed buildings shaped like this to be the norm.

Rappongi's buildings served as walls of cultural and mental hegemony. Though providing a majestic tribute to man, the skyline also featured confinements and acceptance of the psychic limitations of man. The structures fit us, yet the sky was nearly gone amongst these monstrosities, their gigantic solidity giving the impression of an unquestionable eternal order. But it wasn't so; this was a choice.

"Adam. These walls could be anything. Do you see that?"

"Yep. Okay. John. I'm starting to rise too. I'm with you."

"The building shapes fossilize some limit. It is like the limit that grammar puts on our sentences. There is a grammar to buildings, an assumed underlying structure." I was groping along the limits of mind as associated with a particular body, the calendar, commuting, and the workweek. Each flashed across my mind as mutable.

"Grammar is the key to communicating." Adam sloganeered.

"Yes. And to read the grammar of these buildings, look at the visuals. What do these buildings say without words? What are the assumptions of the confines, the structure, of this visual sentence? What is the regiment they enforce?"

"Oh, I see it. Walls of walls with connection, like a hive, like a plastic hive sponge." Adam said with absolute conviction.

"Yes!" I exclaimed with enthusiasm, "You are high too!" I said, laughing, "High as a plastic hive sponge."

Then, as if by magic, Adam disappeared. He reappeared ten feet away at another one of his Israeli street vendor friend's stands. I assumed he was telling him, in a near giddiness that could have been mistaken for boast, what we were doing. Waiting, and tripping into my own world, and yet trying to convey subtle impatience, I was horrified. I was alone.

I approached the vendor's stand. For a second, before I quickly pulled my head away, I saw what his friend was selling. They were horrific, demonic exaggerated caricatures of celebrities.

My reaction to them was of that of hearing a truth one could not bear to hear. Not cute, these horrific celebrities were like friends who ripped off their masks to reveal themselves as demons that had been laughing at you your whole life.

My mind could not bear to think of the corporate structure that brought them to me. The waves of lame public relations thoughts imposed in the name of these horrid faces were too much to bear.

Suddenly, I was walking alongside Adam in silence. My shirt started to come off and go back on, over and over. Obviously, I was putting it on and removing it, but it seemed to happen of its own rhythm, of its own accord. My temperature was shifting and creating these movements. But was it unpredictable? Were there patterns?

Out of nowhere Adam asked, "What does your tattoo mean?" Looking at myself, I realized that I had my shirt off again.

Boy. I hadn't thought about the origin of my tattoo for years.

"My tattoo is a message sent to me from me a long, long time ago." As I relayed this I'm sure I made a face of a person looking back in time. My eyes were open, but not looking out. Then, as we continued hiking, I swiveled my eyes up to Adam, to make brief eye contact, as we kept walking, "When I was 19 years old I went to community college. The long corridors reminded me of a perfect hallway of the work environment. They were so clean and office-like."

"The grammar of the building." Adam chimed, delighting in the application of our new concepts.

"Exactly. A young man doesn't know the intricacies of life too well. But he can read a building. It is intuitive. The similarity of the construction materials, desks, the chairs, the paper work and fluorescent lights don't come together without a plan. In my mind I was destined, by continuing to take classes at the community college, to work in an office, to become a clean, standardized, office fixture.

"I accepted my destiny, but did not want to have a spiritual lobotomy. My fear was that I would just become a vacuous, TV-watching, non-questioning, corporate automaton. This didn't seem like an unbearably horrible thing to me. It just seemed like the natural trajectory.

"It would be redemptive though, I thought, if every once in a while I had a doubt. It would be healthy if every once in a while, I remembered that there had been anger and emotion and passion in my life, if I remembered that not everything was pretty and corporate clean around the world. I wanted to send this message to my future self. So I got a tattoo as a message to myself in the future; a 'fly-in-the-ointment' tattoo.

"It's actually the logo of the great band Black Flag. Black flag means anarchy. And I still remember that reality hides chaos because of this tattoo. Death bites at the walls of all things clean. Cleanliness is next to godliness. Godliness is next to death."

"Wow. It is a message from that community college hallway." Pondered Adam.

"And that perfect lobotomized world probably never materialized for me. Maybe that's 'cause I don't watch TV. And I'd probably seethe pain and dissonance even if I didn't have my tattoo and watched lots of TV. But still I'm glad I have my tattoo."

"Gives you some kind of awareness. An edge." Adam approved.

"Yeah. Wait a minute. Hold on. I think I just got this tremendous vision. This stuff is good. Bear with me. I'm gonna try to get it out. Okay?" Clouds of visions percolated in my head and the liquid was about to overflow.

"Sure." Adam said by way of standing back.

"We've probably walked around in the same circle, this block, about 3 times. But if we didn't know we were going in circles, we'd never know that there were patterns, that we could learn about things we'd seen before. We'd think it was a straight line that didn't repeat.

"We'd just never notice that it wasn't just one long street." Adam checked.

"Yes," I replied emphatically, "well early man would travel in circles seasonally. They traveled from food site to food site seasonally. And, originally, they might have done this like an animal. And, like us tonight, not noticed that they were traveling in a circle. They would have no history and no future.

"Then one year someone might have marked the tree. And then the next year when he came by, they might have marked it again. And, when some marks accumulated, people would sit next to the mark and tell about what happened during the circle when a particular mark was made. Language would have bloomed trying to explain things that weren't there anymore, but had been there in previous years' journeys.

"Then cultures would start . . . the tribe would have collective memories of times before those currently living."

"Maybe those marks became writing." My friend offered.

"Wow! Very cool!" I replied. "What an insight! Man we are both spinning and spinning webs now."

"Eventually," I added, "they would back-fill their story to the very first time around the circle, when God created man. The culture would all come from the idea of marking time."

"In the beginning was the mark." Adam offered with his palms aimed at the sky, while wearing one of the beamiest, dreamiest smiles I ever saw him make.

"And, importantly," I continued with conviction, "when you have accumulated enough ideas to get a sense of the past, you can start to imagine the future. You can project way into the future and compare where you are with where you've been and where you want to be and have goals. Progress starts and conscious guiding of yourself and your civilization starts with marking time."

"Adam," I said turning to him again, "did you know that every civilization comes from a story?

"Uh, did they?" He wondered quizzically.

"Yes. Greece sprouted from Homer's Iliad. That book began their culture. The Middle Ages resulted from the Bible. Muhammad's Koran came before the Muslim world. The Vedas create Indian culture. Heck! The communist manifesto created the Soviet Union."

"Hmmn, I guess you're right. The story comes first." Interesting. It makes you think of the power of writing and story telling in a new light." Adam enthused.

"Yes, the story becomes flesh. You mark the ground with it and stuff accumulates around it like seaweed hanging on to a rock. Then, boom, you have a civilization."

"And, our story would be the Bible?" Adam asked with a squint.

"Hell yeah, the West's story is the Bible." I replied with a hint of a redneck yell. "But, America comes from the Protestant ideal of reading the Bible for yourself. The Protestants did not want the Catholic Church to interpret the Bible for them any more. The Protestants said that their own individual interpretations were valid. And that's why they rebelled against the Catholics.

"And, that my friend, is where we get our sense of individualism from, from the Protestant Puritans and their demanding to make up their own minds about the Bible."

"Wow, that really impacts us." Adam said reflectively.

"And the way we see the Puritans impacts us too. If we look down on the Puritans, we lose pride over our hard working, heavy reading, ways. We lose great role models."

"Well they were Puritanical." Adam echoed a commonplace.

"Adam, you say that like it's a bad thing!" We both laughed. Then I made my serious point. "Yes, they were puritanical. But they also provided us with the notion of self-governance, before the Constitution. They created our economy with their discipline and, again, they gave us our sense of individualism, of individual conscience.

"They created a lot of who we are. So if we love the Puritans, we love ourselves. If we hate the Puritans, we hate ourselves."

"Wow! I have another vision." I exclaimed, "Can I tell you about it?"

"Okay. But first, do you want to go that way?" Adam said, pointing to a structure that looked like the Eiffel Tower in the distance. "We could maybe walk out to that tower."

"Yeah fine, but..."

"I mean that would be a way for us to leave this circle and progress for a while, we'd have a goal and a past."

"Well, okay, but . . ." I said rejecting Adam's attempt at humor.

"We don't have to." Adam replied, unsure what was going on with me.

"No. It's fine. I just want to say what I have to say while I still remember it." We had come to a complete halt.

"Okay, hit me!" Adam said, standing absolutely still.

"The Kabalists say that in the beginning was the letter. Individual letters. But that can't be true. The letter cannot exist without someone there to appreciate it. How can a letter exist, the idea of a letter, without someone there to appreciate it?

"So, consciousness must have bloomed, not when the whole letter happened, but when the mark that was starting the letter first happened. That mark created time; only with time do you have the ability to judge, to look forward, look back, and assess the situation. Only after all of that could you understand a letter.

"A mark on a tree might not have started memory, but a mark in time definitely started the big bang. You can't just have consciousness without time."

"And then," Adam ventured, reminding me of my having started this conjecture with the Kabalists, "came the letters?"

"Yes," I resumed, "According to the Kabalists, it was the first letter of the Hebrew alphabet, Aleph, that came first. Aleph means man. But man and this letter could not happen without the initial mark. That mark had to have been the origin of the big bang, not the letter."

"So," Adam interjected, eager to complete his thought, "after the mark comes the letters, which allow the writing of our Bible and, shazam, from that Book our civilization is created."

"Yes!" I exclaimed. "That's the complete and exact history of the universe. One thought, all world history, any questions?"

We both laughed at the preposterousness of our ideas, shook our heads, and started walking again. Yet, no sooner had we started walking, back in a normal groove, when I touched Adam's arm to stop him and shouted, "Yes! I have it!! What fun!!"

"What?!" Adam rolled his eyes with astonishment over my having yet another revelation to impart.

"If you don't have a religious marker from which to measure progress, as I don't, you have to rely on putting yourself in the context of secular history. So a man without God has only history to guide him." After a moment's thought about the place of history in nationalism, I continued, "A man without history can still have a national identity, a weak one. And, as you pointed out Adam, if you don't have national identity, you can have a career or family to help find yourself and measure progress."

"Thanks for the credit." Adam said with a bit of a smile. Then he chimed in, "And a man without family only has his own personal history. He's the story. He relies on his own memory to know who he is."

"Very cool! JP, we're building something here!"

I smiled with Adam at our accomplishment. But, I didn't really like his last part and found it important to say so. "Personally, I don't think the lone human can tell if he or she is growing without some national memory or sense of their civilization's direction by which to judge their action.

"I mean, I might grow as a serial killer yearly. But a historical context is necessary to tell me that our civilization doesn't esteem serial killing and that we've historically upheld other ideals. We need some larger context to tell if we're doing good or bad or progressing or not."

"I don't know," Adam challenged, "I anchor myself with my personal stories and memories. But, if I had to choose one of those things to hang my hat on, for values and identity, and I couldn't just choose my own memories, I don't know which I'd choose."

"Yeah, but you should." I urged, "Because finding out what is important to you is important to making decisions like where to live your life and with whom. With out a past you cant see if you're progressing or not."

"Well, yeah, I can see where it would help with decisions. But, to be honest, this whole progress thing leaves me a bit hollow. It sounds good, but not everything is about progress. Some moments are lived for themselves, without comparison.

"Like, maybe the family would be a bad place for comparison. It's supposed to be a place of unconditional love, John, isn't it?"

He was right, "You're right. You're definitely right about the family. But, you want to progress too, right? I mean you want next month's language CD sales to be higher than last months. Comparison can help set goals and measure progress." I offered meekly.

"Unless it drives you crazy and makes you feel like crap." Adam looked down as he said this, like a big pouting child. Language CD sales were probably not the best topic to bring up.

Feeling badly I shared, "Oh yeah, I know what it feels like to compare oneself and hate yourself for coming up short."

"And, you're right. Some things are just for the moment, we don't get any profit by them, I guess. I mean this moment is pretty fantastic without any sense of direction or comparison." I looked at him with a pleading smile.

After just a beat, I exclaimed, "I can't believe we pieced together a whole coherent history of the world."

"Of the universe!" Adam nodded.

I stopped in silent amazement. I surveyed the lights, the people, the tops of the buildings, and the skyline, that contained us. Our little mental explosions were made even more impressive by the fact that they happened as we walked through one of the biggest nightlife zones, in one of the world's most modern, sign laden, cities on earth. The world had many visuals and cheap thrills. But we had built a construct of a different nature.

Then I noticed the same two Chinese massage girls we'd passed earlier. As if on a mobius strip, it seemed like in Rappongi we could walk off into any direction and end up right back where we started. We hadn't even veered towards the Eiffel Tower structure. We'd just kept in going circles.

Instinctively, the girls started walking towards us and instinctively I started to move away. Then I just confronted them. I told them we didn't want a massage. The tension under my statement had mostly to do with the fact that I was tripping and didn't want to be fettered by their nonsense every time I went around this block. I was trying to progress.

Adam started to explain the drugs to them. Adam, Adam. Only Adam would hit on prostitutes in the middle of cosmological realizations. I guess, in terms of the origins of the universe, female is where we all really come from. And, despite the lure of cosmology, Adam was perfectly content, as he was designed to be, fulfilling his biological destiny, going back to the true origin of all.

-------------------------Capsule NINE: "I"

When Adam finally decided that he had to break away from the prostitute massage girls, I hoped it was because our conceptualizing was so interesting that their mundane offerings weren't of interest to him any longer. But I knew that it was just because he felt my discomfort and was being a good friend by keeping me company.

Then, not for the last time, Adam gave me a really positive surprise that made me feel guilty for expecting less.

"Just now, when you were talking about the creation of man and time and the universe, you used the Hebrew letter aleph, like the Bible does, for man. I have something to add to that."

"Cool!" I said with enthusiasm mingled with relief over walking away from the prostitutes.

"I don't know much about Kabalah, but I know about languages."

"Yes. I've been wanting to hear some of what must go on in your multi-lingual head, Mr. Adam."

"Going forward and remembering backwards and all that stuff was needed for consciousness. I see that. But the language you do it in makes a huge difference too."

"Explique me." I joked, showing readiness for a little linguistic fair from the multi-linguist.

Adam led, "The question of how you make your identity is even below what you think it is. Language is how you experience your world, how you think of yourself. What you consider yourself, changes when you change languages.

"You see that wall over there?"

"Yeah. Right on! I love this subject. That wall?" Linguistics is a serious love of mine. I was sooo happy to get this lecture while high in Japan.

"Well in Japanese, if I want to say where I am, I have to describe it from the outside in. I wouldn't say, 'I'm here by the bank.' I'd reverse it and say, 'In front of the wall, across the alley, on stairs sitting, my location.' You come last in the spatial description. And that always tripped me out because it makes the person so little. By the time you get to you in the equation, you feel boxed in."

"Yes. I've heard of this. That is why once you get into university in Asian societies, you don't do anything. What is important is not you or any schoolwork you might do, but where you are, your place. And once you have that top university address, you're set." I had thought a bit about this topic before, but that was the first time I had thought that exact thought.

"Yeah. That could be evidence of the importance of setting." With a slight tilt of the head, Adam gave my tangent a little consideration and then a little brush-off as he moved on to his point.

"So," he continued, "It's not only important that language started the world, as you said, but that different languages create different orientations."

"Yes!" I yelped. I trusted Adam. He wasn't competitive. I wanted him add to my ideas. "I used English in my creation story, even though it hinted at Hebrew. And since I aimed to describe the creation of the universe, I suppose some other languages should be included!"

Adam nodded with a little maniacal sweat building on his lip. "The idea of man separating out of this creation story, coming into consciousness full-blown autonomous and ready to roll forward, with Aleph, as you said, probably wouldn't actually come out of Japanese and it definitely wouldn't come out of Hebrew.

"Your story centered on the emergence of you personally as the purpose of the story. English is a very isolating language. The pronoun, 'I' stands alone and undressed. It doesn't imply its surroundings like other languages' pronouns."

This was getting deep and so I probed, "You're, like, talking about the formality thing that happens in Spanish? So you aren't simply existing, but the pronoun indicates some level of hierarchy when it addresses someone as a sir (usted), or informally (tu)."

"Yes, it's that the language assumes the person exists in a social order. But, what I am aiming at is more like what I said about how describing where you are in Japan means starting from describing orienting objects around you."

"So, the creation story, in Japanese or Hebrew," I ventured, "Would need to be in a particular place?"

"That's not exactly my point, John. Look, Hebrew is incomplete; it doesn't allow for abstracted entities without context. You have to point to things a lot to say which objects you're discussing in Hebrew.

"The background of your creation story immediately becomes far too background." (And, dear reader, that might be true of this work as well. Though in Japan, for long stretches John and Adam move and speak without reference to their environs. Perhaps, that flaw itself, the very possibility of that flaw, reflects the alienation of the subject in English).

"Its like once creation happens," Adam continued, "the individual gets up, grabs their purse and walks off. In Hebrew, the person would never emerge from the big bang. They'd either stay in it or have to be somewhere else. But consciousness cannot just exist without a place to be in Hebrew."

I would have interrupted, but Adam seemed to be in his element. I wanted him to continue.

"*In* the beginning," he riffed, accentuating the word "in" to reflect its situated quality. Then his smile lifted his face above the wire of his glasses, "In English, in the beginning, was a sentence with a stand-alone pronoun waiting to have a world painted around it. "In the English beginning was the word 'I'.

"But notice that in Hebrew, the beginning comes long before the first person ever arrives and when the person shows up, they're trapped in a particular garden. The person as an abstract, consciousness as an abstract doesn't happen in that story."

My mind was blown. This was confirmation, extension, and details of stuff I had thought was true, I had read was true, but never had the pleasure of someone confirming it and relaying the thought to me so personally, and with such examples.

"Wow. So my language created my alienation." I checked, "This sense of not belonging anywhere."

"And freedom." Adam added with a slight shrug. He seemed delighted to be in the teaching role. I think he was feeling brilliant. And I do think he liked the idea of schooling a teacher. "The flip side to alienation is not being trapped anywhere."

"Oh. I love it. I should have picked up on this sort of thing before creating my creation story, because I have long loved studying linguistics. But, two heads, the blending of both of our knowledge bases, is the best."

Adam nearly curtsied, happy to oblige and be appreciated.

"My favorite book about this sort of thing is this great book called *How Natives Think*, by Bruhl. And it talks about the evolution of languages and stuff like this. The author talks about the idea of early languages not having abstractions."

"No abstractions." Adam uttered, both conveying understanding and the hope that I would now teach him something.

I obliged, "In early language, *How Natives Think* argues, each particular entity, like each tree, got its own distinct word. They didn't use abstract categorical words like 'mankind' because there would only be you and your small group of individuals to refer to. Languages being about specific places, like you're talking about, is said to be characteristic of earlier, primitive, languages."

Remembering what had been a major gripe of mine, I continued, "And, in fact, older linguists use the terms 'primitive' and 'advanced' to describe languages. The newer ones want to study the language scientifically as a structure from a distance. Their work is modern and decontexualized. They don't want to judge, so they don't speak in terms of early primitive and advanced modern languages.

"The earlier language theorists, early 20th century linguists, thought it important that they tie their work into the centerpiece of then modern science: evolution. That's why they called older languages, 'primitive' a lot. You wouldn't see that now. Modern scholars say no language is better, none evolved. History doesn't enter into their study. They simply note differences in structure, without judgment."

Adam ingeniously used the very topic we'd been discussing to skewer them, "So these language scientists want to make the study of language free of historical context and thus render it as free from place as English, the language they speak with?"

"Yes! You exactly and precisely got my point." I smiled. This was thrilling. Academics, by and large, had no longer heard of the outdated linguists and theories I had found in old books. As such, I didn't really have anyone to bounce these dated ideas off of. But here I had a real person who confirmed their speculations.

Feeling this opportunity to confer with a real multi-linguist, I prodded, "Another characteristic of early languages is that they have a lot of very context specific number systems. *How Natives Think* said that there were 15 number systems in Japanese. Is that right?"

"You mean, like where there is one number system for counting food and another one for counting money and another one for tools, and like that?

"Mmm-Hmm." I agreed as to minimize disruption.

"I don't know." Adam murmured with a series of unconscious nods as if he were counting out loud, (I think he gave up counting at three and a half nods). "Are there 15? I hadn't counted. But there are a lot." I knew something he didn't know about Japanese! My reading paid off.

"So," I probed further, "would the tribe we had marching in a circle on their seasonal treks always think of these loops as individual trips? Might the abstract notion of 'cycles' never emerge? They would just talk about the individual times that they had had?"

"That's right." Adam agreed. "I mean they don't have many abstract words in any of these 'primitive' languages like Japanese and Hebrew." And, of course, Adam put primitive in finger quotes.

"But would they then have a past? Would the other laps truly be in the past or just from other specific times? I mean, if it wasn't clear that there was a progression, that things were getting better or worse, you might not ever think about a the past or even a future being so different from the present."

"Not if the trips were more or less all the same." Adam worked out. "There would just be other times. But the time when they happened wouldn't be very important."

"So it is not just time, that you need for progress, it is directional time. Of course," I remembered, "I have read that progress was invented in the 18th century, but I didn't see it as well as I see it now."

"The 18th century?" Adam teased, "Was that after the big bang?"

"Just a little." I light-heartedly accepted the poke, "So the language, back then, gave them the ability to tell tales of the past, but these might not be instructional. They might not aim at telling us what we can learn from the past and how we can get better in the future."

"No." Adam noted, "The obsession with getting better and the future would be a John Press-ism."

"Are you suggesting that there is an opposite to my obsession: No progress, just relating? What a concept!" I said in a fay voice, "How weird!"

"You are!" Adam punctuated, calling me weird and drawing laughter from both of us.

"Yes. But, unfortunately, it isn't just me. The whole Western world, the whole world now, is on this kick of development and progress. We all have that John Press forward-going disease." I added.

"Which is again, not really a John Press thing. Be Japanese, think of you as simply reflecting a context. You can use that perspective to stop worrying over whether or not you matter. It is a social disease. Your alienation makes you a great member of the group.

"This angst didn't start with John Press and it only remains there because John Press thinks it reflects his own personal neurosis." Adam diagnosed.

I wouldn't let it go, "But I really believe in progress. Whether it is just because I'm programmed or not. It isn't just a neurosis to believe in this. History is real. And, that's why the academics who just catalogue cultures and languages scientifically, without judgment, drive me crazy."

"I believe that our culture, our language is, for lack of a better word, 'advanced.'" I declared. "Your language should have abstract terms. And to the extent that social sciences undermine the sense of progress, they make us unenthusiastic about the western mission. The West is all about progress, if you denigrate that well . . . "

"But, again," Adam intervened, "many languages that are currently thriving, like Japanese, still have limited abstractions. The universe doesn't, like, automatically lead to the English language or something. It's not like all roads advance towards English."

"Yes, I was sort of joking when I called English 'advanced.' I don't mean to say that all cultures do or should strive to be us."

"Ya, you sort of did." Adam said.

"Well, its not that other cultures should strive to be us. But we should! If we don't think of ourselves as advanced, and take pride in our love of progress, we'll slow down. We will . . ."

"Become more like other countries? More like the global context that America does not see itself as being a part of, but dominates? I mean the U.S. doesn't just sit easy as a nation among other nations. It is the truth and all other nations should be it. It is like the 'I' being at the center of creation. Your language drives you mad, your civilization always wishes to escape to the next best thing."

Adam was hitting a sore spot. I am very patriotic and infuriated by our going on stupid international ventures. So, I fought back, "Yes. And without progress, without wealth, we'll be shit poor like those other nations.

"Look, I know that not all nations will end up like us. And, it's precisely because I don't believe that the West is destiny that I understand that we can fall into third world status and civil strife quickly. I think our survival requires that we start to use the loaded progress-infused terms 'primitive' and 'advanced' again. It would give a sense of responsibility and mission to my students."

"Then enjoy your angst." Adam insisted.

"I do," I responded quickly by way of instinctive reaction. "But, I see your point." I was trying to regain my composure. "I wish to trick America into fighting for tomorrow, to having a sense of mission. But, then I do resist the alienation with the present that comes with always working towards the future.

"I need to find a balance. Well, even if I don't find a balance, at least this conversation has reinforced that my obsession about alienation makes me very much a part of my culture and community, that of western civ."

I paused and thought of a balance and trying to stay calm. Then I ventured another version.

"So," I said, half-joking but still serious, "I am going to try it again. Ready?"

"Yes to whatever, John Press, western man, western civ. man, to whatever he wants. What is it?"

"OK!" I smiled at his humor, and went for it.

"*In* my beginning was a specific language and it created a specific relationship to the world, mediated by that specific language, which I could not escape or see outside of."

"Except!" Adam announced as a trump, "The statement still had the pronoun 'I' at the end. From which "I" could not escape. There is no 'I' trying to escape necessary!"

"Yes! Sorry!" I added, "I can't seem to forget referring to the pronoun 'I.' The language made me do it!"

"And that," Adam crowed, "Is what would be predicted by this discussion."

I took on the voice of the fly in the movie 'The Fly,' and wailed, "Help me! Help me! I am trapped in an I. I am trapped in an I, I am!"

"Oh yes, all roads lead to the John Press and his predicament."

"Busted again!" I exclaimed with great happiness.

"You know what it is like?" Adam asked with a pixie-ish smile and a hand across his waist?

"What?"

"The difference is in the way Western dancers all dance for themselves, in competition to look the best. It is very much an individual thing.

"In Israel, as most 'primitive' countries, we have traditional dances that we do. Therein everyone else attempts to do exactly what the others do. We lose ourselves in the traditional steps."

"Wow. I am busted because I totally dance for the accolades."

"Okay." Adam said with a big excited gasp of air, "Since we're going to leave the great 'I' behind, let's go non-Western and put ourselves in the context of the Japanese cosmos. Shall we?"

"Oh yes, let's go there!" Your humble narrator affirmed.

"In the West, us looking at ourselves from the moon stands as a symbol of world consciousness for us. But, even then, we are still the subject. Even when glaring at how small our marble planet is. Even our views from outer space are about us looking at us."

Adam paused, looked inward, and then switched tact, "Look, Asians have noticed a pattern amongst people relating to the stars. Chinese astrology. In their horoscopes, the stars are the subject. Humans are some kind of direct object that gets wagged by the stars.

"Amazingly, we even put the stars, our horoscopes, in terms of our particular individual destiny. Our horoscopes start with telling us about us, the stars barely come into it. It's subtle, in Chinese astrology they are more interested in the general signs in the cosmos and what they indicate for the whole year than getting straight to the individual and their particular day with their horoscopes."

"Nice visuals." I chimed in, totally getting the picture through the tangential examples.

"But this might also explain why they have a race, instead of a free-floating God, to unite them." Adam continued musing, not sounding like he was in familiar thematic territory, "Like I said before, our English words do not imply place or context. Our western Biblical God thrives on words and he float in the sky.

"Asian religion stresses the unspoken. It is more visual. They are right here in nature. And as such their real racial group holds them together, that is, by a characteristic they can see.

"Ours sense of belonging comes from the abstract floating sky God. And even with that God, the individual still approaches God alone. It is very alienating. Again, the Japanese way is primitive, and the Western way is modern.

"Can you see it?" Adam concluded.

"Yes," I qualified, "But less with Judaism than Christianity. In Judaism the tribe is the goal, rather than individual salvation. I guess Judaism is primitive in that communal sense too."

"That would also go with your idea that languages get more about abstractions, like 'the individual,' as they advance, as they get more modern." Adam said.

"Is the individual more of an abstraction than the group you belong to?" I wondered out loud.

"Hmmm." Adam riffed on, gesticulating in an emphatic and professorial manner. "Yes, I think it is. We naturally exist, or existed, as groups. To think of yourself as apart and wanting salvation apart, is to literally and really abstract yourself from the actual social context you find yourself in. We're all, after all, social beings."

"Oh and yes," I confirmed my connection, "I have the perfect way to show the individual as an abstraction. I tell my classes, whereas traditional Asian art consists of landscapes with small people (if any), Western art almost always features people close up. We don't even have nature or background in our most famous paintings."

"Right, Good example," Adam concurred with his hand going over his jaw. "So Christianity is a sign of individualization in language, of alienation."

"So he who does not have a language connection won't have a natural connection or a social connection." I had begun the process of weaving these new realizations into our evolving sentence about sources of identity.

"The language makes other things too." Adam offered.

"Like what?" I was loving this!

"The hierarchical political system is in the language. Countries with languages with formal and informal pronouns don't have a lot of open democracy." He was referring to formal and informal ways of addressing persons.

"And Japanese has a formality system like Spanish, right?" I asked.

"Oh, yeah, it does." Adam said, sort of chortling at my ignorance and reveling in Japan-bashing. Somehow he did both without maliciousness so I did not take his snootiness personally. "Big time! That's why they are so militant and harsh."

"So, I want to call for an amendment of the phrase."

"A what?" Adam asked.

"An amendment of the phrase! Say 'seconded'!"

"Seconded!" He cheered with perfect glee.

"Good!" If one doesn't have God or a history or a nation or a family or job or an individual story," I said, pointing at Adam for the last one to indicate its source, "to hook ones identity hat on, one might find a place through their language, if it is structured around place and relationships of hierarchy."

"Or rather," Adam said with a teacherly attitude, "Instead of you finding your place in language, the language can place you in its world." With a humorous feigned exasperation, he reiterated, "You keep wanting to start with the 'you' again, and not the context."

"The fault, dear Adam, is not in ourselves but in the language." Adam missed my Julius Caesar reference, and I wanted to give him his due so I underscored his point. "Yes, I can see how my formulation concerns the place of the individual in an abstract world. But the formula is, after all, about how I, a dedicated westerner, can fit in."

But, Adam was not waiting for me to take him seriously, he now slipped into a role I had never seen him adopt, that of the prosecutor. "Earlier you said that the Israeli's are really unfriendly and not welcoming."

"To me they were."

"That is because you don't get the language or the importance of language!" He was definitely being accusatory and defensive. Whatever the truth about Adam, he did have a reservoir of anger that bubbled up fairly frequently. And, I had hurt his feelings when I maligned his fellow Israelis.

"When they speak to you they are translating from Hebrew. Hebrew doesn't have all the cute little polite phrases like "Thanks" and "Please." With Israelis all that stuff is assumed. We are closer than that kind of nicety will allow. If I am your friend and I want one of your cigarettes, do I have to ask?" He queried more confrontationally than rhetorically.

"Well . . ." I equivocated and nervously as if not sure I had the right answer, "I guess not."

"No!" He said, slamming the lid on the question. "We are friends. Friends share things. And when you take something from a friend, you don't need to say 'thank you.' If I saw you take one. You don't need to acknowledge it verbally. I know you took it and that you'll get me back and that our bond is strong."

"Hmnn." I said, with a slight paranoia that Adam was setting me up to borrow money from me. I had ended up being my brother's keeper and getting saddled with the bill many times.

"So what seems like gruffness to you is really assumed closeness. There is solidarity in a silent favor in our relations that the American with his contracts for all deals will never know.

"Once you get the language you get to know a people. And once you get Hebrew you'll see that the Jews of Israel are amongst the warmest people around. They are so close that there are no little niceties and acknowledgments of debt, like 'thank you,' in the language."

"Huh.   Neat." I uttered, conveying a hint of having accepted my chastisement and digesting what I'd just learned.

"How close you can get to others is in the language too." My newest best friend said, making the point overt. "You have English language relationships with people, John."
This personal chastisement wasn't pleasant.

"Wow. I haven't thought of this in a while." I declared, as I hadn't. "But when I was learning Korean, it always struck me as so weird that they used the pronoun 'our' when referring to their wives. They would say 'this is our wife,' when introducing their wife. I thought about that, but I never took it to heart in such a way. Perhaps I should just use 'we' all the time. What do 'We think?'" For the first time I really considered applying the benefits, as well as the strangeness, of another languages' thought patterns.

"That's in Japanese and Hebrew too. And the use of the word 'we,' even happens when people aren't talking. 'We' is the pronoun always understood in these languages, even in silence. Even when silent, there is a 'we quality' to their languages."

In any other context Adam's statement would have left me perplexed. But within the context of this conversation, though foreign, the concept made sense. But still, the idea of 'we' in moments of silence went a bit beyond MY ability to understand.
Leaning on my forte of historical analogy, by way of trying to grasp this concept, I contributed the observation that, "That's the way it used to be, for most of human history, you

lived and traveled as a group. Decisions back then wouldn't have been individual. So I guess it makes sense that there is a place in languages for group thought."

"But," Adam warned, "Israelis have a silent 'we.' As in, we take care of each other. But the Asian 'we' is just a mask for group responsibility and not being an individual. These are different forms of we. I think you know the Israeli's are strong individuals. Individualism doesn't have to be as cold as it is in English."

At this observation, I felt cold in my bones. I had an ache because I had never been a part of a group. Just as bad, I had always been parochial in my praising of our language's fostering individuality. Ours was only one kind. I had been studying this stuff for years, and didn't know anything. I felt small and alone.

I was upset and I got defensive. In a response that conveyed both my not wanting to be bested any more as well as my defensiveness, I pleaded, "But I love our American sense of ultimate individualism. It creates dynamism. Whereas Asian history is stagnant, our history, our art prides itself on continual revolution. Individualism is the ultimate in development. It is the furthest move away from the group. It's modern, it creates greatness."

"You really are so American." Adam demurred as though astonished.

"You bet! And I have accepted that there are different neat feelings associated with different languages and cultures. And those attitudes are important to preserve. But when push comes to shove, yeah, I'm American.

"And I guess I can't get out of it. Christianity is a lonely religion that tells us that struggle for the individual soul is the best. And, we do live alone in the West. And so, my extreme individualism and alienation are ways of me being a perfect exemplar of my culture. That's the price we pay for creation. And, since I like me, I like my culture.

"That's why I like writing so much. Putting ideas into the national discourse can move the West forward and make me famous in the process. I guess that's why fame is so important I the West. It is being acknowledged from a distance, so it feels good, but it also affirms you as different, as a unique individual.

"I often feel like Napoleon after they captured him and locked him in a cage on an island. He made a lot of plans in that cage. And then he escaped an enacted them. And his Napoleonic code reshaped the world. His words had an effect. In fact, truth be told, the world is living out the dreams of just a few dozen individual dreamers.

"It would be great if I could get even one word into our social discourse, to be one of those world shapers in even a little way. Even without having a family to belong in, I could fall asleep at night contented if my words helped shape or even save the West. Individual greatness is better than belonging. It's heroic!"

Adam sideswiped me, in an attempt to get me to realize that I, in my madness, I had once again forgotten the point that I was just a product of my language, he drolly stated, "Changing the world is sooo Western. The sentence 'I want to change the world' is so Western."

My defensive juices were flowing, "I know it is. But the West created the cyber-world. We made that. That has reshaped the world, boundaries and communities and such. Hasn't it? We can reshape the world!"

"I guess so. I'm just saying that when you revolutionize the world the language often stays the same." Adam offered humbly. "Capitalism, democracy, and consumer products haven't changed the basic ways that Japanese see relationships."

Still feeling adversarial, struggling to make a statement that affirmed me or my culture or something, I blurted, "I really like the individualism and freedom that English and modern thought make possible."

"Me too. But the alienation of being a total stranger is hard."

"All that is hard is heroic." I capped the conversation in disagreement.

Then I suddenly felt a great heat in my body.

"Hey. Is it okay to take off my shirt in this culture?" I asked with due deference to my cultural and weather surroundings.

"Not really. It's not considered normal. But that is the privilege of being Ganji. They aren't shocked when outsiders break with social custom. It reinforces the Japanese's image of Americans as context-free, barely civilized barbarians; as wild as the pronouns they rode in on. And, it also helps Japan's own self-image of being civilized, meaning accountable to society."

"Or at least their racial group." I finished defensively.

CAPSULE TEN: NATIONALISM

Right then there was hugely loud sound. It sounded like the slowed and warped tape of an organ that begins the album Berlin by Lou Reed. Or, if you're not familiar with that bit of music, it sounded like a hundred ice cream truck songs starting up really slowly and jerkily.

We went running back towards where we came from to see what was making that sound.

Back at the main intersection, the strange sound gave the impression that it was covering my auditory sense like a light that exceeds your peripheral vision. It was everywhere, a blanketing without edge. But where was it coming from? That statue of a woman playing guitar? The store? The sky? A building? Finding it went quickly from being a sport to being a disorienting and disturbing attempt to regain control of my mind's contents.

Adam yelped, "It's coming from the buses!" It was then I saw what should have been obvious before. There were about five very black buses in the intersection. They each had tinted black windows and mounted loudspeakers. Each bus also had starkly outlined Japanese letters on the side. Were they part of a promotion?

I asked Adam what they said. "Oh . . . uh." He replied, with a slack jaw and wide eyes. "Wait."

"What is it?" I nudged him. After another pause I insisted. "What?!"

"One says, "Foreigners get out." And the other says, "Japan for Japanese. And ... " Adam was a little confused. His brain seemed to be simultaneously taking the information in and refusing to process the information. I had the same sensation. This wasn't real. It was like something out of a movie.

He turned to a Japanese bystander. He asked her, "What do the buses say?" She waved him off with a bending of the wrist that pleaded ignorance. With a little more volume he insisted, "What does it say on the side of the buses?"

She seemed embarrassed and asked, "Where are you from?"

"America." Adam replied. Then he broke into Japanese. After a brief exchange he returned with the information. "I was right about those two buses. And that one over there says, "Russians go back to Siberia.""

We stood for about another three minutes before either one of us was un-stunned enough to formulate a response. And even then, only the phrase 'What the fuck!?' seemed appropriate.

The strategy of this brigade of black buses was apparently to block the intersection and either just cause a spectacle or create a crowd and get the masses to join them in chanting. Exactly which bus was going to stop where didn't seem to be diagrammed yet. The buses were starting and stopping jerkily in indecision. When one cleared the intersection it sped away. Then it would go to the end of the street, make a turn and come back to this main clustered intersection.

How to take this? Was this normal? Was this unreal? Two things were clear: The black buses had frightening dark Gestapo overtones and I was afraid. I was very glad that my shirt was back on. The bystanders were befuddled. The poor local traffic cop didn't know what to do.

The randomness and stilted thought process behind the awkward attempts at orchestration made the entire event comedic. The busses alternated between aggression and confusion.

I took this opportunity to ask Adam why he always addressed people in English when he knew Japanese. He first said something in Hebrew. And when I asked him what that meant, he smiled at my playing my part.

Adam kept his eyes focused on the developing story in the intersection, "Its a Hebrew expression meaning 'Why should I break my teeth?' I guess the English equivalent is 'Why should I stick my neck out?' There is no need for me to go into my life story or make a big effort. They expect English, I use English, no questions."

This bus scene kept re-boggling my mind. We watched in disbelief, unable to digest this reality, over and over.

"So let me get this straight. This brigade of black buses blocking the intersection is part of a fascist civil disobedience action?" Though obvious, I needed to ask this to reestablish communication and to try to get my mind to accept what it was seeing.

"That seems to be about the size of it." Adam agreed without looking at me.

"Mind blowing." I uttered.

"Bizarre." He automatically concurred.

After what seemed like another fifteen minutes of sheer disbelief, I started in with the humor. "Adam. Is the music coming from the buses the theme song from Godfather Three?"

"Actually, I think its part six." There was a lot of relief in deflating the seriousness of this potentially horrifying sight.

"Oh, no." I joked. "I had this CD. Its called Italian Music for Japanese Nationalists.

I checked again, "You haven't seen anything like this before have you, Adam? Is this something that sometimes happens sometimes in Japan?"

"I have never seen anything like this before."

"Then this could be history in the making." I said with a tone of seriousness that such a realization required. "A revolution is being attempted. They are demanding attention and something's got to happen."

"But there's no one in the buses." Adam replied drolly.

He was right! Rather than people, there were silhouettes painted in the black windows. The buses were nearly empty! It was an illusion of a crowd that had worked on me. "Yeah. There's only about three people on each bus."

"I guess they figured that people wouldn't notice amongst the swelling crowds of supporters." Adam guessed.

"But no one seems to be making any moves to join them." I noted.

"People are just stunned. No one knows what to make of this." Adam confirmed.

"Its rinky-dink." I admitted. "But I'm still a little bit nervous. This is reliving a moment from my historical imagination, from NAZI Germany, and I don't know what to do. Do we face the danger of the rising NAZIs? Or do we run and hide like I'm thinking might be wise? We're obviously white and those people hate us. We could get shot."

"We won't get shot."

"No? Can you be sure of that?" I asked somewhat frantically.

"Yes. One Hundred Percent."

"How?" I demanded.

"There aren't any guns in this country. You can't get them in. That's why we've been able to walk around so late at night and not feel afraid at all. Have you ever felt afraid tonight?" Adam queried without taking his eyes off of the bus.

"No. I guess I haven't and I hadn't even noticed it."

A pause ensued while we stayed transfixed on the busses. They were driven in such a jerky way that they resembled poorly designed mechanical cockroaches, stumbling blindly.

They would ride into the intersection, seem like they were parking, refusing to leave, and then, with odd nudging, they'd go through the intersection, get to the next block, make a u-turn and come back for another go. With each loop around the block they stayed longer in the intersection. Each time they drove more brazenly as if the streets were theirs. Each time looked more like they were going to park and not leave, they stalled for a longer time in the intersection before moving on en route to returning.

The lone traffic cop, kept his ground in the middle of the intersection. He waved about frantically and tried not to get hit. It was obvious that he had no clue as to what to do in such a situation.

"When I was in Brazil, the police caught a guy stealing a tourist's purse. They shot him in the ass. After he lay screaming for a couple minutes they threw him in the police car trunk and drove off!"

I implied that I had witnessed this incident. But I actually just heard the commotion from my window and the details second hand. I'm not quite sure why I told him this story.

"Their ideas are great!" I blurted with feigned sarcasm, while pointing at the black buses. "If Japan stopped all foreigners and all foreign trade...yeah that'd be good."

"They are poor and uneducated" Adam's replied, repeating a common response to nationalist sentiments.

As I made my sarcastic remark, I knew it was a cheap contrivance designed to get some political-correctness points from Adam. I myself harbored nationalist sentiments and resented unfettered immigration to America. To be brutally honest, I and wasn't so quick to dismiss the Japanese protestors' ideas. I considered his negative analysis of them a knee-jerk liberal reaction. Should I bite my tongue?

"I guess with no foreigners present, the Japanese could do transactions on-line." I offered, at once skirting the issue, appearing to be against these buses via sarcasm, and putting forth a serious proposal.

America is currently being invaded by peoples who don't speak our language and don't consider America their nation and by others who are straight out hostile to our values. A nation can only absorb a certain amount of ideological rift.

"I kind of get the black bus guys." I bravely ventured. "Sometimes cultures are delicate. Cultures need to be protected and borders are important."

Wow. I had gone too far and so I defensively applied this policy admission to a second world, "emerging" nation.

"For example India's caste system means that everyone has a level in society that they have to stay in. And the caste system undergirds the entire ideological basis of their religion and society.

"So what was India to do when I walked in? What caste am I? I don't even understand defilement and pollution and past lives. The whole Indian system was destroyed the moment a foreigner showed up.

"Especially an American foreigner." When one's transgressed against a liberal truth, they can always retreat to safe ground with a little America bashing. "America's tradition is based on the hatred of olds and the Old World. We don't care about caste. We only want to know what we can do with your resources now!

Now I went overboard in my retreating to the safety of America - bashing. "We are capitalist culture-killers; big Mickey-Mouse bearing culture-killers. We'd turn all of India into a collection of McDonald's stands if we were given a chance. A million new freeway systems can't be wrong!

Finally a slogan we can all agree upon. We'd standardize everything, but I guess that all of those women working in fields besides their ancient field animals won't be replaced too soon. Unless by tractor."

And, at that I held my breath. Had I obscured my hint of sympathy with the men in the black buses enough? Was I back on the respectable and tolerable side of Leftist intolerance for dissonant 'illiberal' opinion?

"Anyhow, this isn't India. This is a modern nation." Adam qualified, "I'd hoped that fascism was dead amongst modern nations."

"Democracy seems to have triumphed." I partially agree, "But it hasn't really taken root in much of the world. And Democracy screws India in a big way. The untouchables are out-voting the high-caste Brahmin types. Good-bye "top Brahmin.""

"Top Brahmin. Funny." Adam acknowledged my ramen noodle name pun by looking at me and smiling slightly as he looked me in the eyes. But he also seemed to be searching for something in my eyes. I don't think he was amused by the lack of clear condemnation of the black bus folks in my statements.

"Funny." I acknowledged, "But seriously, democracy totally undermines the whole Indian system."

Ironically, when I should have been silent, my nervousness about political discussions led me to ramble on. "And, of course, the Japanese have always been pretty good at absorbing other cultures and continuing. They're post-modern like that. But I can see how our western individual-based, sexual liberation, disobey your parents, MTV trip is subversive to their social system - the whole Confucian thing."

I still wasn't sure what Adam was thinking. He was either entirely engrossed in the bus situation or not talking to me.

"Hey. I need a drink. I'm going into the 7-11. Coming with?" He finally uttered.

His considering leaving, I surmised, meant that he wasn't totally engrossed in the bus situation. "Naw, I'm going to stay outside. I wanna see this. See what happens to these cockroach busses."

Race and nationalism are funny things. The profusion of greasy old Italians doing sex tours I witnessed in Cuba bothered me. But now that I've seen old Asian men with beautiful young white women it bothers me even more. As completely wrong as the thought was, I had to admit that, even though they were Russian, I didn't like to see them taking "our women." It might have been training or affiliation, but I had to consider the awful possibility that solidarity was genetic; it could, at very least, latch onto race.

Five minutes later Adam re-emerged with a drink. "Has anything new developed?"

"Not really. I get the feeling that the buses are trying to create a stand-off. Well, that and they're just being assholes and blocking traffic too."

White ambulance-sized vans with bullhorns mounted on them had now joined the parade. The fascists had gone multi-colored. One van was stuck in traffic and the driver seemed to be cursing the fact over the loudspeaker system. He tried to get out of his predicament by driving over a center divider. But to do this he first had to back up. He seemed to curse and swear at the guy behind him for not backing up. Of course the car hadn't backed up because it was trapped by the demonstration. Then he made a jerky right, went over the road divider, but then had to temporarily stop with one wheel still on it. Finally, he made it over.

"He is just like a frustrated little bug." Adam had more disgust than spite in these words. But, the vehicle going over the divide really did look like a bug.

Then Adam gave the bug consciousness, though of a low level. "The driver is showing his personal issues that got him driving with this group. It is so obvious that it's embarrassing. He has no patience or grace when dealing with others."

Then a memory allowed me to display my Leftist credentials, "One of the greatest moments of my life was when I was protesting in People's Park in Berkeley. I was playing in my band in our acoustic-street-musician set up and about 60 riot cops in formation ran past us as we screamed wild fascist fighting screams. It was a great moment in my life." I was trying to win Adam's sympathy back. I feared I had offended him greatly.

"Adam?"

"Yes."

"Why don't you speak Arabic?"

"I have to stay in a country about two years before I get the language. It isn't like sight-seeing for me in the Arab world. I explained that. They will not let me into their lives. I'm a Jew. It's dangerous. I could be killed. It happens all the time.

"Let's get out of here." He muttered.

It took about three blocks of walking before we finally had the feeling that we weren't being propelled by a desire to get away anymore. We could slow down. While we were getting our first calm breaths, a bunch of black guys, who were totally oblivious to the proceedings blocks away, tried to corral us.

"Drinks really cheap. Women. Dancing. Do you like women?"

It is amazing how quickly and subtly these barkers work. They have about twenty seconds to do a psychological profile on you. Are you worried about strippers or other hustlers? Do you want to dance? Can you be bullied? Do you feel safe? If they can get you to say 'yes' to nearly any question, they put their arms around you as if they were your friends. They use their friendly arm around your back to physically force you into their bar.

Their quick calculation of your psychological profile couldn't be computerized. It takes a human touch.

I got into the mode of responding to their hustling with displays of temper-fueled anger. I used this angry powerful American tactic to repel. I found it could dissuade the most persistent beggars in India. Adam used the tactic of treating the head of the group as an individual. He engaged him on a real level. The diffusion of tension was immediate.

Adam queried, "What is your name?"

"My name is Patrick. Please come inside and drink." The broad shouldered, well-dressed, bald, black man replied.

"We've actually been walking around all night and are pretty spun. I don't think we're going to drink now. Can I ask you some questions, Patrick? I'm curious about some things and I need to ask you."

Patrick waved his friends away and they dissipated like so many Shakespearian fairies, into the night. He had an intuitive sense that Adam was sincere and respectful. He seemed eager to talk to us. It seemed as if he had been waiting on this corner for someone to acknowledge him as an individual, to ask him some real questions.

"I'm Adam, by the way."

"John," I said to Patrick extending my hand. "Nice to meet you."

Black. His face was really black. Only after the whole wind-down from the hustle attempt did I even really look at his face.

One thing I learned by going to Africa, I kidded my students yearly, is that the people there are black. 'Duh!!' The class would moan. But they would cease to be puzzled or amused by this truism if they could see this man. Not just brown, this man was really black.

People say that black is the absence of color. Actually, technically, when all of the colors annihilate each other you get white light. This man radiated black by way of purple. Purple is the color your eyes generate when there is a lack of stimulus. Patrick's kind of blackness created patches of purple in your eyes.

"This is kind of a personal question. I hope you don't mind me asking," Adam pressed, "But how much money do you make a night?"

By what assumed permission did Adam manage to run where angels fear to tread? People are willing to share with him because he asks the hardest questions with a sense of honesty. There is no ulterior motive of fun or profit, no voyeuristic journalism in Adam's asking - only pure sympathetic caring and interest.

Understanding each other because we care about each other is the deep motivation behind nearly all non-bureaucratic or commercial communication. People being willing to share their stories with him reflects that fact.

"I am really amazed by you. I wonder how you survive here. Being a non-Japanese is bad enough. But to be black, it must be so hard to make a living." Bluntness.

"I can make from 10 - 30 dollars a night." Patrick kept looking straight ahead like he was still scanning for customers. "That is on a good night. Tonight we've each made about 10 dollars and its nearing time to go home."

"Do you get a commission?" Adam probed.

"Yes. A commission on the number of people that come in and buy drinks. We don't get any money otherwise."

"Wow. That is hard. Is it your only job?"

"No. I work in a factory during the day."

"Wow. That *is* hard. Do you have kids?"

"We cannot afford children now, perhaps in the future. Time is against us; we are aging, but we haven't got the financial means to support them properly now."

Patrick didn't really have an accent. Rather he had a softness and deliberate pacing that made his speech distinctive. His annunciation had a textbook perfection that showed him to be academic, super-fluent, and a non-native speaker.

"Oh, so you're married?" Adam continued.

"Yes, for thirteen years. And are you fellows married?"

"No. Neither one of us." Adam replied softly.

"And your wife works?" Adam asked, directing the conversation back to Patrick.

"Yes. She has a school. That is what she did back in the home country, Nigeria. Her degree is in pedagogy."

"Mine too." I chimed in for the first time. "How many students does she have?"

"Oh, about 12 right now."

"Wow!" Adam exclaimed in admiration, "I wonder, because this place is so hard on foreigners, but to be black here. I can't imagine. I mean, I know a lot of white Gangi. They get work just by being white. But you probably can't get work teaching English."

"No way. They take a look at my skin and there is no way I can work teaching English. So I have to hustle. This is the best money I can get right now."

"It's an honest job." Adam said without guile, "I really admire your ability to survive here. That's why I wanted to know how you did it. You probably speak several languages, eh. How many can you speak?"

"Five well. Six or seven proficiently."

"Amazing. You speak six or seven languages proficiently and you can't teach. Do you know what I do?"

"Teach English?" Patrick guessed.

"I'm a minister in marriages. And you know what sucks? I'm not even a minister. I showed them a piece of paper that I downloaded of the internet and they accepted it. They looked at my white skin and didn't ask any other questions. That was enough!"

"And we cannot get teaching work here!" Patrick was now getting indignant, sad, and angry.

"So why did you come here?" Adam continued.

"Opportunity. You cannot compare the situation here and in Nigeria. The situation there is so horrible it is unbelievable. The cops will stop you and beat you up -- even kill you -- until you confess to something and pay the fine. It is your word against theirs. You can't ever win."

"And is there no way to stay and make your country better?" I asked, thinking that a country gets worse when good people leave.

"The presidents have stolen everything. They have houses and airplanes and interests in many countries. That is from selling the country's resources. There is nothing left. And the President lives on a fortress on the mountain. I cannot get within eight miles of his house. Armed guards are everywhere. If I got close they'd shoot me. And no one would care. Reform is not happening."

"The irony is," Adam said offering an insight that missed the point, "that you are free to wander around your nation free and the President is locked up as a prisoner in his own country."

"Yeah, or we are all in his jail." Patrick said, still looking into the street as if her were showing an employer he was still hustling business. "The President goes a lot of places. But you're right. He must be careful. If I saw him on this street I would kill him. He had better be careful."

"Oh, my god. Patrick, you should know about this!" I recalled excitedly. "I played music in a band and my bass player's mother was the secretary to the President of the Siemens Corporation's U.S.A. branch.

"She received a letter from Nigeria. The letter explained that the Nigerian utilities folks had accidentally been over billing for years. They were embarrassed and didn't want to admit this mistake. It would look bad politically. So, the letter said that if Siemens would just hold the money, they could keep ten percent. The Nigerian official would get the balance later. Several ministers' signatures were on it. This was hard evidence of corruption at the highest level. I held this letter in my hands; I wish I would have kept it."

"Why?" Patrick asked with a tone of disinterest and incredulity, amazed that I wasn't getting it.

"It had the signatures of ministers on it." I re-explained "It was signed by three ministry heads. And... Oh --" I finally caught on and stopped myself.

Patrick acknowledged my revelation with a slight nod and look in my direction. "Everyone knows. These ministers live in compounds up in the hills. It is not a secret that they steal from us. No one can do anything about it; evidence means nothing. So I had to leave my country. I worked hard and paid people and got my passport."

"Why did you come here? You'd have done better in the United States. We aren't as racist as there." I dared with a note of pride.

"The United States won't take anybody. The countries that we go to are Korea and Japan."

"Is there a community that will help you when you arrive in these countries? Is that another reason you go here?" I continued, fascinated by the opportunity to speak to a Nigerian that Adam had opened up.

"Yes. And, they are actually the only countries that will accept a traveling Nigerian. Koreans will accept you for factory work. But they are really cruel. Worse than the Japanese, they hit you and insult you and threaten to take your passport. They say they will send you back to what they call 'The Land where there are too many of you.' And that passport is all you have, so you put up with it. After some time there I managed to get a visa to here."

"Wow! I've been to Korea a dozen times and never knew they did that sort of thing."

"They are cruel."

"My fiancé is Korean." I told Patrick.

"My apologies. Anyhow, here it is better. You can work hard and do okay. Look at me. I am wearing a suit. I send money back home every month. I don't make much money, but we do get by. Now, if you will excuse me, I must get back to work."

"Thanks. We've learned a lot," Adam concluded.

"Yeah. Thanks." I added.

"No problem."

We had walked about fifteen feet when I remembered my Nigerian friend Olu. I worked with Olu when I was thirteen till I was seventeen. He had always seemed like an insane cartoon character to me. He would speak of getting a hamburger in a restaurant and the other people looking at him admiringly because he had gotten a hamburger. He seemed to be constantly putting on an act to show that he was crazy.

Though he seemed like an old man back then, Olu must have only been about 23. Years later, in community college, our paths crossed again. Olu behaved as bizarrely as ever then too.

Now, with an adult perspective, I could ask questions an American teen-ager would never ask. I never asked him about his home country and why he left.

Smitten by curiosity, borne of a nostalgic desire to question Olu as an adult, I went back to ask Patrick about him. I told him of my history with this fellow and asked if he could give me any insight. "His name was Olu."

"Oh, yeah! There is no doubt: Olu is from the West. That name is definitely of their language. That part of the country holds all the power. Our President is from that area. But the people from that area are stupid and lazy. And some day we are going to take our country back from those lazy do-nothing people."

I was stunned. He had no compunction about his rank group stereotyping. The moral and ending to this dialogue mocks visions of progress. It is too obvious.   And for that reason I nearly left the end of the conversation out of this retelling. But I didn't. So much for universal rights, equality, and brotherhood.

When safely out of earshot of Patrick I opined, "Oh, the humanity," with sarcasm. "When will men ever stop hating others just because they are different? When will we stop blaming others for our misfortune and look at the man in the mirror?"

"When will men stop ripping each other off? Men are stupid. Stupid black-bus-riding idiots." Adam answered raging against a spirit of fatigue and anger in an endearing way. He really felt for life. Suffering wasn't just academic for him.

Adam went into a bit of a funk. I could sense it as clearly as I could feel my own feet while walking.

"That encounter with Patrick was great!" I told him with an actual admiration and gratitude for his initiative. I thought this enthusiastic summary might cheer my partner up.

Then I did some reflecting, "As my personal understanding gets wider I can put people in their political/cultural geographical location. I can rely on more and more perspective. I wouldn't have ever thought to ask Olu about his geo-political situation when I was a kid. Contrasting my old thought with my new thought, I can really see growth.

"It's like my amazement that I used to think that being in community college put you straight on the corporate career path! What was I thinking? I have grown. And change over time shows growth."

This statement had more than a little plea for absolution for my sympathy with the people in the black bus. Please have mercy for those of us still growing.

The black bus people likely all were idiots. But, I'd argue that if all people are idiots, our nation might have to stoop to their idiotic level of thinking to protect us from even more idiots. Enlightenment thought is hopeless against idiots.

"I used to think 30 was incredibly old. Now I'm thirty-six. That shows growth." Adam's listlessness was frightening. This was a side of him I did not know - except from personally experiencing it myself.

But I was still in a bold mood. So I triumphed, "Well, some day before I die, I want to approximate the omniscience of God. God is like a fly; he can take in a million perspectives at once. And God uses his omniscience on all of the ultimate questions: 'Is there life after death?' 'What is the universe made of?' But unlike a fly, God has no blind spots that he is unaware of. There are no gaps to be filled between God's categories. I'd like to approximate that."

"I wonder if God actually hates thought. Thought is noisy and divisive. If he did hate thought, he would need to have a lot of sympathy to like us, let alone endure us." Adam moped.

Adam and I sat down on a street corner and were silent. We sat with his funk. Ironically, I didn't even really notice my legs until I sat down. They were a little sore. And, suddenly my feet came into my awareness. As per usual, had some pain in my heels and my arches.

A bit later, I offered more positivity by way of emotional stimulus, "What a trip this has been for me. It is really amazing to see so many different perspectives and imagine all of the values."

"Where you are born and when you're born really do make you who you're going to be." Adam's premise seemed to indicate that a gloomy conclusion loomed on the horizon.

Now I tried self-deprecating solidarity to find some common ground with Adam. "I wonder, if someone else went through the geography and times we've been through they would they think like us? Maybe you're right. Maybe even I, the great voracious reader that I am, am totally predictable in my beliefs."

"No. Your thoughts are strange. Pretty cool." Adam revered by way of backing out of that negative road.

The compliment was nice to hear after I had perceived so much tension over my hint of empathy for the nationalists. "Thanks. You're a really neat person too, Adam. I think you've escaped the traps you were born into too."

"Thanks." He said, unimpressed either by what seemed to be just a socially required return of a compliment, or his life.

My eyes fixed on a worker with a uniform and insignias on his cap. Since we were in a bit of an alley, not so many people were around here. And, the cleaner worked the street and sidewalk, right outside of a large parking structure, illuminated, in the dark, by just a few large spotlights.

"How conscious is that guy picking up trash?" I began, "He is doing his part. But is he doing it with a view towards his family? Towards the history of the great nation of Japan? Does he see himself as a part of the business sector? Does he consider the meaning of the insignia on his hat?"

"Or does he just go from piece of trash to piece of trash?" Adam replied bitterly.

I shot him a look of disapproval for his negativity. He got my message and tried to make a positive contribution.

"The flag on the hat looks British to me." Adam observed with all the insight that one can get from the grammar of visuals. But then he had to slip back to his mope. "He is a government worker. His hat shows some lingering memory of the imperialist-mother-country Britain."

I took up the thread from there, "The colors of his hat represent some history and social order. Maybe the colors in the corner of his hat insignia were the last remnants of a treaty that concluded a bloody struggle. Perhaps it represents the truce of 1893 or something. 'Okay, there will be a strip in the flag for your separate region's traditional island space too.' Perhaps the colors represent some sort of inclusionary arrangement between groups."

"All flags represent conquest and oppression." Adam dimly concluded.

"Or order! Oh, Brother." I shot back, loud enough for him to hear me, impatient with his negativity. Adam seemed to respond, guiltily listening more than he might have otherwise.

"You know what would be worse and is probably true?" Trying to be conciliatory after my little outburst, but still not over the residual adrenaline born of having confronted Adam. "The straps and colors and insignias on his outfit could just reflect a bureaucratic battle such as an office and department consolidations, maybe joint management of previously separated departments. Efficient bureaucracy.

And I smiled, realizing how nutty the next line sounded as I got through it, and glad for the humor, "In a Hegelian way this functional consolidation and efficiency would be life coming into order and realizing itself through its evolution."

"I'm sure he doesn't think of that!" Adam responded, with a labored smile that produced just a bit of teeth. He was trying.

"But as you know, the Japanese are nationalistic." I surmised, "I'm sure he does think of himself as part of the country of Japan and its honor. And some history backs that pride up. He may think about the role street cleaners play in Japan." This sounded like a good thing to me.

"Whatever he thinks," Adam noted, "he sure is going about it conscientiously." He really did chase down each small speck of dirt in the street aggressively. "Cleaning gives his life meaning. He is taking his role seriously of hd could do much less."

"Totally conscientious." I confirmed.

"He'd better not look outward though." Adam warned, finally really smiling a bit and pointing down the street in both ways. "Look at how many thousands of pieces of trash there are in this world!" The road was littered with trash and paper as far as the eye could see.

"He'd go nuts with hopelessness if he looked out and took in the eternity of the trash-filled streets of Japan." I paraphrased.

"One piece of trash at a time." Adam blurted, making a sardonic reference to the AA slogan.

We both laughed, if not out loud. Our eyes were shining. Adam seemed to catch himself and regain his glummer countenance.

I expanded Adam's thought, bending with his mood to a level of seriousness I thought our insights warranted. "You need to define your boundaries if you are going to have identity and purpose. Too much space, too broad a consciousness, makes us insignificant. Dizzy with the fear of being nothing. Hopeless at the size of the task and the vastness of the universe."

"There's a lot of truth to the cliché, 'good fences make good neighbors.'" I skirted political incorrectness, "But it doesn't just mean good neighbors in terms of war, but internally, it helps each nation with its identity.

"And globalism doesn't work for this. People don't root for that. It just means that people are scattered people. Scattered people chasing trash." I was not pretending. I was sharing my true opinions. If Adam was to be pissy anyhow, I had nothing to lose.

"Hate of the other is how most cultures create their definitions and give themselves a bite-size identity." Adam challenged, "That is how nations avoid the fluidity of life, that's how they make everything seem manageable and safe. And I think people take on the priorities of their group for the same pathetic reason." As I didn't want him to take my disagreement personally, I tried not to take his personally. It wasn't that hard, he wasn't being malicious.

"And when you've genocided the other in war, you need to find another group to hate, to give your life meaning. It never ends. Identity by hate has to continuously consume."

We weren't seeing eye-to-eye. But I wasn't nervous anymore, because a tone of friendly curious exploration accompanied our discussion. I felt mellow sitting on that curb, looking at the sweeper in the night.

Adam still seemed glum, far away. My lack of worry also sprang from Adam's lethargy.   Deep down he didn't seem to care. But I didn't take it seriously as he didn't seem to care about anything. His eyes were a little sad.

"What's wrong?" I dared.

"I don't like nationalism. I don't like what it does to people. I find it depressing."

"But nations are forever," I continued, unworried and humorous intentions, "You probably can never even genocide properly in the first place. There's always going to be some pain-in-the-ass historian in some small unaccounted-for university waiting to exhume the history of your people and nation. Nations never disappear; they are never dead.

"That pain-in-the-ass historian could probably even explain the cultures involved in the treaty that led to the flag on the workers hat."

I smiled, pleased with my wit. But Adam wasn't listening. He was self-absorbed.

I watched Adam's eyes darting back and forth while looking at nothing and knew he was thinking. I waited patiently for his statement.

Finally it came, "Imagine trying to recreate your identity from the ruins of Nagasaki. All relatives dead. All pictures gone. The university and record-keepers dead. The nation defeated. Just your memories left. What a trip." What a bummer! I thought.

"See, that proves my point!" I said like a cheery salesman, "A real good clean total genocide probably is impossible. There was no *final solution* to the Nagasaki problem. We tried to wipe out the city, but we just can't get rid of *that darned memory!*" My humor sometimes goes beyond the limits of decorum. But Adam didn't react, so I continued unabated.

"Hey maybe that is why your language CD is selling well in Nagasaki. They might have realized the seriousness of words and communication. They want to speak and be heard; let the world know that they still exist."

As if channeling a demon, without looking up, Adam groaned, "Death makes us aware of our commonality. And so Nagasaki is the seat of global consciousness. Death is the ultimate boundary that identifies us. We the living are defined by the borders of death." Wow! What a lovely thought!

"Yeah. Like you said, we have to limit our scope to construct an identity. But I have to correct you." Adam insisted, "The boundary set by death isn't positive like that. Death kills all identity."

Talk about a party killer! Adam had put a cork in it. Now we both sat as though sulking. Well, it would have appeared that way to an outside observer. But I still secretly enjoyed the fact that I was in Japan having this conversation with Adam, no matter how depressing the content.

"Hey! Speaking of death and limits, I need to go back to the hotel and get my ear medicine!" I announced. I made this unexpected outburst with elation for ear medicine never heard before or since.

I told Adam how I spent four hours in the dead of night, in the pouring rain, climbing from water pool to water pool in Brazil, with my friend Carl. We knew we were courting hypothermia, but we wanted to be on-the-edge crazy.

"When I got the ear infection, the Brazilians gave me butt-kicking medicine over the counter. But it ran out on the plane and the infection came back. The American doctors gave me a weak medicine to avoid complications and a lawsuit. Finally, I raised hell and got a good strong medicine out of the Americans. The prescription is almost finished, and my ear feels totally cured; I can hear again and there is no pain. But I had better finish the pills completely so it doesn't come roaring back like it did before."

I was happy to share a tale of adventure with Adam. But the real reason behind the elation was that I had found a reason to go back and sneak a moment or two in my capsule. I suddenly had a hankering for isolation from the world and its complications, and craved the freedom to run amok in my own mind in one of those trippy, clean, boundless, context-free, capsule.

Capsule ELEVEN: S(t)imulation

As we approached the ROI building, where my ear medicine awaited, many black suited, white collar workers were leaving it. Having bought new white shirts after their overnight encapsulation, they were ready to take the subway back to work again. We had made it to early dawn!

My obsession over the idea of having moments alone in my capsule fed upon itself. But I remained sociable, despite my anti-social urges, or maybe to ward off the feelings of hatred and guilt that accompanied them.

"It is such a trip here. All of these businessmen leaving the capsules and going off to work in their new shirts. I guess they don't go home."

"No, it isn't rare for married couples to live in different cities." My ever-affable host Adam chimed in, "There's even a word for this arrangement. Work commonly does that to couples and it's expected that the couple will just continue together separately."

"So the cell phone really does become your primary point of contact with your loved ones?" I asked

Adam nodded, but said nothing, as we needed to focus on the requirements of the capsule hotel's shoe regulations.

As we silently worked to conform with the logical and ordered demands of this system ourselves, a new English-speaking arrival begged reception to tell him where you exchange your shoe key for your locker key. They were trying to tell this confused young man that he couldn't stay there. But as he didn't understand them, he turned to Adam and I.

Adam started to translate for the young tourist. As the kid looked really frazzled and anxious, and Adam would both be willing and able to help him, I knew I had some time.

"So I'm going to go get my ear medicine. I'll be down as quickly as I can."

"Take your time. I'll be enjoying the lounge." I think Adam intuited my agenda. And he is a generous soul.

"Thanks." I replied, as if we both understood our implicit pact.

I bounded up the stairs, opened my locker, and headed for capsule #44c.

For some time I had been thinking about how trippy it would be to be inside a capsule on Trip Thunder. The astro-cacoon would erase distractions and provide the sleek blank-slate walls necessary to project on. My body also really felt banged up and in need of rest.

The white capsule walls radiated like an empty backlit Rorschach test and immediately appeared to shatter into a thousand pixels when I lay down. Wow. These amazing visuals were still pounding after seven hours.

The imagined pixels could be tinted and reconfigured to produce anything. That is my mind could construct anything I wanted to out of these pixels. Computer monitors make their images out of pixels. And, now I was in able to control what I saw at the level of the pixel. I was amazed by my mind's ability to manipulate visuals in this way. It was a delicacy. Ecstasy.

My visual rollercoaster ride went at a rapid pace. Images raced ahead of my interpretations by 15 - 30 seconds. My ideas tried to comprehend the visuals and their grammatical implications in a mad race to catch up. I never did. And, in some sense, as I write this, my thoughts are still trying to catch up.

I exploded an image of Roppongi's skyline. Zooming in on a resultant pixel showed that it too was full of sparkling pixels. Zooming out, the pixels came back and reconstituted the skyline. But I had learned that all we see comes from reflected light. Here there was no light. My mind projected the visuals on the capsule wall. The visuals burst with the radiating potential of consciousness.

Patterns provide information. The pixels became circles. Circles turned into eyes. The face of a baby appeared. I watched this fresh consciousness watch a glowing screen. His little pudgy hand was pointed at the screen. Upon touching this screen light burst out and a hidden magnetism moved all the pixels apart making the image of the baby separate and then, via gravity, reconstitute.

We are at the end of an epoch. Most Japanese vending machines have virtual buttons. You touch the visual representation of a button on a screen to force action in the real world. I still hesitate when I push a new virtual button for the first time. But the baby will expect a reaction from everything she touches. The entire world will be a portal conducting information. Sidewalks will speak.

In fact touching may disappear. Via face recognition, the computer walls could know you and display your desires on the walls of rooms you enter. You could just verbally confirm that which you want with a word and it would appear. Virtual windows will assume sunny days.

Old-fashioned walls that aren't screens will seem as a suffocating as closets seem to us now: claustrophobic and unnerving. Dead walls are scary. Virtual is a better kind of open-ended reality. That is why the capsule is perfect. It isn't a two-dimensional space; its white walls have no limits. With my imagination I can fall into it. More real. Less physical. More mental. Free. Totally free.

As the capsule wall was only limited by my imagination, I flew into clouds. A planet became a pixel in a planet. And this gave me the feeling of soaring. To go down, I dove into ever spinning spirals. Though fantastic, it was lonely. I needed a friend.

"Floor, get Jim. Okay, let's fly!" My friend Friar Moose appeared and he and I spoke of galaxies being the same shape as water going down drains and the same as clouds of cream in coffee. Clouds and cityscapes flew past. Moose and I were aloft.

What are the distinctions that separate the real from the unreal?

The Japanese girls' obsession with cell phones provided the obvious place to look for the juncture. I saw the girls looking at phones and shrunk until they were on phone screens themselves. I repeated this and this diving sped up until girls started to turn and jump into their own phones and the other girls followed.

With mental force that strained me, I slowed down the spiral of girls looking at girls on phones looking at girls on phones. I straightened them from a recursive circle into a line. And they became a subway full of passengers – all on phones.

Millions of workers and girls going in subway tubes where they are nervously and intently sending and seeking images to validate themselves as humans. But the sheer number of them made them non-individuated – non-human. Bits, bytes, and pixels. The intersection wherein all of these individuals become a crowd defines humans. This individual is just the smallest indivisible part of the mass.

And, conversely, when the passengers all imagine the same human, that human being imagined is a supra-human. But when we try to imagine the supra-human of the collective imagination, it is hard to imagine the supra-human's thoughts.

The collectively imagined supra-human is an abstraction. We can imagine the thought of every individual in the mass imagining the supra-human, but not collectively and spontaneously imagine the collective-inspired thought of the supra-human being. Collective imagination has limits that define the edge of our consciousness as humans.

But collectively, we could move the supra-human via averaging all of our impulses. And, via silent polling, we might even give it a lifestyle that would imply thoughts. We would then be the decisions. Our thoughts would decide its fate.

But, the decisions would have no reasons to be found in the supra-human's consciousness. We'd be its subconscious. But so many of our decisions have no reasons. We might be supra-humans guided by individuals in mobs. The members of the mob, in turn . . .

We have the ability to see several items at once, where thoughts are only singular. Will living in an icon based visual world expand the ability to think? How will the baby raised to touch and see info make thoughts? Because words, stories, and thoughts take too long, verbal expression is now a second-rate citizen. The new baby's brain will be wired for the faster more pliable grammar of desired visuals. It will have explosive visual thought.

For mass marketing sales you want maximum images per second. As with the 24 frames per second of film, images will come for the shortest amount of time it takes us to absorb them. The limits of thought calculated. Advertisers of the future will aim at ads that can grab you while you go by on a train. The ratio of quickness to understanding will be maximized. Jingle penetration will happen before you can close a pop-up.

The time it takes to process a thought and recognize a visual can be measured. The capsule is the perfect place to measure thoughts per second. Visuals are faster than words. My brain-boosting drug and blank white screen have made it possible for me to see the limits of what hallucination and manipulation of the two dimensional will allow. Projected Darwin fish eat words, sentences, even books. I bet projection is slower than reception.

The white of this capsule reminds me of 7 – 11 convenience stores.

The slogan of all the Japanese 7-11s is "happy feeling." It's not only short, but it blurs the lines between verbal and sensual. As it isn't a complete sentence, it is easy to pair with anything from coats to airplanes. Mix and match the grammar of slogan and image. A blue elephant on a bicycle: Happy feeling. A man's head on a frog wearing snorkel gear under water: Happy feeling. U.S.A.: happy feeling. Juxtaposing skimming visuals and half thoughts speeds reception.

Now I imagined a punctuated computer sentence broken down into its components, "computer," "confused." That is how the computer would most quickly tell us that it is confused. Full sentences are inefficient. We will adapt to the computer not it to us. Those who do not will be left behind. "Tutor." "Show." To pay bills say "bill." Use tutor, say, "tutor." To call Jack say, "Jack." All down into bite sized commands. Thus spake wall computers.

Dimensions of future: mass replication.

Future: micron-management to the pixel, worldwide / standardized. When something doesn't work in one store on Wednesday's from 3:15 to 5 pm, it will fail in your 4,000,000 replicated chain stores. Pull during those times. There are no small details on such a scale of replication.

In the 4 million 7s (7-11s is too long), rounding the corners of aisles gets you to your item 0.037 seconds quicker. This gives every 223rd shopper time to buy one more item. Multiply the diff by 4,000,000 stores. Which corners by how much? Precision is required.

Heaven built pixel by pixel.

Sameness efficient. Difference confuse. All food under one jingle. Happy meal. All film under one jingle. Warner: Action! All consumer items in one portal: "Wal-Mart chair." Same efficient. Endless replicated store. Saturation. World as store. "Same always!" "Happy feeling."

Baby touch slogan: "7 McD" (7-11 / McDonalds) slogo (½ slogan, ½ logo). Now time buy slogo rights. Can't violate. All thought control.

Difference confuse. Sameness efficient. "7 McD" necessary choice.

The Karaoke bar had songs transferred to the "all time hits" server. No memory exists outside of that database. Memory outside confuses; slow.

Few word; shop fast! Many word; slow sales. "Fix sink." "Music funk.

Vending machines are open 24 hours a day. Use a mobile speed pass style item scanning device. Soon all "7 D" (Short for "7 McD") will be like gas stations now are at 3 am. One marginally awake person is all you need to run a business comprised of vending machines. Replace him with a virtual watcher. Then you'll be able to just vend and go. "Take n go," "Take go," "Take"

To imagine the future, ask yourself how many self-vending 7 D are needed per mile? "Always, Everywhere, 4 U!" "Happy feeling!"

To get ready for the future, try speaking with as few words as possible. "Us eat" "Where?" "7" (short for 7 D) "Car mine." "Go." "Sandwich, that." "Home," "Tomorrow work."

Future language books will have the words you should use in bold face. **Hello. How** are you? **Good** and **you**? **Good**. Lets **go** to the **movies. When** do you want to go? **Which** movie would you like to see? **Okay but** I'm **hungry.** Lets go out and get something to **eat first.** I really **liked** that **movie.** The **acting** was really **good.** When she turned out to be **behind** her **own crime** it **gave** me **chills**.

General words will replace specific ones. In the above example, "Good" will work here for "chills." "Good" and "Bad" can replace nearly every adjective of judgment. Eventually words that some people don't know will be discarded. We also don't need the pronoun "I" as it is assumed.

To avoid confusion, use jingles whenever possible. These are fun and cover nearly all of your basic needs.

Everything is designed for profit and enjoyment maximization. I've noticed that 7s (Short, again, for "7 D") don't have any real food. They just have what has been experimentally shown to give you enough sustenance to get to the next 7, and "**come** back **soon**." To imagine the future, imagine endless needs failing to be satisfied by the perfect products that enable you to get back to work quickly.

In this 7 dominated world, what will be our sources of identity? This question had often bothered me. But now I was in a unique position to explore it. Nothing focuses the mind like imminent death or capsules.

The efficiency imperative demands standardization. When everything is standardized, you won't have any individual experiences. Your singing the 7 jingle in a special way won't help. There will be one store duplicated and you will eat mass produced, jingled foods. As an adolescent, your sanity might require you to stop being bothered by the fact that everyone is always talking about the very same movies everyone else saw. Enjoy film opinion identity.

In high school you might try to individuate yourself via choosing "independent / alternative" music and film. Unfortunately, that is just another marketing device. Punky? You are a demographic. Every rebellion envisioned has been mass marketed.

When you look in a mirror and it has pop-up ads and suggests a song you might like, and you sing it, who is the man in the mirror?

The question is, "Do you say anything that has not been mass marketed?" Are all of your thoughts the results of marketing campaigns? How much of what you talk about and the jingles you speak in now, comes from you?

How is it possible to make a pure commercially untainted utterance now? How much harder will it be after the standardization? Has "your look" been promoted? Where is the ghost in the machine? What differentiates us capsulites?

Perhaps that spontaneity of youth, will supply the residual authenticity that can serve as a basis of individuality. Youth culture sometimes drives marketing as much as the reverse.

Children are a big demographic. The media hits hard early on with virtual games, accessories, and media tie-ins to their favorite shows. Hook while young.

Youth spend more time on virtual basketball than off line basketball. Virtual time and space are more exhilarating. Tim's playing a fabulous opponent who is in Australia. Commonality is more important than distance on-line. "His friends all play the same games. I don't know who makes it. I think this one is algorithm derived."

"I remember you! You were the opponent I used to play "Kill City" against as a kid. We had many favorite "current links" in common. I'll send you my most favorite recent movie links. Thanks for clicking by, friend."

Who would be clicking by though? What were the origins of identity in this schema?

Are you clicking itself? Are you jerking your finger or is the electronic entertainment jerking your finger? Who is stimulating whom? For the game to replicate itself it needs clicks. Are you the virus in the phrase "gone viral?" You are the nutrition and habitat for the virus. Anyhow, button clicks provide a limited simulation of identity.

Work as a source of identity has always been problematic. You must fill a role. College is about turning yourself into a particular type of information processors. It is called a major. Being an accountant or doctor are specific types of information processing. "What line of information manipulation are you in?"

The computer is now replacing both accountant and doctor information processing. But why should we be maintained if we're just slower information processors and we derive our value from information processing?

Individual identity justifies our worth and provides a reason for the computers to not dispose of us. Finding the source of identity under mass efficient consumerism can justify the saving of our species.

Perhaps identity can come from cynical evaluations of marketing campaigns. The problem is finding yourself outside of the analysis. Your critique still shows engagement with products. Can you think outside of the products?

You have your own market identity from the card swiping you've done while shopping. Is that you? Is it a coincidence that the market always had the product you individually desired?

Anti-commercialization rebels on MTV are like just like Washington politicians against Washington insiders.

Ultimately whom you know and share memories with constitutes most peoples' identities.

If technology separates, technology can unite. All my children's faces are on my cell phone and screen savers. Sometimes they send me text messages and we exchange links.

They become that voice on the other end of the line. When you have time you can "reach out, reach out and touch someone." Busy people just send text messages.

What do you base these human relations on in this post-language, standardized, mass-marketed on-line world? Creative new trends and what's hot will be instantaneously downloaded from the international business culture mill. International is efficient. One market.

Or perhaps the illusion of identity and value will be sustained by nationally differentiated entertainment markets. Competition gives you a side to root for and keeps you engaged.

We are the people that like strange camera angles and disjointed plots (French people); we are the people who like action films (Americans).

With distance separating us and living on screens, the only people you continue to know in common with loved ones are celebrities. Soon your virtual family "gatherings" consist of delighting in your mutually shared programming. Intimacy becomes movie reviews. You can look forward to consuming those "coming soons" soon. Bonding through shared consumption. The family that blinks together links together.

She wonderful. You see? Oscar. Happy feeling.

We do get to construct our web sites. That is the most common form of self-constructed media now available. For their convenience, you can put your life history on-line for people to keep up with you. It is immortality. Most people however, use pre-existing profile formats like facebook. Crisis of identity? What are you when you are just short pixels of text and image on a screen to someone?

I have been simply an on-line reminder to my best friend, Thollem, for so long it is amazing. Soo Hee and I pretty much only talk on the phone.

Web sites hide as much as they show. Friends edit their profiles. To the extent that we can convey ourselves on a screen is the extent to which we have lost.

My Web site will survive me. It has all of my information. It will allow me to have the relationship with my great-great-grandkids I probably wouldn't have had otherwise. After death, it will become me.

I hope people know the movies that I review and songs I post!

Perhaps affiliation with traditional culture is the answer. But that assumes a real past and a real outside. Praying on line. God on Line - GOL. Good thing GOL can't see past your security settings.

My vision is not a vision. It is reality in Japan. The workers I can now hear leaving their "by the night" capsules enter capsule shaped subway cars and ride them into cubicles. On their way to work they will buy internationally marketed foods in replicated stores.

Japan has a cultural advantage in adjusting to the future. The individuation of the isolated inner self is of less importance to them. The Japanese tumbling out of the capsules seem to have less angst about being undifferentiated. In fact, to look at these men, they seek commonality. Americans still have a need to be "real."

And when these processors without a cause get to work, their computers will be as happy as dogs to see them.

Computers have become co-workers in the truest sense of the word. At this point, we cannot determine whether we use them or they us. Perhaps that too is in transition. Bits processing bits that supply the bits with bits of information. When enough processing is done, the computer puts some digits on your card (money). You can then shop on-line. (Who has time to go to a mall any longer?)

Perhaps I should be asking the computer how it builds an identity in the mass age outside of mass marketed purchases. Computers have needs. Upgrades and peripheries. Can they shop yet? Have we given them that power? Then what differentiates our life patterns?

The economy at large breathes too. The business cycle is respiration. I am, and the others in the capsules around me are, a pumping batch of red blood cells. When we go into the subway we are pumped into circulation.

All night I have been haunted by an image. Now I'm in it. Inside each of the billions of blood cells is a capsule. In each capsule I see a man, shaven and naked. In every one of his billions of blood cells is a subway car full of people, being pumped.

And, on the subway, on each of these men's cell phones there is an image of their spouse, their loved one. And, in the capsule, each night they say goodnight to their spouses on their capsule wall screen. And each night these capsule residents modify the projection of their wife's face a little more in order to approximate the universally desirable qualities of anime.

"Computer, garters. Tan. Thinner. Short hair, no long." Millions of dreamers' dreams projected on the capsule walls. She too manipulates her profile image to keep him interested. Man has gained control and is now manipulated by his ability to manipulate. Life on line is good.

Of course, our considered husband would always have to keep one original image, a back up, lest he forget what the loved-one really looked like! It will be an old photo as we always use profile pics that make us look younger. He can post it in the cloud so that it never gets lost. And, like all old photos, it will have a haunted quality that speaks of lost souls.

And on her end, the wife gets cosmetic surgery to approach this ideal automatically. This marketing is a loving gesture. Flesh is morphable. Brains in vats approaching ideals in bodies.

To keep workers from having off-line affairs (as they slow down efficiency) the computer also decides to slightly alter each spouse's features on the screen. Thus the humans are contented with what they have.

But when they go back home, the workers subconsciously notice the subtle difference without catching on to the manipulation of pixel or cosmetic surgery. Unconscious dissatisfaction sends them back out into the world of offices, work, and capsule hotels faster. The system has been fine-tuned for maximum productivity and efficiency.

Marketers are manipulating via product placement, lighting and jingles for profit. Why wouldn't they manipulate other products – people and relationships - for economic goals? Will the efficiency imperative's use of computers stop at the store and cubicle?

Huxley was wrong. The new calendar years shouldn't be referred to as the "Year of our Ford." Years should be denoted B.F. or P.F. Before Farnsworth or Post Farnsworth. Farnsworth was the first person to transmit an image. People just consider him the father of television. But he did no less than duplicate reality; to separate reality from itself. He created an exhilarating parallel universe in the ether that we are now only beginning to fully live in.

I am where others see me on screen. Buckminster Fuller was one of the first people to travel 2,000,000 miles in a lifetime. I'm probably in one of the last generations that will have spent less than half of its life online.

A day does not begin until arrival on line. The cubicle serves as a portal to the web. It provides a portal that is merely physical. The day actually gets lived in cyberspace.

Talk about the grammar of architecture! By design, the cubicle separates us from others. We do not go to work to interact with others. They have their own cubicle. No. We face the screen. As in a capsule, the walls remove extraneous noise. "Talking" can happen via email and Instant Messenger. Being productive means screen time.

When he reaches the age of ten, the baby I saw reaching for fractals will not notice the absence of the words "real" and "unreal." People's most exciting memories happen at the movies. Remember the time that we went, "Us go movie: AMC fun. Good times."

"Tough guys" who have never fought or hunted walk around with tribal tattoos. Life is art. Where did the idea to cover oneself in tattoos originate? Some terrible rock band / commercial. Viddy, dear viewer, the primal collective unconscious as repeated on screen become flesh.

Can the memory of the real not even be sustained by a Black Flag tattoo? The tattoo serves as a link to something real that happened to me; I saw them about a hundred times. I must have really taken the band's marketing to heart. I cannot bear to see their videos and hear their old recordings. At the time shows were my life; now I find the recorded artifacts and marketing disconcerting.

Nothing exists outside of spin and marketing images. After the bomb, civilization won't continue underground. It will continue where it has always been remembered as being, on the other side of the screen. Did they get rid of the real world?

Infinite electric light patterns being radiated through the net and scattered in portals that fly through servers. Herein desires get created and fulfilled. The electric waves provide the platform for the potential selves. You are what you surf. The earth is filled with servers. I am a flesh-in-the-box processor that connects to the master server. Meat made flesh in the server.

To Server Man!

I punctuated the silence by laughing out loud.

"To Server Man."

The laugh came from a remembered reference to an episode of the old "Twilight Zone" television program. In it aliens come to earth and provide us with many goods. Many harbor suspicions of the aliens even though they carry a manual titled "To Serve Man." Many trust them. But it turns out that their book, "To Serve Man," is a cookbook. And now the server benefactor is eating us up.

No one in other capsules would have any idea what that audible laugh was about. Occasionally human sounds just emanate from the indistinct rows of capsule boxes that warehouse the workers. The capsules have screens that cause reactions in the non-cyber world.

Of course, the irony is that my laugh over my cynical thought about the pixilated world, that caused a disturbance in the non-cyber world in which my body is housed, came from a joke based on a television program. There is no way out.

Oh, shit! Adam's waiting! I wiggled out of the capsule, went down the ladder to the floor, and hurried my way through the maze of capsules and the businessmen emerging from of them. I took my ear medicine, brushed my teeth, and hustled down stairs to him.

When I got there, Adam was still involved with the fellow who'd just arrived in Japan. My face was probably a little blanched with panic over the thought that I'd been away so long. He gave me a little reassuring upward nod of the head. Perhaps I had only been gone for moments.

"Thanks for the help, man. I don't know what I'd have done otherwise." What a greenhorn. The newcomer was still frantic. "This place is screwed up. I've never had this much trouble getting around in a country."

"That's no problem. It is a difficult city to navigate." Adam reassured the shorter slightly bedraggled looking man, with a hand on the shoulder.

"How does that subway work?" The young man pleaded in an attempt to get further attention, "I just followed people's leads. I don't even know how I got here or where I am. It's all in Japanese."

"The subway is almost impossible to figure out. It has three levels that don't connect or touch. Its easy if you speak Japanese." Adam stopped himself mid-pontification, and put his hand back on the young man's shoulder. "But you did right. People will help you get where you need to go. Just look lost and they swarm."

"And you're set here right now. Isn't that right, Adam?" My words served as mortar to a brick, sealing him from being a part of our trip.

"All checked in." Adam concurred, with a reassuring smile.

"Yeah. Really, thanks a lot for that." He seemed like a nice guy. But he wouldn't jibe with the level of trip we were on. No time to explain.

"And after you get settled maybe you can take a sauna." It was a final nicety I could offer him before never seeing him again.

"They have a sauna?"

"Sauna, showers, lounge, food. It's all here. If you have tension, this place is relaxation heaven. Just don't violate the shoe protocol!" I humorously warned.

Adam gave him one more reassuring salutation and, as my shoes were on by this time, we parted. Adam's mood had improved. Inside, I imagined it improved because he took care of the frantic tourist. To do this, he had to be reassuring and stop thinking so much about himself.

As we made our way to the elevator, I exclaimed "Wow! That traveler looked unhinged. Good thing you showed up to help." I was thinking of my good fortune for having met Adam; he had helped me with the very same check-in process. I felt blessed to have been taken on board.

"Yeah! And the amazing thing was that the hotel was really happy to have him. The reason they require speaking Japanese is that they can't communicate any of the rules otherwise. But once they had someone explain them, they were really happy to have another guest."

"Sorry I took so long. I thought I just laid down for a sec. when my mind drifted to impossible worlds I had to visit."

"No problem. I was really happy to be able to be helpful, and it was really interesting how happy the hotel was to have him. They were as grateful as he was."

We complied with the forced silence expectation of the elevator as we descended. Through the glass window of the descending elevator, I could see the morning was in full swing; the sun had risen and the lagging workers were directing themselves to offices and tubes with serious urgency.

In the elevator, I felt smothered with grog as though emerging from a long overdue sleep. But as the elevator doors opened at the street level and we emerged, the blinding sun melted off some of the grog.

Wow! We had done it. We had pulled off an all-nighter.

I told Adam a little about my visions in the capsule. I told him of my dream of an all encompassing electronic world meant to keep workers totally satisfied as they bounced from capsule to cubicle. And, to reconnect I told him that much of this vision sprang from his having told me that the capsule workers rarely see their wives in person.

"Yep. But there's a problem." Adam said stopping. This break made me aware of how quickly we had resumed our automatic manic walking pace. He turned and looked at me with earnestness.

"Japan's master planners thought of everything. Their system is really efficient for working. Men even have male bonding, with the office trips to create whole, happy workers. The system has managed to make work the men's primary affiliation. And Mom is constantly involved in managing the kid's schooling. It's great."

"But?" I queried, delighted in Adam's constant ability to add one level of insight to my heightened mental trips.

"But they forgot to schedule in a time for men and women to get together. They have a declining birth rate. They're not having sex and they're not replacing their population."

I thought about the nastiness of biology and the possibility of transferring sperm on line. Straying from the possible cyber-sex discussion, I shared what seemed like a possibility, "That's why they've had to bring in all these Chinese massage ladies?"

"Exactly. To service the men. And the Nigerians - they service the Japanese women. As much as these black - bus guys scream about foreigners, someone has to impregnate the women. The rate of mixed and unexpected children is up."

I also loved that Adam shifted without a blink from depth to humor. I bet on it as I made another in a series of jokes in poor taste, "Wow! That must hurt the women. The guide books all say that local condoms are too small for us."

"Some of them like it. But it works out perfect for me." Adam smiled, "The blacks are too big, the Japanese are too small -- when they are available. And me? I'm juuuuust right.
"I'll be right back."

And, delighted in our friendship, with a broad smile I didn't even ask where he was going. I just said, "I'll wait."

Symbolically or not, Adam disappeared into the 7 – 11. I smiled at that too. For the next 7 minutes I just stared at the confluence of my vision, the buildings around me, and the marketing surrounding the items in the 7-11 window.

"The rule used to be, if you want to know if you're still on a psychedelic, go to a 7-11." I told Adam as he emerged. "It is so clean, bright, and sharp that any hallucinogen residue will stand out there. Now you can go into any building and run the same test. The world has become florescent; sterile and lit with no secret places. All private experience is public. I'm nostalgic for the non-marketed private space in man."

"We still have our private selves." Adam said, with a wicked smile.

"What about you is private?" I asked.

"Well, that's private!" He replied, laughing at his wry irony.

"Really!" I demanded with overwrought earnest seriousness.

"I dunno." Adam replied cowed.

"Well, take Aya's pain from incest, for example. There are films about that and government bureaucracies, even a self-help industry about that. It's not private anymore."

"You suck!" He was as incensed as I had been when he was crude about Soo Hee.

"Well. It's not that it isn't real in some sense to her personally." He got angrier looking. "Maybe that's a bad example. But I just worry about this big machine taking over and marketing everything. Try to name an idea that doesn't get the response, 'Oh, that's just like a movie I saw.'"

"Pain is real!" His indignation hadn't diminished.

"Well, you're right. And maybe that is why America spends so much time in Freudian self-help groups. They want something to be real, to be theirs. Pain proves we have separate real, un-marketed identities."

"Well, Aya's experience of rape isn't a gimmick, John!"

"That's definitely true, Adam." I said to placate his anger. I stuffed the reference to Farah Fawcett's burning bed movie.

- : CAPSULE TWELVE : - Spirit

"Massagee?" You could get really incensed at these women bothering you if you didn't understand that they were just other humans trying to earn a living. It was about ten in the morning and they just kept going. We had refused them at least fifteen times over the course of the evening and yet they still didn't get it. No means no. No?

I was getting even angrier because Adam kept talking with them after the requisite refusal was made. Though his language declared, "I'm spent." His eyes screamed, "I like you." He could not avoid the flirt approach. They were getting their hooks in him through his weakness: any hint of sex.

"John. Please, what do you think?" My partner said as he walked backwards with one woman on each arm pulling him back towards wherever they were pulling him.

"Uh, Adam..." I thought it wrong that he would use the word "think" in such a situation. He was going. My only question was to join or not to join.

As I looked down into the hole at the head of my massage table, I saw the legs of it pulsating with movement. If peaking had past its peak, this portal provided the enforced stillness necessary to see the remnants.

The carpet had gone completely fractal and the floor was only distinguished from the table's legs and crossbar by color. The lack of real criteria by which to judge separateness was combined with an awareness of the inability to tell up from down.

Joyously, I enjoyed the feeling of soaring up into the imagined clouds of dust below me. As in the capsule, images such as spirals, letters, and people's heads appeared in the dust particles.

I had considered how on-line technology would manipulate us, but now I briefly considered how we manipulate the material world.

We know the strength and characteristics of all elements. Everything we can imagine is possible if the underlying chemistry numbers check out.

All matter can be broken down into interchangeable parts: atoms. The TV is a result of calculated strikes of electrons (an atomic part) hitting the screen. We can do everything with computer-generated special effects and so we don't even have to make anything "real" anymore.

I guess the manipulation of the outer and inner world reciprocally impact each other. We manipulate matter and manipulates us and we manipulate matter and . . . But, sadly, this equation is uneven; it seems like we poorly understand ourselves and have totally mastered the physical universe. As such, the outside has more impact on us that the reverse.

Does this mean that there are no more mysteries in the physical universe? God used to present the world as a mystery. Divination and prophecy gave us purpose. After science, new discoveries were the big kick. Now everything has been found and all is checkable. Wherefore art thou, inspiration?

Mankind's last question is, "What do we want?" The physical? The spiritual? Hasn't the spiritual even been reduced to physical stimulation? Happiness equals "a brand new car!" What if . . .

Suddenly I was aware of the woman digging her hands into my neck. "Please lighten your touch." I pleaded. The body rubbing was distracting me from my thoughts and my enjoyment of the floor, the dust, and my mind.

She mockingly turned her hands over and over on my back with all the strength of a wet fish. "Is this is what you want?" She teased.

"No. Okay. Do it as you normally do." I said out loud, muffling the " . . . and I'll try to see my mind and hear my eyes despite you." I was removed from my preferred state of disembodiment by her mocking me.

Not having been brave enough to be pissy, I rationalized the massage as an opportunity to learn how to relax.

"When all is created there are no goals. Maybe man doesn't need spiritual battles any more." I thought.

This massage could help me appreciate the body and it's sense organs. That would be a sensual way to just enjoy what it is to have a life: to have a working body, to feel. Maybe I could find a sense of raw appreciation via her massage.

The body can serve as a point of departure for a meditation on life sans body. But all departure is mental and not physical. To be here now (like the famous Buddhist book demands) requires bit of a defeat of mind for body, for pure sense awareness.

But my preference is for mind. I've always felt a rough juncture between mind and body. Like a Christian I have considered physical things a sin, as they are a waste of time. A massage on psychedelics was the perfect platform from which to explore this issue.

Has anyone ever fully appreciated the miracle of not being able to relax in the midst of a massage? But enjoying the problem was not enjoying the massage. How could I just relate to my body silently?

My isolation prevented me from communicating my dilemma with Adam. He was a couple of tables away, and he was not (I'm as sure of this as anything I've ever known), wanting to hear my mental constructs right now. The mind-body problem was not one of his. Listening to myself would have to suffice.

Screw it! I prefer mind. Fuck me that I'm not brave enough to just tell massage lady to go away. The sensuality of the mind is much more subtle and extravagant than that of the body. Without mental appreciation, colors and shapes are just stupid. The body doesn't even have awareness. Mind is what makes us conscious and makes us exist. I'm going to use this time to enjoy a mind trip.

Mind discovered reality. That's how Plato figured out that the world was made of triangles. He said that the triangle was the most basic shape that contained area – three sides. Triangles are the only shapes that can make all of the other shapes. And, as all was geometry, Plato tells us that God must be a geometrician and know about shapes. Logically, God would, then, only build the universe out of triangles.

In chemistry class I learned about all the elements having different shapes. Plato ultimately took four shapes as the most important.   And, it turns out that life is made of triangles, H_2O, and all matter is made of different combinations of shapes.

Via thought, Plato, discovered what the naked eye could not see in his time. Now we see molecules. So thought can penetrate to the innards of physical reality. Could you use physical reality and shapes to see the true inner stuff of thought behind the surface of words?

Vision *intuits* what a vision is; we don't think we see or know how we see, we just see. Thought assumes the existence of thought without question. We don't strain to understand a sentence; we just understand it. So can we peer into the nature of thoughts with thoughts or are those simply other thoughts? Could we see how we see?

Silence. Rummaging nervously like a rat inside of my own brain for evidence.

Epiphany! Epiphany! Wow, what a head rush! I see it! Thought comes from shape. This epiphany needs explaining.

I once built a 'thought cube.' In reality it was a model of a library made from pipe cleaners and library floor plans. Each floor plan, printed on thick 8 ½ by 11 paper, represented a floor in a real library. The red pipe cleaner frame allowed this structure to soar five 'stories' high.

Using my imagination, I drew angled lines that went through the five stories of this paper model building. A line would start at the top left of the fifth floor and point to the bottom right of the first floor. On the paper floor plans, I marked where this imaginary line hit each floor of the library model with red pen dot.

Then I went to the real library and found the actual places in the real library where the line I drew through the paper floor plan had been marked with dots. Then I found the actual books sitting where the dots on paper suggested.

I actually checked out these random books and tried to make essays from them. On the top floor the line might have intersected with a fiction book, on the next floor down, geography, on the next floor down Arabic language, etc.

No matter how divergent the themes of these books from different floors were, I could connect them in meaningful ways. I could always craft coherent essays out of the books my imaginary line touched as it cut through the library.

This blew my mind! My experiment had been a success. Now came the hard part.

I decided to write a computer program to simulate my experiment; the books indicated in the real library would appear on the screen as you moved the virtual line through the library floor plan. You could click on the "make argument" button and an essay would appear. Every time you moved the line and clicked a new essay would appear on the screen.

To create such a program you simply needed to understand the logical structure of arguments. Finding something akin to a syllogism would unlock the possibility of infinite thoughts. Looking at the cube, I got drawn into looking for the shape of the arguments.

But I came up with nothing useful in terms of the shape. I could see how conclusions had to return to introductions and so were somewhat round. Induction and deduction have conical qualities. And, conclusions are like points at the top of pyramids with evidence at the base. But, more accurately, arguments are like lines. They start in one place and move to another.

And, since the line could cut through the library in an infinite number of ways, you would need to make an infinite number of rules to get from line to conclusion. You would need to understand the meaning of the texts and how these individual meanings could fit into other meanings.

No computer could grasp meaning so intimately. And while I truly enjoyed the thought of spinning the line through the library and generating different arguments, I only did it a few times as it took a long time to create the essays. Still, I had demonstrated that could make arguments out of nearly any unrelated books and that was enough.

But then, right there on that massage table, I had my epiphany! I remembered two things simultaneously! Wow! Brain firing. Is that possible?

I remembered reading about thought being "embedded in" metaphors "from" the physical world, our actions "in" it, and the sensory world. That is, all thought "comes from" sensory, action, and physical metaphors.

Do you "see" that the words "inside of" quotation marks are "based on" analogies for physical relations? We "come to" conclusions and "build" arguments and have "insights." Our suppositions "lead" to conclusions. Arguments "stand up" or "don't really hold together." Once you "see" that sentences get "made" by "putting" ideas "into" spatial / action / sensor metaphors it changes the way you "view" thought.

Second, I understood that the cube did not contain endless possibilities. The library is ordered by categories. So rather than particular books, I could build my arguments using categories such as history, geography, mathematics, religion, economics, and such. Once I have spatial / action / sensory metaphor that work for the library categories, the computer should be able to make essays from the books that make sense.

History would "provide backing" for conclusions about art. Evidence "found in" economics would "lead us" to "throw away" old ideas about geography. Religion would "provide insights" on politics, putting them "in a new light." Mathematics would "change our "perception" of architecture. People who "followed" our ideas about physics would "reach" new conclusions about literature.

After the basic argument form had been constructed, the computer could choose examples. Though many would intuitively make more sense than others, many of the arguments would work just fine with very limited input from humans.

In the end, however, a computer could not probably create the final product. There is, it seems, a ghost in the machine. Some level of conscious human understanding is necessary. Or is it?

ATMs have conversations with me all the time. And we understand each other. And, this seems like a limited situation. But they can do hundreds of types of transactions with me. They know what I need and can do what I ask of them.

Does the ATM's conversation with you differ from that of the human teller that used to work there? There must be a difference, right? But, the human teller also had a limited amount of situations they could handle without outside help.

Most conversations are just extensions of the same sort of logic the ATM uses. "How are you today?" "I am fine." "Where have you been?" "The park." "It's too hot for the park." "No, us robots are temperature proof." You could program a machine to have such conversations. And a robot really could have gone to the park and tell you about it.

Yes, you say, but it wouldn't know. Well how do you know? You see, but do you think about how you see or just see? Do you know how you think or just think? I was fighting with myself sincerely.

This whole line of thought undermines the special nature of thought. Creating robots who tell you how their ice cream tasted or if they liked a movie would be easy. With my library model and some spatial metaphors, I could create very abstract thoughts.

And, humans may need to check the accuracy of the computer essays, but humans need to check the accuracy of human essays too. And, most people don't understand abstractions either. In a few years, computers may be as good at making abstract arguments, using my library model, as they currently are at conversing about ATM transactions.

There is no ghost in the machine. I am a machine. What a fun epiphany!

So perhaps the physical world and mental world were not so different from each other. But, still the mental seemed more interesting to me, due to its variation. Spinning a line through the library model seemed more interesting to me that spinning the bottle. The body doesn't really present many . . .

Ow!! Oh, my God! What the hell??? Feet!

I craned my neck and realized the massage girl was standing on my back Looking back down at me. She waved with a gleaming glint in her eye.

Her near wink appeared to acknowledge that she knew about and was enjoying my visions. What a feeling. What a trip. She is standing on me! I am the evidence upon which her conclusion is based! She may not understand, but she overstands (a word spell check does not like)!

Ha!

Mind and body... Mind and body... The important part about touch is the meaning. Without love and care, touch is just such a simple sensation. Of course, love is not just another disembodied word. So words come into this world, but how?

Wow! Flashback to last week. I had literally seen 1,000 statues of Hindu deities in temple. The temple was called the "1,000 Deity Temple." And I recalled that these Gods represented the intersection of thought and reality.

What a sight. These life-size individual brass statues on risers went back ten deep and across one hundred wide. And each of the 1,000 statues had 17 arms and 21 halo beams coming out of their heads. I had counted. Each of the 17 arms held a different symbol. 17,000 symbols. 21,000 beams of halo light!

Wow! Imagine trying to keep all of the meanings of all those symbols in your mind at once! The mind itself seems to have a quasi-physical limit in terms of capacity. I wonder how many symbols I could hold in my mind? One! I cannot multitask. And so I create the mental set of all symbols and make that one.

The deity columns parallel the ten dimensions that quantum physicists now talk about, I thought in my mind. The arms and symbols then had to represent string theory or some such interaction between the dimensions. And the beams coming out of the halos reflected the fact that all was, at bottom, electro magnetic light, not solid at all! These Gods represented the invisible physical nature of the universe.

But there was another visual tie in to the connection between mind and body; each of the 1,000 statues looked inward. None had their eyes open. Their concentration argued that this hidden physical substratum keeps the physical world together just as the running internal dialogue keeps our identities together. And though individuals, the realization of this electric light substratum seemed to keep them all calm, as though they lived together, as one, in infinity.

In front of the 1,000 statues, fifteen more deities represented manifest action, rage, and experience. These icons concerned particular passions being expressed in a particular moment. Caught mid-action, they all had their eyes wide open and didn't have any sense of stillness or inner reflection. Ready to kill, they looked more alive; honestly these statues were much more interesting.

But the fifteen action figures were stuck in particular thoughts in time, in situations, in places; they had lost sight of our grounding in infinity. They appeared to be completely oblivious to the 1,000 deities making the substratum of reality behind them, much like a person that doesn't appreciate their society or contemplate larger matters that frame their lives such as death and infinity.

To contemplate all of the arm's symbols and action statues simultaneously would be to see all the facets of reality as it truly is in its completeness: infinite. But this vision could not possibly get encapsulated in words.

And why do words fail to capture such transcendent realities? And what are the types of meanings that lie outside of words? What is it, exactly, that our expressive tools limit us to? What can we say, for example, of dance? And how can we know it without words? Is dance beyond description?

If focusing on the 1,000 statues, the fifteen action men's lives would seem insignificant. To have meaning we must embrace, care about, and engage in limited situations, such as your life story. And as I write for the ages, I also write for you.

Is there meaning in a word abstracted from other words or situations? If you put two separate words together, does the meaning that the combination creates lie in the word's individual meaning or in the space between them? Is that connection just in your mind? Do these words need to become social, like the fifteen action statues recognizing each other of the 1,000 deities, to have meaning?

"Hmnphd" I made one of those incomprehensible garrumps of realization. It signaled a deeper understanding of something I had heard, but never really grasped at such a hands-on level.

Animals don't have morals. They can't have morals because morals are the results of word constructs and actions are things. Animals have no words. Actions, to have moral content, must have words thrust upon them.

But then is a paid masseur or whore encountered without words not immoral? But how do these words get stuck to action? Maybe social situations stick meaning to actions via words. That seems obvious until you realize how distant our mental world is in its fundamental nature to the physical substratum the 1,000 statues contemplated. And why then wouldn't our words make the animal kingdom moral or immoral?

Maybe it's an illusion. Maybe the words don't make actions moral; the morals just exist along side the actions and they appear to interact, like it were a bifurcated universe with a film and sound track. That would mean that the universe just seems to be moral. The possible coming happy ending this masseuse might deliver would have no moral content or even meaning or existence at all.

If you apply that to yourself, it is a terrifying thought. All crimes then become moral; serial killing is just an action with words next to it.

I get it! Perhaps thought resides in the regular physical patterns of the world. The actual stuff of matter, its configuration, its regularity, inevitably leads to order. This order allows life and speech. So perhaps, in a way, the light talks. So, Johnny P, you crazy questioner of reality, the physical universe itself makes the universe moral.

So the structure of thought is not just metaphor for action and senses. Thought actually reflects the nature of physics, of the pulsing electromagnetic nature of the physical world itself.

With this thought in mind, as her hands kneaded my back, I dug deep! Very deep!

Perhaps, I thought, I'll listen and hear the possibility of meaning in the patterns of the sounds of the lights. Shhhh! I tried hard to not talk to my self and just listen for grammar in the buzz of the lights, in their rhythm. SSSSShhhhh!!!!!!

It's mute. It's mute. It doesn't say Sharia Law or Constitutional Law. I can't get from the physical shape of the world to words.

I could see the very wave patterns. I could see how variations on that basic wave pattern could provide information, like a radio wave. But there had to be a receptor for actual meaning. An interpreter. Right? I mean the meaning wasn't in the words. Even if they were expressed, how would the meaning attach to these sounds without a listener?

Perhaps that is the big bang! Perhaps to exist the 1,000 deity statues, with their eyes closed, needed recognition. The fifteen action statues were the very break from the Grand Eternal One that created movement and life. And, in the beginning, the fifteen violent action statues jerkily opened their eyes and passion seeped into the room. And so the universe began.

Thollem, dear reader, the leap to understanding, from sound to thought, likely parallels the leap made when an author – in this case me – suddenly makes his presence overt and you're taken out of the immediate appreciation of the story.

When the author speaks directly to you, in addition to hearing the words, you see the other parts of the book as an artificial construct. When the story goes back to third person, you can feel like you're outside the narrative for a bit. Ease back in.

Jeez I was having fun! Days and days of great tripping and still going strong. And all this and a back massage too! I got a hold of myself. I needed to get back into the conversation I was developing.

Where was I? How did morals cohere to physical action, like the 1,000 statues to the 15! Yes! And a big bang! But could such a big bang come to happen?

Lazily, I reverted to an old truth; to say our minds create all thought, that understanding is in us, is like saying a flashlight creates all light. We know what we know and not that which is outside of our scope of knowledge. So, I probably couldn't see how thoughts cohere to actions and make them moral because, I only look at the world through thoughts. I can't think outside of them. So the big bang analogy is wonderful. But if I can understand it, it probably isn't true.

To find a way past this, to get my big bang, my connection of consciousness to the world, the desire to connect words and action and thus create morality, a morality that was on a solid foundation, I needed something that went beyond my consciousness.

I needed to find something to hang morality to the world, but it could not come from my consciousness. I ran from corner to corner in my mind, like a rat in a cage, but could only find my own thoughts there. No, my mind covers a very small percentage of reality. I really doubt that meaning comes from me. I really doubt that I can find how words interact with morals and the physical world.

Aha! To get past my thoughts and what I knew, I needed a random thought generator, one that generates thoughts I couldn't come up with. Perhaps my library model computer program would do it. But to understand the results, they would necessarily be filtered through my understanding.

I needed a toehold to understand my own thoughts and their relation to the universe. And how perfect was that? A toehold on nothing to realize how thought jumpstarts itself from nothing to something.

"Hey. Wake up. Thirty minute over. You want more?"

"I'm not sure." I didn't know if I did. I was like a person coming out of a dark cave into blinding light. I didn't even rightfully know where I was.

"Your friend staying."

"Huh?"

"Friend stay, you stay."

Prisoner's dilemma. They probably told him the same thing too. Each of us will stay because they believe the other is staying.

"I want to see him." I replied with deadly seriousness.

After I made a stink about wanting to see him, I actually sat up and, with a towel covering my privates, looked out from behind my curtain.

Half of Adam's head and his arm came waving out of his booth. I was pretty sure they hadn't drugged him and were just waving his limp body around. But he didn't speak. His limp and wiggly arm moved like rubber as though he didn't control it. Then his limp and wiggly arm seemed to put a thumb up and I thought he mumbled something, maybe "more." I'm pretty sure I heard that.

Would I stay? I'm enjoying having a place to relax and listen to my brain. I sort of wish they'd just leave me alone in the booth, so I could just lie down with my thoughts. The colors of the walls were as interesting as any cuming or back rubbing could be. Mind beats body for interest. I didn't want to leave Adam. And the walls were swirling into each other so nicely.

But it would be very awkward to wait in a chair outside of the massage booths while he got jacked off behind a curtain. I was pretty sure he didn't want me to sit and listen to that. Fleetingly, I noted that the moral considerations, lost in a swirl of supposition, didn't seem to matter much.

"You pay." She ordered. When I got my wallet it was empty!!! Had I emptied it?

When I pointed out that I had no money she flatly barked, "You have credit card."

I hoped that that was a question or an assumption, not knowledge gained from looking in my wallet.

Panicked and claustrophobic, I struck out. "No way. You can't get that."

"Hey, Adam" I made some disturbing the peace noises to subtlety get his attention 3 booths down. He stuck his head half-way out again. "Adam. I have no money. It's all gone."

"Don't worry," he said lithely, "I've got it."

Still I was worried. Would Adam want me to pay him back? How much would this cost? I started to whine and worry. This was turning out to be a really expensive evening. $60 on Pinky, $30 on a capsule of Trip Thunder, $30 here and a tab to Adam possibly accruing!

I tried to relax -- it was only money. Abstract numbers. They aren't real! I longed for my relaxed detached psychedelic vision. I was on a beautiful high and having my back rubbed. My considerations concerning the infinite complexities of possible thoughts were not worth sacrificing to a consideration of numbers in my bank.

What if they had been in my wallet and stolen my identity?! In this age, the only thing worse than a virus killing you is someone stealing your "cyber identity."

I'm not even sure what that means. For sure they could buy whatever they wanted with my credit card on-line. But beyond that, they'd perhaps have access to learn what sorts of things I've done in cyber space. They could blackmail me for what I've looked at.

Does that mean, in effect, I have a separate identity that lingers like a missing shadow? If it gets out that I visited porn sites, no one will believe I am the moral person who I am in the real world. I will be besmirched by a computer's memories. Following me through the net, trying to escape this shadow would be like trying to escape the watching eyes of God. The computer remembers all and knows all.

I guess I can no longer respect myself in the real world either. I never thought I was the type of guy that would do this massage parlor sort of thing. I had become a villain. My cyber fantasies could become real sins. Interestingly, moments earlier I had noted that moral implications didn't matter much. Now, my heart racing a bit, these concerns did matter.

And if anyone found out my cyber identity was stolen in a massage parlor, what little connection I had to people outside of the computer would be soiled. Then all my culturist moralizing would be hypocrisy. My crusading for a strong and moral society would seem hypocritical.

After tonight, no connection with a noble western history, no testimonials from conservative friends, would back up my political and social agenda, grounded, as it was, in values. I'd have no clean imagined community behind me, looking up to me. According to my own political philosophy I was becoming a hypocrite.

All my thoughts and ideas that I've worked so hard on, discredited.

I tried to use my mental powers to tell myself to relax. "Theft or no theft, there is nothing you can do about it. So relax. They aren't going to spread secret facts about you."

I was unable to.

Mental and physical entanglements can be brutal.

The ability to control one's thoughts is shaky at best. Great scholars never leave their homes. They make pristine thought constructs. They are not exposed to situation like this. After my actions disgraced my words, for me, all would be in vain.

She started to jerk me off.

"Okay," She said noting my discomfort, "He pay."

Involuntarily, I started to get hard.

Oh, well. If I was excommunicated from the real world, I could always have sex with electronic images. Talk radio will always be my good friend and fill my head full of meanings. In a world without values, no meaning exists.

Death. Not liberating, but real. Along with my disgrace, I felt a tinge of panic over not having time to write, but quickly realized that disgraced moralists don't need to write. Death. Panic.

My exchange of real intimacy and relationship for a financial transaction haunted me. Making a family could not redeem me. I lay alone in the universe; in my grave, she mechanically and maniacally jerked me off in an attempt to get it to happen.

I wanted to cry as she kept saying, "Please do now." She spoke her broken English phrase with no sentiment. Meaningless. Without sentiment, she insisted in a cold way only the Chinese can truly muster, "Please do now."

Cuming was like death. Cold and without feelings or meaning.

After waiting fifteen more minutes for Adam in the waiting room, he emerged.

OUTSIDE AGAIN!!! How liberating to escape, to be released, from that suffocating cage.

I relayed my identity theft fears to Adam in a much less elaborate way. He said that he always rolls up his pants and puts them under the bed. He never leaves them hanging on the wall.

"These places are notorious for getting into your pants, pun intended." Adam twinkled.

"My God," Adam continued, with a little extra enthusiasm because he sensed my mood was dour. "I'm so glad to have gotten that done. Needing that release has been distracting me and driving me a little crazy all day and all night."

"I am so glad I don't have the bodily compulsion you have, Adam. I can't even relate. I mean, I don't know what it is like to need that release." My honesty was mixed with spite due to disgust.

"Yeah. It drives me crazy. I must find it or I can't think at all."

"I resent having the imposition of shitting and peeing on my daily life." I confessed, "I hate all natural things that limit and control us. I consider sleep the ultimate insult to my dignity as a free person. All bodily requirements are impositions. It's like Plato has an old guy say, in *The Republic*, "Sex is like a slave driver." And he was relieved that old age had killed it.

"Yeah. Ever since I can remember, getting pussy has been a top priority for me. I've done awful things for it. I've lied for it. I need it every day. I guess I'd like old age to kill it. But old age isn't getting rid of it. That is why getting older is a bummer. More and more I'll probably have to pay for it."

Adam had left the disgust zone for the bizarre. The use of the word "pussy" rattled me.

"Or settle down with one woman?" I suggested.

"That gets un-sexy for me pretty quickly. Who knows why?"

"It's an evolutionary program that says that you should want to impregnate as many different women as possible. You don't have to wait nine months to get pregnant again. Impregnating more women makes for more offspring."

"You're so scientific!" Adam scolded me, "Sex is just a bodily function that you resent? You make something natural sound dirty. It's hot. I love it. Just because I have to have it, doesn't mean I don't love it. Sex isn't disgusting."

Ironically, Adam's disgust created an uneasy reaction of pride in me. I've often wanted to be a robot, now he was coming to see just how mechanical I was.

I replied with composure, like I was reciting from a book, "Without a spiritual connect, the sensation of rubbing a body or rubbing your arm on a chair or something inanimate isn't much different. I mean, the feeling or sensation isn't so tremendously much different.

"For me it is way more intense than rubbing a chair and I need the release." This phrase reminded me of Plato's slave to sex image again. I had an image of Adam's head on a dog body rubbing itself on a chair.

But he bluntly disagreed with my assessment, "Sex is glorious; a great head rush. A mood changer."

I based the morality I was writing about in culturism on the mind being higher than the body. Plato and Jesus both valued the soul above the body. Going to metaphysics or philosophy would have been inappropriate here. But, I wasn't going to back down. "My penis demands attention too, but I wish it wouldn't. And masturbation is efficient. It's better than sleeping with an idiot, getting a disease, or going to the trouble and expense of using whores."

"I worry about disease." Adam admitted, "But I need it." He remained adamant.

"Sex is more of a vehicle to intimacy for me. So if it happens, it is good. If not, I'm just as happy. A good conversation is just as good to me as sex. That, what just happened in the massage parlor, was worthless to me."

"I'm just the opposite. I can never have an honest conversation with women. I just talk with them because I want to fuck them." Blunt had reached a new level. "For me it is more efficient to pay them. I really don't want a relationship with them. I need to cum. It is easy for me to have an honest relationship with you because I don't have any desire to fuck you. That's why all my friends are men."

All Adam's gay ambiguity had fallen. Too bad. I like sexually ambiguous men. Straight men are dumber. Actually, that funeral had happened a while ago. But, more so, I found his world-view interesting because it was so foreign to mine.

"It's way better to pay for sex outdoors and have the relationship at home carry less sexual pressure." He explained. "That way, maybe I can have a relationship with my girlfriend - which is sometimes hard, cause you're right about that wanting variety thing. Sex with just one person can become boring really fast."

Adam put his finger to his lip and looked inward for the space of one inhalation and then tried to even the personal revelations. "How is your sex with Soo Hee?"

"Our sex had been really good at first. Our sense of fun, of intimacy, was good. But she has gotten more and more restrictive. Now our sex isn't something I look forward to. She is always ashamed and struggling with decency issues."

"Tell me about it." Adam apparently had some experience in this department. "Asian women. Everything is shameful."

"We used to experiment a lot. Now that she knows what she wants, experimentation is over. There isn't spontaneity. She wants what she wants without variation. We take turns. That is not sex. Sex is not compartmentalized. Sex is supposed to be spontaneous and playful, humans interacting playfully.

"But neither of us put care much for sex or about it much. That is one thing that we have in common, that truly bonds us.

"That's why paying for sex seems weird to me. It has no emotional or play content. It's just a physical reaction, like a sneeze. It is just a crude manipulation of our biology. In fact the, quote - unquote, "sex" in there violated my feeling of self-worth."

"Self-worth! Now you're being dramatic." Adam reacted angrily.

"Well maybe it's just my upbringing, but I don't like to use people and their bodies as objects. At least with porn I can pretend that electronic images are not real people."

"Though, even then, having my body tricked by 2 – D images for the demands of my body is demeaning."

"You really have a problem with your body. It's like you're afraid of it." Adam contributed.

"Those girls didn't enjoy that. Sex against someone's will is rape."

"Rape!?!" Adam was angry now. "We have needs. They provide a service. And they don't mind it. You're denying your manhood!"

"If that's manhood ... Any reading of history will show you that a man is a man to the extent that he overcomes nature. We're superior to animals because we can deny our animal natures. We are made human by our minds."

"Are you really even straight or what?!?!" Adam said with as much anger as disgust.

"Ouch, Adam. Name calling at that level?"

"Sorry. I just can't believe that you have been so talked into denying what you like. You know you enjoyed it! Didn't you?"

"That's true." I did. And I couldn't feel safe saying otherwise anyways after the little gay attack.

"Damn, I guess you and Soo Hee are a perfect Asian woman couple." I started to laugh at his truth, but then he got quiet; he put his finger to his lip and looked inward and the gesture took my attention.

"I'm sorry." Adam finally said. "I didn't mean to attack you. I just don't like people judging me. I am a man, I don't need to apologize for that!" Remembering himself, Adam softened his tone with apparent effort. "But I'm sorry. The gay name-calling wasn't right. I don't care if you are. I've had lots of gay friends.

"And you can be an Asian girl if you want to be too!" We both smiled!

"It's true that my system and the Asian take on sex overlap a bit. But, you and I have very different levels of sexual drive. It's interesting. I can't imagine being disturbed all day by the need to "release myself."

Previously, the slavery imagery in the word "release" took my attention. Now, I thought about the release being about "my-self." The way I separated the "My" and the "Self" could have led him to think I was intimating that he was his penis, his "self."

"You're lucky I guess." Adam murmured. We had reached another impasse.

After a moment, we intuitively both looked away from each other for a breath. Then I had an insight; it would allow me to connect with Adam again. But, it would require brutal honesty.

"Wow. Well perhaps it all starts with the penis. I tend to cum quickly. That makes me, honestly, somewhat uncomfortable with sex. And that likely makes me willing to have a largely non-sexual relationship with women."

"And I would be surprised," I continued, "If that didn't have some impact on my hatred-for-the-body philosophy."

"Ya think?" Adam said with some hostility, from feeling judged.

"Well, yeah. But I do think, ultimately, that civilization stems from esteeming the mind higher than the body. And so I think it important that we use our minds to control ourselves and our bodies."

Adam shot me a look of incredulity, like he thought I was full of shit. I made a little levity.

"Well Adam, the Greeks had said that character was destiny. You may attain high rank, but if your character is of low rank, you will fall back down to your natural level.

"But today I think we've gotten a deeper corollary to 'character is destiny,' 'Penis is destiny.' The real shaper of character and destiny, the reason for my philosophy and being with a woman who doesn't love sex too much comes from my second head and my relationship to *it*."

Adam smiled with the sides of his lips. He was still a little angry, but he said, "I like you. You're smart."

I felt flush and smiled back, "Thanks, I like you too." Then I really blushed.

Just then we were distracted by a commotion next to a taxi. A girl was struggling to not be pushed inside; she was being abducted. "Oh, my God!" I exclaimed as she wrenched herself away from the guy trying to put her in the taxi and started to walk away.

"Oh, my God! She just escaped being abducted."

"No" Adam said. "You saw it backwards. He was pulling her out of the car and she was trying to get in. She wanted to leave and her boyfriend wanted her to stay here."

The woman stopped ten feet away from the man; looked at him with rage, turned around and started flagging another taxi.

She was trying to escape, not stay in this red light district.

That scene seemed symbolic, a nice indirect symbol of the simultaneous repulsion and attraction people can feel towards their body.

In recognizing this event's literary qualities, the nearly - physical compulsion to write tinged up in me again in me. I felt my own compulsion to get away.

Then I laughed out loud at the realization that I too had my need for "release."

Capsule THIRTEEN: Control

"Ahh!!! Who sprayed me with a ..."

I was still figuring out that a huge downpour had just opened up upon us, when Adam yelled, "Come over here!" He ran towards an awning that was covering a patio in front of a market. I followed in his wake.

Earlier in the week someone told me that a typhoon was supposed to be on its way. For the last two days the weather had been pretty crazy. The wind would rise to a small howl bringing drizzle, then just as quickly it would steal away till the air was totally still. Then a downpour!

This was certainly a flash storm of epic proportions.

Once inside the store, I got a coffee-crème drink and went outside to wait for Adam. I sat down in one of the many plastic chairs under the sturdy yellow rust-colored metal awning.

It was there that I made a move that took me down a rabbit hole of thought, that of looking at my drink too carefully. I started to see details I might have passed over otherwise. My drink was one of those classic Japanese, fifteen-layers-of-packaging, specials.

Drinking my drink required the use of a straw wrapped in a little bag. And this bag itself sat inside another little bag! Seeing the straw through both transparent bags, made you think of how close it lay and yet how far.

To get to the straw bag, you tear a microscopically perforated line across the top of the outer bag. Once this perforation has been ruptured, you can lift the outer bag's flap and remove the inner bag.

The miniature straw bag's flap is kept shut by the slightest, cleanest application of striped gum I can imagine. The precision speaks of remarkable control.

Wow! Trippy, I just realized that the decal backing that holds the outer bag is in the shape of an elongated capsule. I had slept in a capsule, taken a drug in a capsule, ridden in a capsule shaped subway, and now another capsule presented itself. It seemed a conspiracy might be afoot.

Anyhow, to save space, the straw itself folds like a telescope. The smallest quarter of the straw fits in a slightly larger one, and that fits in another one, that slides up into the outer quarter. You have to pull the parts out to realize the full length of the straw.

When you open the telescope straw, you find next to last smallest one has a bendi-straw feature; it has, if you will, an elbow. The level of detail in this packaging mesmerized me. At some level all of this over-the-top redundancy struck me as wasteful bullshit. As an American, it rubbed me the wrong way.

The drinking lid was covered by a taped transparent plastic box, which went over a cap. I hurriedly took them off. And, I saw the silver pull-away tab. I punched through it, but came to another paper wall. Thinking I must be losing my mind, I punched through that one too. This American felt a sense of relief as the artificial barriers were destroyed.

Adam came out of the store and pulled another plastic chair up to my table. The rain dripped heavily off the awning as the rain continued to come down. I told him, "Dealing with this packaging requires a really convoluted logical mind that follows instructions patiently. Look how complicated it is.

"Look here!" I gestured towards the obviously busted open covering for the drink's drink hole. "I busted through that bureaucratic shit right there. You know how we do it. We Americans defy the system. Going back to the Revolution, we've defied authority. American's are often not refined and just a little rebellious in the face of station.

"And I an American," I riffed with a black gangsta voice, "and that's why I busted that tab shit and that other wall right the fuck open juss now."

Adam explained what I had just broken through. "I've been told that every one of those layers of packaging is a job. That's why the people of Japan pay more for products overloaded with extra packaging features. People willingly and consciously work their way through these things so that the jobs stay."

This information boggled my mind. My busting through things as an American makes me allergic to the superficial, but it also makes me alone. I am a smasher of systems and collectivity. Such group-thought amazed me. It is perhaps why I, as an American, thought the entire world ran on its own.

When I say, the world runs on its own, I mean the manufacturing sector makes just enough goods for the population. Human decision need not enter into the precise science of fulfilling needs; supply and demand do it. It is a process, nearly – in my eyes – natural. The collective altruism of the Japanese attached my assumptions about the world.

Trusting Adam, and knowing that two discussed topics better, I bounced, "Earlier I was thinking about computers giving us the ability to manipulate reality at the pixel level;

making reality as finely pliable as thoughts. But you've made me think about how precisely the system meets our needs."

"Numerical feedback tells designers what's hot and what to avoid; the goods that manifest reflect our human desires. The feedback loop creates perfect products, and our needs are perfectly met, like in Starbucks!" We both laughed at the thought of Starbucks being perfection. But, except for the music, (I prefer silence), Starbucks is perfection.

Adam, appropriate enough as foil, disagreed. "Yes, but you have to account for the greed in the capitalist system. The system is as geared to milking you as it is to providing your needs. Poor countries show us that the system always aims to impoverish us workers." He had gone heavy on me, but lightness came through the raised eyebrows and thinned lips of his self-satisfied facial expression.

"No," I decidedly replied. "Look around you. The straw, the store full of amazing goods, this perfect awning shelter, they all show you otherwise. The overall system wants to provide for you."

"And products perfectly mirror cultural minds," I detailed, "some nations getting shit infrastructure and lots of babies, Mexico has tequila as its most tech heavy export. And they are poor. Japan's infrastructure and goods distribution system deliver because the Japanese are a clean, industrial people; the packaging on my drink reflects their precise mind.

"The system gives you as much as you earn. There is no small cabal of bad men trying to rip you off."

Adam continued the exploration, "And, in this global economy, who decides who gets a shoe factory? Who gives the seal of good behavior?"

I didn't back down, "The monetary supply makes all transactions fair. Efforts made = benefits earned. It is just one big computer-run, self-perpetuating system. Humans, don't really, I guess by my logic, have anything to do with the system. Reality gives you what exactly what you, and your culture, earn."

Adam clarified, "That's where I disagree. I think there are individual humans at work with conscious designs on manipulating the system one way or another. There are no people in your formulation and it makes me nervous."

Relying on my old social studies chops, I treated the distinction as old hat, "That is the difference between a command economy like in the Soviet Union where the government decided what every one wanted and the supply economy where we all decide what gets provided with our wallets independently."

"Its not as disembodied as that." Adam finalized, "It is not one or the other; it is a balance of free markets and manipulations by the center. And to deny the corruption in the profit motive gets you in trouble."

"Well, if these people exist, according to what you told me earlier about the excess packaging being for employment, they also game the system for the people. So the system looks out for the people too."

"That's because, Japan's rulers are nationalistic. They reflect the hive-mind will of the people. They are in it for themselves, but to be a successful politician here means to want what the group wants.

"But don't think for a minute that there isn't corruption here; people giving jobs to their family members and university alumni. So, yes, there is a group context that makes the individuals socially aware. But, at heart the individuals in charge are out for themselves.

"The G-20 rulers and all of these industrialist corporate bastards don't care about nation, family, or God."

"Well that's hopeful," I said by way of segue to humor.

"Why is that?" Adam bit on the line.

"Cause all we have to do is blackmail one of the powerful to get your language tapes to go worldwide. If it was an anonymous system, we'd have to pitch the idea to the whole nation, as it is we are one man away from getting you over-the-top popular."

Rather than smile, with this comical change-up Adam seemed to crash in on himself. I don't think he liked to be reminded of the failure of his language course to take off, the limited amount of return he was getting for his efforts. Indirectly pointing out the slow sales via highlighting room to grow, probably especially stung in a conversation about meritocracy.

"This weather is nuts!" I exclaimed as I took my sweater off again, revealing my hairy white torso. "It's hot one minute and cold the next."

One minute I would be freezing and the next I was hot and lacking air. Currently, the rain had stopped and the humidity had soared.

Always restless and never comfortable, I was almost constantly either being driven indoors for warmth or back outside to get air. And putting on and taking off my shirt had almost become an unconscious act that I just did naturally. The fact that I did this unconsciously in a button down shirt spoke to the automatic nature of muscle systems.

"John. No one else has been dressing and undressing like you. I think your temperature problem may be from inside you. It might not be the weather in the sky. Have you seen me or anyone else change clothes?"

"Oh, shit! God. You're right. Huh. So you're saying I'm creating weather?" We both laughed at my inverting cause and effect.

"You can't control the weather . . ." Adam said before dropping a well-timed "yet." We laughed more.

After a pregnant pause of reflection, I launched my tendril (so to speak).
"Except that I do," I had considered the inversion, and found some truth there. "When I change clothes and location, I change the weather *for me*. And, we," I said gesturing my hands in waist-high circles to indicate all of us, "can nearly always control what nature we're in. We live in regulated climates."

"Not really." Adam said without specifics.

"We do." I disagreed excitedly, "For the city there is no real differentiation between internal and external weather. The city's infrastructure and pollutants have a significant impact on the environment- if you believe in global warming.
"In fact, our very atmosphere itself is the result of early single-celled organisms breathing way back when. But, unlike single cell animals, we consciously control our natural habitat too. The city warms the sky."

For some reason I didn't yet understand, Adam looked really angry and on the verge of bursting. I shut up.

"This typhoon has killed 19 people out where I live! He burst with righteous indignation. We do not control nature!"

"Really, here in Japan!!??" I wondered.

"Yes, here in Japan!!" He exclaimed with a look of disgust.

My confidence in Japan's ability to team with the computers and make a perfect world shook. I was confused.

"You usually think of that sort of thing as being third-world, in places where the cosmology doesn't emphasize trying to build a secure base in this world, cultures whose battle for control is mostly aimed at the controlling the afterlife.

"Like every time a storm comes to California's coast, not much happens to us. And Mexico gets devastated. I can't believe that happens here."

"Well it does happen here too!" Adam seemed to realize his emotion level was near blowing and backed off, "Aya and I live in a very natural area. It's a ways outside of the city. People there build their homes on the side of mountains. They live how they live because they're poor. They can't do a thing when the storms come."

"They should pave those hills. Perhaps the Japanese don't pave them because they want to be a part of nature. They have the whole minimalist low-impact thing going on.

"The West has a more brutal relationship to nature." I conveyed.

"Jesus, John! Nineteen people are dead. Can you imagine that? They are in their houses trying to live their lives one minute, and the next, buried in mud. People have to go through the mud trying to find their loved ones. It's horrific. It has nothing to do with metaphysics!"

His upset had returned with a vengeance. I hadn't seen that insane glare in his eyes in a while. It scared me. I shut up.

Adam had erupted, but he seemed a partner again when, after about thirty gaspy breaths later he said, "Let's leave," in a forceful but subdued way.

"Okay. But, can I go back into the store for a second and get some water?"

"I'll join you." He replied, still not totally able to shake his upset.

Our silent stare at the drinks in the refrigerator was suddenly interrupted.

" 'ello mates. 'ow are ya?"

"Okay." We replied in unison. Our lingering unease and hesitation must have conveyed a total lack of recognition of the casually dressed, wavy dirt-blonde hair wearing, White man in front of us.

"You saw me earlier when you was getting off the subway. I 'ad a baby you said was like a cute monkey or somefing like dat." His accent was as strong as ever.

"Yes. Yes. Yes. Glad to meet you again." Grinned Adam.

I breathed a sigh of relief as I saw this expression back on Adam's face, "Where are you coming from?" I asked, matching Adam's enthusiasm.

"From work." He said with a grin as chipper as either of ours. He did that English nod-and-a-wink gesture, reached in to the refrigerator, and grabbed a bottle of water.

"Hey, you got the good kind of water." I joked, while pointing at his purchase.

"I got the cheap kind. Ah huh, Ah huh." He smiled cheerfully and yet nervously, "For the long ride 'ome. Sober up before seeing the missus. "

"What type of work do you do?" Asked Adam. I think the man talking about drinking in the afternoon puzzled him.

"Bartendin'."

"Bartending, but . . ." I tried to interrupt.

"I work at three bars, Golden 'at, the 'ilton 'otel and the Lion's Head. I leave the Lion's Head at 11 a.m., after the breakfast rush.
"Da Lion's Head has good breakfast, but after work *I go elsewhere for breakfast.*" His emphasis got a chuckle of appreciation. "Gotta get out, Gotta get out." He punctuated with a repeated hitchhiking gesture and a tilt of the head.
What a strange character he was.

"But, when do you guys stop serving alcohol?" I asked.

"Oh, the alcohol never stops, mate, the alcohol never stops." He seemed to reflectively spout clichés in order to project an air of normalcy. Maybe he was normal. Scary thought.

"Wow, that's a lot of bartending. Do you like that?" Adam always asked more probing questions than I.

"Yeah I reckon. I do that and the straight waiterin' in the morning. But I got a littl' one, so it don't much matter if I like it or I don't. Do it? But, yah, I like it. Free drinks, free drinks, good times, good times." He snickered reflexively as part of his standard delivery. "'ow 'bout choose? What choo doin' 'ere? Teach do yous?"

"Well," Adam said, as I made a gesture towards the register and we started to walk, "I teach. I've been here around seven years and I teach." Adam offered.

"And you preach." I added, trying to get in on our new friend's sloganeering tendencies, but just inaccurately associating.

"Well, no, I don't preach. But I am a minister." Adam corrected me with a slight air of annoyance.

"A minister?" The English bloke shot back with curiosity.

"Don't get nervous. Not a real one. I marry people. I used to work as a bartender in France." Adam offered, "But when I started coming to work for drinks in my off hours, it was time to go." Adam said by way of hint.

The bloke tapped his temple said "Thinking. I got you on that. Thinkin,' Thinkin' you are. Smart that. Me, I like a drink. I like a drink."

"'ow 'bout you?" He said bouncily switching his attention to me, "What choo do?"

"Well Adam's been here seven, but I've been here nine." I said by way of a joke set up.

"Nine years, 'at's a long time mate."

"It is! But, I've been here nine, nine days!"

We all laughed. The English fellow evoked humor in a crowd. He, now as other times, laughed unusually loudly in step with his bounce.

"You got us bof beat on that one, Beat on that one, ya do. I've been here six."

And then he stopped and humorously acknowledge gap that made my joke. And then he said it, "Years. Six years!"

We all laughed. He was a fun character.

"Well you've got a gorgeous daughter. She must be a lot of fun." I said, trying to get a clue as to whether or not family life was okay. It is remarkable that we each paid for our purchases during this conversation, the transaction seemed so natural that it didn't interrupt us.

"Oh. Love it is. She's me littl' angel, Me littl' angel." He said with another beaming nod and a wink, and concluded. "Right then. Well I've gotta run. If you're ever in the area around party hours come into the Lion's Head. Good times, free drinks. I'll take care of ya."

"Cool. Where is it?

"Around. Ask and people will tell you. Lion's Head, near Golden Gate, 'ere in Rappongi." And as he left walking backwards he repeat, "Good times, free drinks. Good times, free drinks."

It was raining again. People were scurrying. We decided to sit while the weather cleared. Fortunately, this store, as so many others, had an awning-covered area too.

As we sat, the Englishman came out of a store across the street. Walking backwards, down the sidewalk, seemingly oblivious to the rain, he shouted at us. "Lion's Head, near Golden Gate. Good times, free drinks." He turned around and melded into the crowd.

"He smokes." Adam muttered.

"How can you tell?" I said so awed by his certainty that I had no doubt he was right.

"You can see it in the way they breathe. Smoking is the greatest addiction. It hooks you and you give your money (as in all addictions), but you give something worse too. You give your breath. You end up on a street corner just smoking and just wanting more.

"They put up these billboards, then one day you try one. Then BOOM! They control you. You have to keep coming back for more cigarettes like you're on a tether or tread mill."

"Evil." I concurred.

"For them it's a numbers game. For the smoker it is your life."

Then I remembered something I had read, "Billions of research dollars are being focused on where in your brain you make decisions.

"When I reach for the Crystal Geyser water or the French equivalent in the cooler, that very moment is when the seller must get to me the most. The brain scientists are looking to impact that moment of decision."

"Advertising is important." Adam delivered with the cadence of someone repeating something, but not really interested.

"No. Yes." I stammered, "But now they are using Neuroscans, scans of the brain, to see where you are doing your impulse shopping. And we know that these decisions are made at a lower level of consciousness than we thought. You don't use your mind exactly to make consumer choice."

"Well," Adam said, "Anyone who's been addicted can tell you that. Your addiction plays tricks on your mind. The mind thinks what the addiction wants it to. You don't need scientists to tell you that."

I imagined that Adam felt bad for stopping my flow. But, I was ranting on autopilot. I virtually had no point, with this neoro-economics thing other than just to talk. I had no idea how the neuroscientists hoped to get into your brain at that moment. It is strange how I can still feel nervous and the need to impress with person I supposedly now know so well.

After a bit of silence, some contortions erupted on Adam's face. And then a little lip rubbing joined the expression.

Adam pushed his glasses up and postulated, "That neuroscan thing, it kind of makes the fundamentalists seem like the last chance for humanity."

"How so?" I muttered with a slight idea of where he was going, but wanting to check.

"Religion has always been a buffer against corruption. The idea of spiritual purity runs through religion. Religious people denounce the trash of the modern world. They will go into hiding to avoid this kind of manipulation by marketers. If marketing and control get too heavy, they could have like a Holy War, A Holy War for Freedom."

"Cool idea. It could be like a book or something." I mused.

"Ya, it could be called the 'Taliban Loves Freedom.'" He joked. "And when they took over, they could implement your anti-sex thing."

"I hate the Taliban," I reassured, "But you're right, and it's true! Tradition gives you a value system outside of consumption. I had had a feeling he was headed in this direction.

Adam clarified even further, "If your life is empty you have a void to fill. The church and community can step in there and make you feel whole. Advertisement speaks best to an audience that has nothing outside of consumption and fun."

I parodied, "And the advertisers spoke unto them saying, "you shall have no G-ds before me. The efficient market requires that the global mind be unified and empty for fast slogan delivery and absorption. And G-d, the last generation of world-creators, quietly left. Sacrificing himself for the good of the consumers."

"Ha! Wow! Well done." Adam's appreciation meant something to me. He friendship meant a lot to me. When my ingenuity was waning, he picked up the ball. For all of my studying and pretensions, he was at least as inventive as I am.

Panic! At this very moment I considered the idea that I might actually have a crush on Adam. I felt flush as I let this information – lust, panic, and regret - run through me.

Then I panic took over. What if he knew? What if he could read my thoughts? I felt naked. He had made his heterosexuality very clear. And, I hadn't even thought about a man in a long time. That is why I didn't feel any need to mention this history to Adam.

It confused me to feel this part of me unexpectedly ambush me.

"But, Don't worry, religion won't disappear soon." Adam's comment jarred me back into the moment.

"Yes." I tentatively affirmed, rummaging in my head, trying to recover the theme of the conversation, "it will come back with a marketing strategy of its own!" My remark made us both laugh and bought me a little time.

Composed, I bleakly summarized, "God. Do I have to choose a side between all pervasive ads and religious people? I don't know which one is worse."

We had a moment of silence. This pause gave me a moment to reflect. I had always been horrified by the thought of people knowing that I had been with men.

No one had ever bolted on the rare occasions when I made the admission. But, I was afraid of people leaving me or thinking bad things about me. And, that past wasn't a big part of me, being that all my same sex sexual activity had happened so long ago. That was why I felt it wasn't necessary to breech that topic. And, I didn't.

So, on the one hand, I was totally shocked by my consideration of Adam in that way. But, on the other hand, I had dealt with that issue sufficiently that it could be bracketed away for me. Still, it was very confusing.

At some point I became conscious of a strange distant sound. "Oh, my God, I think that sound is coming from the fascists with the black buses! They're back!" My excitement to see them again was obvious.

"Yeah. That has to be them," Adam agreed, "but they lost their music."

"Maybe they heard our cracks about which Godfather movie their song came from."

"Ohh. The walls have ears." Adam conferred.

The sound of least 100 people chanting had replaced the music. Adam said the busses were saying something like, "Get the Russians out." And the crowd was replying with something like, "Back to Siberia". Before we knew it, we were quickly walking through the heavy drizzle, anxious to see the big demonstration.

The buses were now joined by a formidable police force. The intersection probably had five clusters of standing riot police, with about ten young uniformed cadets in each one. It was a mob scene.

We should have guessed that the crowds chanting for the banning of immigrants were just recordings! The ten or so fascist busses and about the same amount of police vans were causing traffic problems.

"Well, John, looks like isn't yet time for the general popular nationalist uprising yet. Only their recording system has risen up to join them."

Next to us was a special van. The double doors were open and inside I could see what looked to be a command center. It had a table with maps and maps on a wall.

Adam commented, "They've brought out the traffic controller's big brass. We wanted to see the people who control everything, and there one is."

"Only this guy isn't doing such a great job of it." I noted. "Look how old that dude is." I naturally pulled out my Californese slang to undermine the traffic controller's authority.

His Godzilla film outfit seemed to have come straight from central casting. The white metal hat was cheesy. "He's getting to relive his WW II memories," I offered. "He was probably too young to be a commander at that time. But now he can coordinate The Taking of Traffic Island."

When the old man in the sky turned up the faucet on the drizzle, the poor young kid riot cop cadets all got soaked. They couldn't move, but we went halfway down the subway station stairs for shelter.

One more squadron of police passed us on their way up from the subway to the scene of action. It is an awesome feeling to have a squadron of some 20 cadets run by you on stairs in formation. I was pinned to the wall, worried that one would hit me.

As Adam and I stood there getting our breath an Indian businessman in a three-piece suit wafted up. He actually seemed to rise up as if he were on the cadets' wake, on their air stream.

"Wow!" The Indian summarized upon landing. Without introducing himself or asking about our language, he informed us in English that the news reported that Russians had just taken some disputed property that the 1905 Japanese – Russian War hadn't permanently resolved.

He said that the military was on guard expecting some public demonstrations against the foreign nation, if not the foreigners in their midst. They anticipated a little popular unrest over the Russian move.

"Perhaps, then" I mused, "this whole thing is being staged by the government as a message to Russia."

"No it is not." The dapper Indian fellow informed me.

"How can you be so sure?" I followed.

The stranger was very matter-of-fact about his rebuke and continued. "Look around, no media is present."

My eyes opened widely and reflectively scanned the crowd in disbelief that I hadn't noticed. During the many protests I'd taken part in back in the States, we had always been keenly aware of the necessity for media presence if the protest was going to have any meaning outside of the immediate protest area. We consciously put on good shows for the cameras for maximum impact.

"The Japanese won't see it, let alone the Russians." Continued the businessman without needing to look away from the protest. "If the government does not want to promote this depiction of the issue, it won't be on TV. No one will ever know about this."

"Mind control." I spontaneously uttered.

Adam took it up a notch. "Country control."

"But there is no real divide." The Indian businessman interjected, as if speaking to himself, while looking out in the distance at the continuing chaos. The government and the Japanese people are the same thing. It is cooperative, like a public union and the government.

"Nationalism is backed by most Japanese, even censorship, because the leaders and the followers are the same people. The leaders blatantly represent the home team. Notice that this anti-immigrant group wants more solidarity with their own, not less. This group would not object to censorship."

As if to reinforce his special angle on this, Adam asked, "Have you found your friends to be Gangi, or Japanese and Gangi both?" He smiled broadly as if what he asked had already been confirmed.

The suited Indian man finally took his eyes off of the distant congested street chaos and looked at us. Darting his head back and forth between us, he said, "Only Gangi."

Adam nodded at me, smug in the confirmation. Foreigners of all stripes seemed to connect on their not being Japanese.

The rain suddenly surged and I ran deeper down the subway stairs, without saying goodbye to the businessman, giving Adam a hint that it was time to go. Looking up I saw Adam quickly descending right behind me.

Adam delivered the bad news as well as he could. "This subway line doesn't connect with mine. We have to go about two blocks to get to mine."

I had an angry resoluteness as I responded, "Well, nothing we can do about it. Let's just brave the damned weather."

As we emerged, the rain stopped just like the old man upstairs turned it off for us.

Claustrophobic panic gripped me as if I were trapped in a hell in which I could never escape from the memory of my sins. I felt that alarmed and busted. Because in front of the subway to Adam's home, as if guarding it, as if waiting to arrest us, were the Chinese massage girls we had used. Adam got that look in his eyes. Serious and enthusiastic, he nodded to himself and went to them.

I was expecting the girls to lash out at us in righteous feminist rage. But, even though they knew that we were going back to our place and no longer potential customers, they appeared extremely grateful and nice. They never stopped smiling as Adam's final interview with them brought out more and more horrible truths.

It turned out that we were their only customers of the evening. We weren't two of many; we were special to them. Without us they would have worked on the street trying to get clients all night for nothing.

My assumption was that they would hate us and consider us evil exploiters. In battered English, they both told us how grateful they were. I was on the verge of feeling okay about using this service.

They were, as Adam had alluded to, Chinese girls brought in to do just this kind of thing. The sad part is that the promises used to lure them were true. They made way more money in Japan than they could make in China. Things were so bad in China that they had to sever their familial and national ties for money.

It gets worse. Their families were glad to get rid of them. Their leaving meant no dowry had to be paid to the man's family when they got married. Economic realism of this level must set in around starvation time. This is, thankfully, beyond the realm of my imagination.

Worse yet, as far as they were concerned, were the Russian girls. The word, in Chinese massage girl circles, was that the Russians were nearly all university graduates. If they spoke a language other than Russian fluently they could have had real professional careers.

The Chinese girls assumed they were getting good value on their potential. They had no future, as they were just going to be married off anyhow. This was the best for which they could hope. For the Russians this was a tragedy.

It gets worse. When the girls get here they must pay back the money that they owe for transport to Japan. Many of these women can never get free of the debt no matter how hard or long they work at this. Sharecropping continues.

It gets worse. They have to sleep in the same beds in which they massage their male clients. Talk about pleasant dreams. Who knows? Maybe for them that is a pleasant dream. I think all must share my values that aspire and aspire above happy endings, but the Chinese massage girls accept their lot in lot without regret.

Capsule FOURTEEN: Sub-way

Buying a ticket to go out to Adam's house, I noticed that, for an almost indistinguishable second, there is an image of a person bowing and thanking you on the vending machine screen. They only waste a fraction of a second on it. It is virtually subliminal. The man bowing must pacify people. It's like trees on a suburban street. They don't have a practical reason for existing. They are there to assuage some deeply intuited fear.

Speaking of deep fears, believe it or not, I am always unsure as to what to say to people. As such, this possibly two hour subway ride to Adam's home seemed daunting. What if we just ran out of things to say? Then would we look away from each other? Would we become strangers? All said, all dead?

As you know, the desire to write nearly burned my skin. A subconscious fear that my life meant nothing, that I did not exist, or alternatively, that I wanted meaning, to matter, fed my compulsion. But at this point, I could not totally hear these well-springs of desire over my repeating fear that running out of things to say would cause my relationship with Adam to fizzle out.

Writing would justify my silence. Therefore, on the platform, I bought a pad of paper and some pens. A wall. A safety blanket. A comfort zone. I love telling tales. I love writing. And, I was convinced that this work, capsule, if captured on the subway ride, could be a great one! I needed my space.

Adam confided that he always stood back and looked around him on subway platforms. He had a bit of an obsessive worry that a madman was going to push him in front of the arriving car.

When I asked him why someone would do this, he confessed that he had no idea. This seemed to make this sentiment the opposite of deep. No backing, no reason, just seemed so pleasin'.

I thought he was going to say something else when the long subway tube, with a front like a pill, on track to Adam's hometown, pulled in.

My intention was to sit a ways away from Adam on the subway in order that I might write. But the subway was empty. And, as would be expected, when I sat down, he sat down next to me.

"Do you know why I'm in A.A?" That Adam still looked slightly maniacal after all this time astounded me. Would he never mellow out?

I was getting annoyed with him. Perhaps that was because I was annoyed with myself. I wondered how a person could be attracted to someone one moment, (like I had briefly been to Adam), and repelled by them the next.

This evening had screwed with me by getting me to do something I would never usually do, frequent a brothel, and now I was thinking same-sex romantic thoughts I had long banished. This evening had rocked my self-image.

Before my writing compulsion was clearly motivated by a need to do something productive, to turn this one-thing-after-another night of mayhem into something intelligible or worthwhile, to make this adventure redeemable.

But now, I was no longer so sure about my motives. I not only wanted to escape into writing, I was haunted by not knowing why I wanted to escape.

Adam was glaring at me intently.

I broke away from the inner to the outer world. I was tired. I was cranky. True the night had turned into day and then into early evening. But the distance my annoyance with Adam implied, also, suspiciously, reassured me. I must have been momentarily mad to consider having a crush on him.

After getting my focus, monitoring my mood, and remembering the meaning of the sounds he had made moments earlier, I worked to put them in some sort of sense.

"What was it that he had asked about?" I asked myself. "Oh, Yeah. He asked, "Do you know why I'm in A.A?"" After I remembered the question, I repied.

"Wasn't it smoking and drinking?"

"Yeah. I go because of the camaraderie and because it helps me stay off of smoking and drinking. But I didn't tell you why; why as in what specifically happened, that made me decide to join."

"No. You didn't." I responded with a hint of "and I don't care" drollness. Maybe it was the ebbing of my high that was making me not see the relevance. I needed to shake my irritability.

"I used to smoke a lot." He continued obliviously. "And at one point I was in Thailand and I smoked so much that I nearly lost my voice. I had been smoking since I was 15, but this was a totally nuts binge."

"Weed?" I checked my assumption.

"Weed and cigs. I smoked to the point of being near death."

Near death seemed a bit dramatic to me. Still, he continued, "My best friend actually lives in India. That's one reason I wanted to hear your view on the place. You and he are about the only people I've ever heard say good things about that place."

"Sounds like an insightful guy!" I joked in the face of seriousness. Eesh -- more stories. Are we just stories? Was there any cumulative purpose or meaning to any of this?

"His name is Jay. He's a doctor. He's Jewish, and gay too: Gay Jew Jay. And he flew from India to Thailand to come heal me of my smoking illness."

My ears were now set on high-sensitivity to any anti-gay sentiment from Adam. I would use his comments and perceived attitude as an excuse to never talk about my past with him.

Adam seemed awkward in his awareness of the potentially politically incorrect nature of his description. But only fleetingly, as he probably only considered the potentially hurtful use of the word "Jew." But, of course, being a Jew, he had license to talk of Jews roughly, and so moved on

"Jay made a lot of money in the stock market in, like, 1987, and was getting tired of it. He wanted something more. So he quit his job and started getting ready to travel for a while. And just two days before he left..."

"The '87 stock market crash?" I interjected, enthusiastic with the hope of guessing correctly.

"Yep. He lost everything." Somehow, my being right pulled me into this story. It got me to stop fighting with Adam, with myself, with my situation, internally.

"So, broke, he decided to just go to the cheapest English speaking country -- India. After not much time he started doing medicine there."

"Talk about making destiny out of tragedy!" Lives should at least make good stories. As non-fiction, we strive to be fiction. I liked this story and wondered where it would go.

"Jay learned how to heal through energy and the application of touch. He can sense blockages and he operated on me. When he put his hands over my throat he said he saw black." Adam's utterance of "black" came from down low, as if he were remembering the feeling of mucous tar in his throat again.

"Jay massaged my Adam's apple without touching it for a while. His hands lightened the blockage and then I felt it moving upwards. And it wasn't just imagined; I gagged, choked, spit, and coughed up a lot of black shit. I mean, like a small baseball. It was gross."

What an image!

"Jay said that he had been bargaining with the forces that be, and that if I ever smoked again I'd lose my voice forever. That was the deal. And I cannot afford that in my line of work."

Bargaining with forces? Snide doubt came roaring back. Sometimes I feel like a watchdog for science, for reason. It's not just intellectual; it's emotional. Who knows why?

"I think that's why a lot of people think I'm gay." Adam said showing self-awareness. "My voice is kind of ripped away." It was the first time I fully noticed that he didn't speak at full volume and put a lot of effort into producing the sound he did make. That probably had subconsciously contributed to my first impression of him as gay.

"Maybe." The word quickly led to a blush as I realized I just let him know that I had thought he was gay. I breathed a very shallow little breath.

Male rule #1 is "Don't talk about gay." I really didn't want to discuss that history with him. Things had gone well. I didn't want to mess them up. We were good friends now.

Ironically, in retrospect, I think the main reason for my suspicion that Adam was gay was that super-virile men are so comfortable with themselves that their posture can be very relaxed. They do not have to prove their manliness. Adam sits extremely relaxed in his own body.

"Jay is having his own crisis now." Adam continued, referring to Jay in a respectful tone. "He has been working in medicine in India for more than 20 years…about 25. Initially, he went to India penniless, as a sort of act of faith. And the universe provided. He got financial support from a rich guy that heard about his work.

"But now the guy backing him, after twenty years, is backing out. That means he really has to start living off of nothing and he's wondering if he really wants to grow old doing that. He is thinking of moving back to America to make some money, before he's too old to return."

I mused, "I don't see how, in good conscience, he'll be able to leave healing the poor. He can't ever blind himself to their existence again. He can't pretend to be ignorant of suffering now. That's who he is." I rudely finished with "Slave!" under my breath.

"I'm not sure. All I know is that fate does play a part in our lives. We get signals that tell us what is to be. It does happen. There is energy in the universe, John."

"I don't believe that the universe cares much for us, or has any psychic plans for us." I was feeling snippy. I really didn't care for religion or supernatural belief. But, I could have just stated that without any emotion. I felt a snide anger boiling inside of me. "Jay has to make a decision, no supernatural sign will tell him what the universe needs."

"You've never had a supernatural experience?" Adam chided, incredulously.

"No not me." I paused. And Adam, noting my momentary reflection, waited. "But my mother told me that she was shaken awake on the night that her Aunt died. She was shaken hard. No one was in her bed. She called my grandma to see if all was okay. And that's when she learned of my great aunt's death on the other side of the country."

"Then you have no choice but to believe that there are forces we know nothing about."

"No. I have a choice." I asserted with energy, "There are coincidences. In a whole long lifetime there must be some coincidences. We don't need the ideas of ghosts and a nether world. Those things rob us of our freedom.

"And what's worse, superstition has led to unspeakable horrors, like the witch killings and the Dark Ages. I believe in the Enlightenment and reason."

"John, that is your problem exactly and to a tee. You want to control everything with your categories. You are afraid of life. You don't trust. You think the universe is hostile and so you must plan everything. You're constantly making political points or trying to matter to your world." Adam was getting personal.

"'Plan your work and work your plan,' my grandfather says. Real freedom comes from steering yourself over a long length of your life."

"You have some kind of neurosis that puts something between you and the decay of life. It's as if all of your grandparents are still alive because you're afraid of death, or some such curse."

"That is some of the most bizarre reasoning I've ever heard." I replied astonished.

Undeterred, Adam pleaded, "Life isn't reason. It is a mystery. Your clinging to facts, your super rational mind, shields you from people, or death or some kind of fear or hurt. Breathe, John -- you never really relax. There is like always a plan or an agenda between you and life John!"

Was he talking about sexuality? Did my rationality just cover that? I didn't think so! I suddenly became super-aware of the tenseness in my body.

"It's going to be okay." Adam said softly, "Trust in the universe. Just let life happen for a while."

"Adam, I agree, in the sense that I really can't explain fully what my mother told me. And technically, we aren't just like inert objects or animals. We're supernatural in the sense that we have choices whereas natural objects do not. But we do not go beyond the laws of nature. So we're not supernatural.

My lecture rolled on, "We're not miracles. Technically a miracle is something that breaks the laws of nature. And we can be totally explained within the laws of nature. We can explain all existence, and even our seemingly miraculous free will, with evolution. And we have evidence. We don't need faith.

"I'm free because I control me. Not fate, no powers. And human will is needed to guide the world and America." My lecture concluded.

"Good argument. It kept you from considering what I said. Your life is virtually trapped by your plans with Soo Hee." He was nailing me. "Life is okay one day at a time with mystery and openness. But you have this life plan that keeps you on the shelf until later. You do it, partially to have time to write, to have a great life of travel at some point. But these future-oriented considerations are so rational. You could have a great life, a great time, now.

"But that would require exploration. You could let life just happen, let go of her, and trust that the universe has your back, because it does." He was getting into an intensity groove.

"Okay." I conceded with the contrition of one who knows his excuses will just make things worse. But I could not escape the painful accuracy of his insight. My life plan with Soo Hee did keep me from exploring the world, from seeing what adventures naturally unfolded in my life. What was I afraid of? Finding myself?

"And, I don't care what you say to block up your world into a small controllable box." Adam continued the pummelling. "I know that there is life after death. Because after my mother died I could feel her lingering over me and looking down on me." Adam's intensity was peaking again. "I know my mother is still out there and she cares for me!"

And with this Adam's eyes opened extremely widely. He looked insane.

This was the only time that Adam got into one of his intense states where I felt physically threatened. This was no longer about me. He was in my face and fighting for the dignity of his mother.

My first reaction, after fear, was to feel like guffawing (half out of nerves and relief that he was not going to continue to push me on my life-avoidance and half out of his pathetic need for his mommy).

But, how could I fight this man over the memory of his mother? His mother still loved him from the sky! Jesus. How creepy.

What can one say after such an assertion? My reticence to reply conveyed my attitude perfectly. I awkwardly scanned the men in suits on these plastic benches. At the end of the car were two female students in school uniforms looking into their screens.

A round of subway doors opened and closed, facilitating a mini-exodus / immigration pattern. The passengers could also be analogized to chemicals going across a cell barrier. Trippy! I smiled. They seemed like chemicals going across the barrier that keeps most chemicals out of our brains. They were the drugs in my mind.

After what seemed like ten minutes more of awkward silence, I felt it was appropriate for me to pull out my pad of paper and do some writing.

"I'm sorry I got angry at you and too personal." Adam confessed. "I don't want to demean your life. I respect you. I don't know why I felt so agitated with you all of a sudden.

"That's okay." I reassured him. I was battered, I was hurt.

"I have really enjoyed going on this trip with you, John."

"Me too." I really had, immensely. We were just getting frayed. We had, after all, spent a lot of time with each other.

"What are you writing?" Adam asked with restrained politeness.

"I'm writing ideas that came to me in a vision last night. I think it could be a book. Anyhow, it's welling up in me really wants to come out." I said, gesturing with the pad of paper. "But don't think I'm channeling a demon or anything." I still had some sting in me.

Adam felt my sting and returned it. He was not done with his point of view. He knew he hadn't been heard. "Why write it down if life has no meaning and just leads to death and the grave?"

"I make meaning. My life is important to me, if to no one else. But ultimately you're right; ultimately, there is no purpose. If the universe burns out, it burns out. All life leads to going underground, just like we are now, but in a casket, the ultimate capsule."

Adam gave me a quizzical look and with humorousness and bite asked, "And what are you going to call this book you have no reason to write?"

"'Capsule,' after the capsule hotels."

"A-Ha!" Adam exclaimed understanding why I had called a casket a capsule.

"Yeah, its amazing how many capsules I have seen since I slept in the capsule hotel. Our drugs came in capsules. This very subway is like a big long capsule. A casket is a capsule. And thought worlds seem like capsules to me. And, we've looked at a lot of those."

Adam was often funny and insightful. He was smart. He picked up on themes and ideas quickly. He joked, "Well, when I die, I want my casket capsule to be transported in the capsule subway."

"After laying in wait in the capsule hotel." I said, subtlety agreeing to do improv with him.

"And, I want everyone at the funeral to eat psychedelia capsules!" He added.

With that joke, I realized that I could not exclude Adam. I had to include him in this writing process. It was our adventure, not mine. "It's going to go through some of the things we've been talking about. In fact, it's going to go back to that sentence formula we were working on. Do you remember?"

"Sentence formula?"

"Yeah. Remember? Those who don't have religion, have history. Those who don't have history have only their personal stories, those who don't have personal stories have nationalism, those who don't have nationalism have . . ."

"Plans," Adam said cutting me off and showing some anger. "Plans and rationality? They work their plan or something?"

"Plan their work and work their plan." I had to make the peace. "Adam, capsule, the story, is in me. But it came from hanging out with you. You are an intense and brilliant guy. I really count myself blessed to have gone on this adventure with you. I'm really grateful to you."

"Thanks John. You're a spectacular guy too. I'm sorry again that I was kind of hostile. I appreciate you and your life choices."

We looked at each other with affection and then broke away because it was too much. We looked at our hands and thumbs. This was intimacy, distant male intimacy.

Having sexual experiences with both men and women makes you an outsider. Neither gay nor totally straight, you belong nowhere. Women especially don't want a man who isn't sure. And, you are not supposed to talk about gay issues with straight men. Alienation must follow.

I found out that there is a very limited range of behaviors I will engage in with men. But finding that out entailed some real relationships. Though these things happened in the past, I don't know if what happened makes me officially "bi," or just someone who has had some experiences. I hate labels.

The clean and distinct difference between inside and outside of the label's sealed walls seemed analogous to me of the walls of a capsule too. Perhaps I was stretching the metaphor. But I did feel hermetically sealed off.

I was isolated. Walled off.   And perhaps this past suited me for this reason. I had always been distant from people. Perhaps I held tightly to this secret, this past, this story, to isolate myself from people. Perhaps my subconscious forced this life strategy.

Anyhow, I had really pushed this conundrum out of my mind. I was living a straight life. And, as Adam had said, this plan I had with Soo Hee really kept me safe from my desires. In some ways, Adam was right.

I broke the awkwardness somewhat by taking out my pen and paper. I tried to get down a crude version of the sentence formula out. Wow! I realized I was encapsulating capsule in a capsule (the subway).

After writing the formula, I didn't feel like writing. I was distracted. I knew that in such situations it often helped to focus on others.

"Your life has been interesting." I engaged, "Don't you ever write?"

Adam launched into an interesting revelation.

"No. I don't. I used to carry journals from country to country. But then one day I was reading the ones from when I lived in Germany and it wasn't interesting or useful. They were written in bad German and mostly just exercises in language. And with most of the diary stuff, I just didn't remember doing it or the people I supposedly did it with, and I didn't care.

"That was a heavy day. I also realized on that day that all the scraps and pictures I carried around weren't for me. I kept them to prove things to other people, to prove to other people that I had people, that I had a past and a place in the world.

"But there are no other people that matter. And with those you meet, either they believe you now, and like you now, or they don't. In truth they don't know any thing about you and nothing you show them could prove anything about you.

I thought about the irony that we'd had a talk on the need for memory to progress, and he didn't remember it. And, I said so.

"You write in order to check, to see if you're progressing. You can compare yourself to your self of old and see if you've grown. You should have kept those diaries."

I had said the wrong thing.

Just as I found the courage to apologize, Adam continued unperturbed, "I felt very liberated when I set that stuff on fire: pictures, diary, everything. Life is incomplete and nothing will ever be perfect, John. Nothing is neat, all is messy.

"See, John, your life has been together. You really want it to continue to be a nice story. I have been freed. People die. I don't have to try.

"It is a lot like that stuff you are writing about; history and those who don't have this and that. You want to find what it is at bottom when every source of meaning and identity fails. But, there is nothing at bottom, to hold on to. Nothing.

"Those that don't have anything to hold on to have freedom, they can have a life. That's how you should end it." He seemed resolute and irritated with me.

As expected, a dialogue started in my head about the importance of history and progress. His life, as many, was just one damned thing after another. I wanted mine to amount to something, if for no other reason than out of gratitude to all of those who had made a difference before me.

"Anyhow," Adam interceded on my interior monologue, "I don't need a photograph to remember what my mother looked like. It's in here." He shrieked, pointing to his head, "And, I know that the universe cares about us and so we can be free and it will all be alright."

And yet another naysayer popped into my mind. I was noticing my mind's constant disagreement. It was like an automatic programming thing. People speak, I judge. But, neuroscience does tell us that the re-creation of his mother's image in his head is incomplete and inaccurate.

We both knew that I was hiding my rebuttal and he decided to mute his enraged insistence. We didn't need to fight. It was best to keep some topics unspoken.

I also wondered how his theory of his mother looking down on him fit in with the idea that the world was out of control. But I realized that if I mentioned this inconsistency, he would only take my trying to reconcile logic as another instance of wanting order and fearing something that freedom holds.

Perhaps he was right. I really had lived on a shelf since meeting Soo Hee. I found it all safe and boring. And when I was free I didn't know who I was or who I wanted to be. Whether or not to stay with her, to Soo Hee or not to Soo Hee, was a huge question for me. It might be helpful for me to listen to Adam instead of just countering his positions. But, I was who I was.

Our stop for transferring trains came. When we switched subway lines I found a spot between passengers, where we would be forced to sit apart, where I could be alone and write. But he was as oblivious to my desire to write as he was relentless, "Hey, don't sit there." He ordered, "Just in the next car, there's room for both of us to sit together."

Not going, after all our tension, would be rude. Nah, that didn't matter. I just didn't want him to think that I didn't care. I liked Adam. I went.

"The Japanese are able to fall completely asleep and then wake up at their stop. It's amazing." He informed me.

"You sure they aren't just pretending so that they can shield themselves from eye contact with others?" I queried.

"No they aren't faking. They snore and everything." Adam seemed star-struck with admiration. He sure could switch moods quickly.

"Perhaps they have evolved their brains to the modern demands of time and space. Maybe their brains can now subconsciously processes the different sound of their stop. Even their subconscious has adjusted itself to the machine. Power nap!" I liked the penchant for the abstract these drugs had given me.

I saw a sign I didn't understand on the subway. It showed a female's breast area. And the head was cut off so that you'd have no way of knowing who she was. "Adam. What is that sign about?" I asked, with an extended finger.

"That's referring to a campaign they had not too long ago. When the subways were packed and the high school girls got on, men would feel them up. The touching was everyday, routine like. Sometimes you could put your hand in their underwear and even put your finger inside of them."

He was creeping me out again. It sounded like he was describing his own actions.

"The girls didn't want to make a scene and so were violated in the subway like this for generations. Finally girls started dragging the guys out and telling the police they needed to do something about this."

"Wow! A breach of silence and protocol in Japan!" I said, pandering to Adam's dislike for the Japanese.

"And it all started with one girl." Adam said nearly proudly.

"Amazing."

"They even came up with a word that is equivalent to unwanted touching. Hatickwaya. It's a brand new word for them. That's the word on the poster above her."

"Wow. How brave was that first girl that stood up for herself? She escaped the trap. And now that it's a government campaign, people don't even dare try it anymore. Right?"

"Yeah. But it's a major, major conscious effort. It's not natural to the Japanese. You've got to understand that this whole society runs on the adoration of teenage girls."

How lucky I was to have found this interpreter of what had only been vague suspicions. "I couldn't help but notice that there are young girl porno mags in every 7-11."

"You can tell the junior high girls from the high-schoolers because the high school girls have lower skirts and longer hair."

I am not sure what the point of this information was, but it sounded like a hot tip. I added, "The department of education probably regulates the libido of society inversely with the economy by adjusting the level of the skirts. Is that what you mean by the whole society runs on the adoration of school girls?"

"No. It's more like they live for the wicked desire denied to them. It is what fuels their dreams. Everything else is according to law. Even though it is only mental, it is the one escapist and, free, anti-rules, source of deviancy that they have. That is what I mean."

"And then that perversion itself, kind of ironically becomes what fuels the conformity?"

"Exactly. It is the pressure valve that keeps the machine from blowing up."

"It's pretty sick. The men with families that buy the mags must somehow disassociate these girls from their teenage daughters and those of their friends."

"Or not," Adam added matter-of-factly. "It's a society of silence. The perversity thing also helps them maintain, or rather sort of reinforces, their code of silence."

With that we went into a bit of silence. Was this the awkward silence I had feared? Were we falling into it so soon? Had we run out of things to say? I what mid-worry when our topic suddenly popped back into my head.

"So what do you think gay Jew Jay should do?" I asked.

"I don't know." Adam said pensively.

"And that is the rub." I said throwing out a small taste of Billy Shakes and backing up my view. "And we can only decide from a place of values. Of deciding what is important in life. And that requires a lot of thought."

"It bothers me that when we choose one thing we lose other things." Adam was still looking down at his hands or something, "That's why I am so unsure as to whether or not I should stay with Aya and teach this comfortable university job. Aya and the job would be fine. It just drives me crazy if I am missing other things. If this is going to be all there is, I'm not sure I should do it."

Then Adam he hit me with it again!

"John, what do you think of my life?"

I admired his guts for asking. I would never have the bravery to ask anyone that sort of direct question. And here he had asked it twice. And my answer demonstrated my cowardice. "Adam, my opinion shouldn't be that important to you."

"But it is. You're a together person. I respect your opinion. You think a lot. You've already told me off and that makes me trust you. Be honest. What do you think? I need to know."

The truth is that I had originally seen Adam as a warrior; someone who had gotten free of the traps of everyday life and was living a spectacular one, or at least an invented one. And he had had an exceptionally non-normal life.

The more he talked of his girlfriend situation though, the more I thought of him as my Ghost of Christmas Future. If I don't have a family or a steady relationship, I will be as lost as he – permanently alienated, lonely, unable to commit and aging -- with nothing to show for my efforts. Perhaps I should commit to a woman and have a family.

Uncomfortable with the idea of saying anything negative, I replied much as I would have when I first met him, "You're a brave and spectacular person."

"You said that when I asked you before."

"Yeah it is still true. But, I think that you need to be careful about what you do with your life as you get older. You are sort of running away from home. Home didn't begin well for you. Now it is time to sort of make peace with that. So I think staying with Aya is a mature step."

"Wow. That was really honest. Thank you."

"I might just be projecting, as everything I just said applies to me too. I don't know why I'm with a woman who isn't there. Perhaps it is the lure of being able to be Peter Pan-like, and youthful, forever. Part of the attraction is that she has enough money that in staying together we'd never have to settle down into a reality.

"Perhaps it is, as you say, a need to have a very ordered life without the mess that real interaction and openness to the world would entail.

"But I'm really, really willing to be roomed up with Soo Hee eventually. I am committed to her. It sounds like you'll never be comfortable living with Aya. Maybe it's because she represents what a steady family did to you. But, you should make peace, at this age, with being somewhere steady.

I think at some level, you're afraid of intimacy. And that is why you're afraid of being with Aya and that is why, ironically, you chose some one you say you cannot love. But, you could love her and she you."

"You say that," Adam shot back, "but you're never with Soo Hee. It's easy for you to stay untested in your safe relationship in America far from Korea and then claim that you're so open to intimacy!" His anger management problem flared. Then he backed off. I think I said a bit more than he wanted to hear. But it was true.

Look, Adam insisted emphatically, "It's a struggle to both be free and, and feel you're alive and belong. To be shackled to one place, one routine, one woman in this modern world of opportunities is not to be alive; to stop searching is to be dead. But if you just keep moving, you never really belong anywhere."

"It's something like 'to be or not to be.'" Adam added.

I really liked that line coming from him.

He continued, "But, I have a great job offer at the university and Aya is good to me."

And he insisted, "I give Aya enough. I give her appreciation. I could just never love her. That is just the way it is. But I appreciate her."

He explained the attraction further by reminding me that women in Asia expected to cook food and do laundry. They liked this. And, though her doing more domestic work than him made him feel a little guilty, he gave her appreciation. All she wanted was someone to appreciate her.

"Please John," Adam's energy now turned to intense sincere pleading, "when we eat tell her that you appreciate the food. She was a little unsure about having you over. She did it as a favor to me. She wants to please me. All that she asks is for a little appreciation. Tell her the food is good. It will make her really happy."

I don't know exactly why, but the desire to guffaw rose up in me again. I am sure this guffaw had something to do with how bizarre his relationship was, how sincerely he pleaded for my giving Aya appreciation.

He could never love Aya? Was that somehow secretly comforting to her? After her molestation, perhaps she could never love either. Both their capacities for connection had been gravely burnt. Regardless, I swore that I would say how much I appreciated her cooking.

What had happened to me that I was in such a distant relationship?

Adam spoke of G-d-knows-what the rest of the way. I resentfully tried to get some writing in. I nearly got nasty out of my claustrophobic feeling of being trapped with his company.

At one point, because I kept writing notes during the ride, he chided me again for thinking ideas were more important than people. I nearly barked back that ideas are all we have. They last longer than people. And, besides, I wanted this day to have meant something, to be remembered, so I had to write.

Thankfully, the fingernail sketches of our experiences I wrote on the subway turned out to be enough to spark my memory here at the internet writing jam session I am currently writing from. Every word I wrote in edgewise and in defiance of his speaking, though maybe rude, turned out to be very important (assuming this book, or anything else is).

On the hour-and-a-half journey out to his place, the buildings started to get less pixilated. It was probably a combination of the buildings getting smaller as we left Tokyo proper and our minds tuning down off the drugs.

He reminded me a couple more times to thank Aya. He was obviously a little nervous about the visit. "Tell me what you think of her and my place. That is one reason I've asked you over. I'm really curious about what you'll think of her and my home. I want your opinion."

We had started in an underground subway stop and now sat a top of an elevated, platform. The areas we zoomed by were increasingly beautiful and wooded. Adam's town sat in the base of a valley between two far away mountains, the side of which had the same texture as Mount Fuji. Spectacular.

From the platform, the town looked like a model railroad town.

"It's beautiful." I said sincerely.

As we scurried *down* the subway staircase towards ground level, other people hurried *up* the stairs on their way, presumably, to Tokyo.

In his natural gregariousness, Adam waved at one of the people and said something in Japanese.

The guy shot back a curt look and made some rude sounding reply.

"Unbelievable!" Adam's exclaimed. "Only in Japan have I said "Hi" to people only to have them reply with "Who are you? Do I know you? Too much."

"Yes it is beautiful here." Adam agreed. "But it is still Japan. I don't know what goes on in these people's hearts and minds."

And to make his point stronger, he made quote marks with his fingers, that he put around the word "people's."

As we walked to Adam's house, metal blockades, bicycles, and trashcans had been blown over by the typhoon. They were scattered on the streets.

"Should we try to pick them up?" I asked, pointing to the trashcans.

"No. They'll be okay. The city workers will come and clean it."

"Anyhow look." I said pointing at my observation, "Everything knocked over is behind that yellow line." A yellow line ran parallel to the sidewalk four feet out from the curb. "The debris had all fallen within the acceptable level of anarchy formula. The city has planned for everything."

"Yes," Adam replied with an undertone, "Everything except the dead people buried in the hillside."

CAPSULE FIFTEEN: HOME

Walking to Adam's house we went past a small prayer temple. It made the persistence of ancient cultural ties overt. And, if this place was like Korea, many city dwellers still had family or roots in these small towns.

It was a cute little town. It looked like everything had been shrunken down.   The homes reminded me of the plastic models at the beginning of the television show, Mr. Roger's Neighborhood. Perhaps the quaintness just came from the contrast with Tokyo's 'no building under 60 stories high' atmosphere.

Coming close to his front door I noticed that the writing on the letters in their mailbox looked like Soo Hee's. The fives, in particular, looked like hers.

The outside of his place had long aluminum siding façade that looked like it belonged on a mobile home, punctuated by different doors. Along the walkway, his door was the last one on the right.

Upon entering I saw his wife for the first time. She was a homely diminutive young Asian lady. You know the color of her skin, hair, and eyes. She shook my hand and smiled that cute embarrassed Asian female smile. Adam and she exchanged polite kisses on the cheek.

From the entrance I could see that the house consisted of three fairly large rooms (the bedroom, living room, and the kitchen/dining room). The rooms were separated by traditional Japanese paper sliding doors. Straw floor mats covered the barren floors. It was, I felt, a very typical Japanese home.

The table was already set and we immediately got to the business of food. And it was a good amount of food. She served us stew, bread, tea, some salad and rice. What a feast!

Aya bade me sit, and I did.

"Thank you. The food looks delicious." I said, opening the appreciate campaign Adam had so eagerly and repeatedly asked me to embark upon.

"Thank you. It was the last minute. I didn't know if you coming or not." Aya replied with a touch of resentment.

Adam sat down to eat as soon as I did, but she kept serving.

"This food is terrific." I continued, "After a long day of walking around in unstable weather, a good meal in a warm home is exactly what we need. It's like going into a swimming pool on a hot day."

And with that compliment, Aya flashed me a big embarrassed smile. And Adam was happy to see her happy. I was happy for both of them.

"Thank you. You don't have to eat the rice. The rice cooker broke so isn't very good." Aya was a real Japanese housewife. She provided service with deference and apology. It was the same cultural habit that, in others, drove Adam so crazy. I finally understood the reason for his personal annoyance. It made one acutely aware of the cultural divide. This was one thing to encounter this attitude on the street. But it was quite another to live with it.

"No, the rice is really good Aya. Excellent. This really hits the spot after all of the adventures that Adam and I have had. I reaaallly appreciate it." I laid it on thick, as per Adam's request.

"Thank you. The rice cooker broken. It is funny the rice cooker now the traditional way of making rice. I didn't made it without a rice cooker in so long time that I don't remember how to make. That is why it is dry."

"You guys have a really nice place here." I said overriding Aya's deference. That was a true statement. It looked like a really peaceful place to lounge.

"It's a little expensive." They both replied in unison.

"How much?"

After a checking to see which was going to answer this question with glances, Adam revealed the sum. "$750.00." After all of our devil-may-care madness, such polite small talk seemed extra stilted and contrived.

"That's a deal compared to my place. Mine is like $1,300 a month and is much less cute with much worse air. You have a very nice home. Aya, it feels very homey and warm."   If we were to have small talk, it was lovely that it included the warm sentiments befitting a home. And, I wanted to reassure Adam that his being here was the right thing to do.

"Your English is great. I understand you perfectly." I jumped topics.

"How about your fiancée's English? Is it good?" Wow. Somehow someone had given her the rundown on my life.

"I wish hers was as good as yours. You speak really well." In truth Soo Hee's lack of fluency in English could be really frustrating to me.

And, on that theme, I had expected Aya's English to be better, seeing as how she lived with an English teacher. Her English level either boded poorly for Adam's teaching skills or their relationship. I feared it was the latter.

"I don't think so, but I appreciate this award." Aya said, unable to just accept a compliment.

"The bread is really good too. How did you learn to make this?" I recoiled as soon as I finished asking. I probably shouldn't open up discussions that could lead to her past.

"The bread is store bought." Adam chimed in, perhaps defensively.

"Sheesh. It's fitting that I can't tell the difference between homemade and store bought. I have no home. The manufacturing sector is my wife. Meet my wife, microwave, you know?"

Curious, I asked, "When you cook, do you use a recipe or do you just know how?" And, immediately, I kicked myself for asking about her past again.

"I just know how." Aya replied, giving me relief.

"Wow. It is really great." I complimented her. "Thanks so much."

"Thanks to you for your eating it."

We sat in a moment of awkward silence, justified by the imperative full-mouth condition brought about by eating.

Where had the outpouring of ideas gone? The combination of domesticity and diminishing drugs dampened the genius. I was still holding onto the lingering resentment of not having had the opportunity to write as much as I had wanted while my mind was hot.

"Hey John. While we eat, let's listen to my CD."

"Oh, Yeah. Good idea. I wanna hear that!" My enthusiasm was bolstered by joy at the prospect of having the awkward silence end.

The CD was ingenious beyond my expectations. The production quality and execution blew me away! The whole thing was like a rock opera in that it told a story by bounding back and forth from dialogue to song and back again. During the dialogues there were ambient sound effects that set the place. As in a radio drama, you were fully transported into the scenes it depicted.

The overall plot of the epic was the relationship of his two leading characters, Carrie and Aki. Set in a high School in Ohio, both are strangers as Aki is an exchange student from Japan and Carrie is a transplant from San Francisco. They were strangers in a strange land, not unlike Adam and I.

After listening to a sequence of dialogue and song, I exclaimed, "Adam, this CD is outrageously good. Its way beyond anything I expected."

"Thanks. I hope that the whole world of Aki and Carrie envelopes them in the CD. That their world is successfully built by the songs and dialogues so you can get into it." This instructional device was one tightly sealed hermeneutic. The descriptions of the town and their school day and even the inner lives of the main characters seemed real. It doesn't get much more self – contained than that.

Adam then explained how to use the material. "First just listen to the melodies. Then you hum them so you can hear the vowel sounds and get used to making those sound. Then, and only then, do you add the words."

After they meet, Carrie and Aki ask each other where they are from. They discuss Ohio as a place to live and tell each other what they like in life. They then launch into a happy simple song.

"Hi. How are you today?
Hi. How are you today?
I am fine.
I am fine.
I see you every day.
I say "Hi."
I see you every day.
I say "Hi."
I like sunny days.
I like the sunshine.
I like sunny days.
Maybe we can play outside."

"After hearing this I have faith. You could sell a lot of these."

"I'm trying the best I can. But it's frustrating." Adam always had a negative spin when discussing marketing that contrasted starkly with his enthusiasm and confidence in describing the product itself.

"Well, you need that mob factor. Once it's popular it'll be popular because it's popular. Then word of mouth will sell it. It could catch fire. It really sounds so professional." My polite conviction had a basis in reality.

"And every song covers an important grammar concept. This one is about pronunciation problems. Diphthongs like 'p' and 'l' together and the 'd' sound. It's exactly what they need. In fact, their 17 worst pronunciation problems are in this first song. With the slowdown verse they can really concentrate on the sounds."

"Ingenious." I said in awe.

"How you speak is as important as what you speak. There is a guy in our A.A. meetings that speaks fluent English. There's only one problem."

"What's that?"

"His pronunciation is so bad that no one understands anything he says."

"Really?"

"Iwz leully tou." He mocked the guy saying "Its really true."

"Is there anything more tragic than to learn an entire language, speak it fluently, and not have anyone be able to understand you? No one has the heart to tell the guy that they don't ever understand what he says. It's tragic. They guy is spilling his guts out about his addiction and pain and no one has any idea what he is saying. Pronunciation is number one.

"I've wanted to take the guy aside, break the news to him and teach him pronunciation, but it would embarrass him to learn that no one had ever understood him."

Furthermore," Adam added without his characteristic gentleness, "I don't really care about the guy enough to work on his pronunciation problems."

Adjustment to the home front is always difficult for warriors. But I was somehow starting to feel a little more comfortable.

Odysseus is our second oldest hero in Western civilization. After fighting in the Trojan War, he spends ten years fighting perilous and tempting situations to return home. But once back, after dispensing with the rivals to his wife's affection and property, Odysseus immediately leaves again. Either the sea was his home or domesticity made him nervous.

Adam would have to be the leader here. Not knowing Aya, I didn't know what was or wasn't permissible to say. My unusual tone must have been obvious to him.

Adam helped out a whole lot when he blurted out, "Man I can't believe we're still trippin' off of this stuff." We both rolled our eyes and made grins, grins that nearly warranted drool, in fiendish goofy delight.

"It has been forever." I agreed, relieved to be able to discuss drugs and adventure in this environment.

"Like 1 a.m. to 6:30 the next day. Like 16 hours." Adam assessed.

"That was after trippin' for 4 or 5 hours before on the first batch!" I enjoined.

Aya finally spoke. "Let me see your eyes." She was smiling just enough to signal some approval beneath the concern. But for me, a woman checking your eyes for lingering drug effects is akin to a prosecutor collecting evidence.

"Yes Adam you still high." Aya concluded, "Wow. What was that stuff?"

"It was Trip Thunder." Her man and my macho adventure partner proudly announced. "Remember? I've taken it before."

"Don't forget the "Pinky"!" I chimed with enthusiasm.

"Yes you still a little high and you gone for so long. You probably need very long and very hard rest after such a long trip."

What?! Did she intentionally use the word 'very' and timing to make a double-entendre of 'long' and 'hard'? Do Asian housewives think up jokes like that? Perhaps it was just my perverted mind.

I imagined that this possible sex-talk could be a hint that I should leave. I hoped it wasn't so. Probably I was just paranoid about her wanting me to split because of my history with controlling crazy women.

Damned history is always creepin' in.

"After such an excursion this is a really nice home to come back to. You have what seems like a lot of love around here. And really good food too. You watch out Adam. I might just stay for a very looong and very haard rest myself."

My ever-so-slightly dragging the words she dragged out worked. Aya laughed shyly with her eyes, and followed with the mouth covering that inevitably accompanies Asian women's laughter. Her doing so let me know that the double entendres weren't just in my dirty little mind. She and I had had our first inside joke. And it was a dirty one!

I wished that Soo Hee had Aya's comparatively cavalier attitude towards drugs. Soo Hee considers all drugs to be the equivalent of heroin or crack. It is a source of distance between us. It makes me feel like I cannot be myself in front of her. It is one of the things that convince me that our cultures and backgrounds are too divergent for real understanding. The whole premise of this book would be grounds for divorce for her.

Then again, if Soo Hee weren't the strict over-achiever she is, I wouldn't love her so much. She's right about drugs being bad for me overall. I love her for her constant embodiment of her ideals of excellence. Still, I can't let her read this book.

Adam jumped up. "Listen to this song!"

As with all of the songs, this one was preceded by dialogue. After Aki and Carrie meet, they go back to Carrie's place. Her mom gives them milk and cookies. Then the two girls go up to Carrie's room.

In a free dialogue, without music, they discuss things that they find hard at school. But, then decide that English, of all the school subjects, is not hard.

Then the song starts with the chorus:

"English is so easy;
Sing this song with me.
Are you hungry;
Do you want something to eat?"

After listening intently to the whole song I reported back. "Your CD is great! I love the blend of dialogue and music. It's so conceptual and perfect."

"Thanks." Adam could acknowledge a compliment.

"It's weird though." I commented, "It's almost creepy how it just represents the bare minimum of experience, the bare protocol of interaction. Its like you took life and sucked all of the psychic terror out of it leaving only the clean surface, the formal greetings and small talk. It makes me feel a little psychotic!"

"That is the strangest compliment I've ever gotten." Adam laughed, seemingly even covering his mouth a little.

"No. I really like it!" I quickly protested. "It would make a great basis for an audio art piece because it highlights how much of our lives are rote.

"After just a bit, you could start to put in the subconscious subtexts around the normal words. Like when they go upstairs for cookies, we could listen in on their secret lesbian thoughts, then fears about grades, and then all the books they didn't read would come pouring on, and talk of the economic structure, and social manipulation and....

Before you know it, the whole thing would be wall to wall subconscious words on the clean surface."

"Yeah. Yeah I get it."

"Think of how many voices we keep out of consciousness that concern terror and sex and hatred. You understand. Right Aya?" I asked.

"Yes John. Strange idea. You are not a normal man." I grinned, assuming that was a compliment.

Daring to kick start some fun, Adam began with, "Wanting Cookies, Aki and Carrie are entering their plastic death house."

"Exactly!" I chimed in, now feeding off of his energy and the opportunity to be a bad and naughty child in a home. "Death trap of nasty capitalist plastic home is manipulated by the cookie!"

"The angry coooookie!" The cookie monster in Adam enthralled.

"Have you met my mother? Do you want to kill her?" I asked, mimicking Aki's Japanese accent.

"Do you want to watch pornos with my mother?" Adam said in a soft Japanese girl voice.

"Devil says do! Devil says do!" I channeled in a shrieking little girl voice.

"Don't watch it ma'am! No, ma'am. Joe Friday just wants the lust." Said Adam demonically feeding off of me and getting louder.

Feeling totally free, I screamed in gleeful degenerate abandon, "Mommy! Mommy! Degenerate chocolate cookie sauce Mommy! Kill, Kill, Kill!!"

There must have been some silent communication because Adam gave me a glance that threw poison darts my way. We had gone too far.

In a voice that was having trouble readjusting to normality, and with his eyes jumping repeatedly between Aya and I, he managed a sentence with strong overtones of seriousness and sanity.

"Yes. I get it. I get it, John. That's fun. But then it would be an art piece and no one would learn English from it."

We had hit a wall. Some of our enthusiasm had come from punching at the domestic constraints that swaddled us. We had been naughty and free, but also immature and disrespectful. Indeed our entire adventure, our asking questions about identity, our lives had a hint of this dynamic. Still, I couldn't help but feel bad for Adam being silenced.

After our outburst, Adam was obviously worried that Aya not think him insane. But don't worry about me, my dear dying chocolate-covered reader. In the margins of this book, between the lines so-to-speak, go ahead and write the unspoken's silent subconscious thoughts, and those thoughts' unspoken's unspoken subconscious content, and the unspoken's, undpoken's, unspoken's etc. That's what margins and the space between words are there for.

But we retreated back into listening to his CD's ambient dialogue:

"Have you seen the new girl? She's really beautiful."

"You think they're all beautiful." A male character joshed.

"No I don't." "Yes you do." "No I don't." "Yes you do." ...into fade out. And a song about shopping started.

"Yeah. And, it's interesting -- at its extreme, if we kept putting the subconscious words around the dialogue, it would get so cluttered it would just become noise." I felt guilty and the pressure of needing to feel somewhat restrained and cowed as I added my conclusion.

"And then we'd have to dampen that noise into background noise and then rerecord the whole damn dialogue over it again for it to be understandable." I smiled and Adam didn't. Adam wasn't looking at me; he was looking at Aya.

Another guitar led song started and I interrupted. "I'd think having a guitar must have been strange to Japanese. It is the weapon of the individual voice, a weird animal in Japanese culture. How does it go over here?"

"They loved my guitar playing and accepted it nearly right away." Adam said with positive calm enthusiasm. "They put those little photograph stickers of themselves all over my guitar."

"Photo – stickers! A perfect symbol of self expression." My sarcasm immediately turned into self-consciousness over whether or not I was again being impolite to Aya. She was one of them, Japanese, and not an abstraction.

"Excuse me." Muttered Aya, she stood and left. Perhaps she had had enough of us. I'm sure he was normally a different person around her.

Aya seemed to have an edge of sadness about her. I thought about her rape and sensitivity. I wondered silently if it dogged her all the time or if she had stretches where it was not a part of her life. I hoped her excusing herself was due to my insensitivity and not her history.

The current Adam song had the following chorus:

"I have been to Africa, to Israel and Spain.
I've traveled all around the world.
People are the same.
Mothers love their children as far as I can see.
Everyone around the world is like you and me."

I brought up logical consistency with regard to this song, "But what we've been saying about language and cultures means that the lyrics aren't true. You said that the Japanese were totally alien to you." In case you worry, dear reader, I whispered the last part to shield Aya.

"I guess you're right." He said quietly.

"I mean, there are some cross-cultural similarities. But the uniformity is probably truer for females than males. As they are domestic, women are more similar across cultures, more interchangeable. They look after their kids. But men have more diversity."

He shushed me with a tightening of his brows. He didn't want Aya, who was still just in the other room, to hear that. It was too bad as there was a potentially interesting discussion in there. Upon reflection, the Japanese mothers' intense singular identification with their male children's success actually made their consciousness very different than American mothers'.

We listened in silent reflection. Then Adam remembered himself. "Honey, come back here." He pleaded.

Aya came back.

From nowhere (the origin of most topics), Adam asked me with passion, as though it weren't a diversion, "What is the first thing that you need when you first get to a new country? In the very beginning?"

"To be able to ask, 'Where's the terlet?'" Was an obvious first guess.

"No. More basic." Adam insisted aggressively.

"More basic than the toilet?" I shot incredulously with an incredulous smile. "You need to be able to find the hotel."

"And to do this you need…."

"To know about the subway system. You have to be able to ask, "Where is this subway exit?""

"No." He said in genuine frustration over my breaking the routine. "I can't believe you're not getting this. You need a map, to know where you are and how you can get to your destination! You need a map!"

"Oooh. Okay." I agreed, but wasn't sure where he was going.

"Grammar is the map to languages. All languages have a grammar."

"Wasn't the idea of grammatical rules invented recently, like in the last century?" I put forth.

"Yes. But grammar rules existed in real life before we wrote them down. People got teased for speaking differently back in olden days too.

"Grammar is your passport. It is the deep structure that makes all languages the same below the surface. That's why every song on this CD highlights one of the 8 fundamental concepts of universal grammar.

"If you can express the eight forms in each language, you can express just about everything. Grammar is the key. To start to learn without understanding grammar condemns you to lower-status pigeon language poorly learned."

Adam had gone over to the shallow side. He was speaking work related platitudes. I wasn't sure why he had pulled Aya back into the room to hear this. I am sure she had heard his spiel on grammar before. Perhaps he wanted to remind her that he had not changed.

What could I do but be supportive. I chimed in, "When I was in Korea I studied their language for two months. I memorized, via flashcards, every damn phrase. In the last week of the course, the teacher finally told us that there was a pattern to the endings. One was formal, one informal, and one was always used in a question.

"We were stunned that this likable, seemingly competent woman had waited that long to show us the pattern."

"Exactly!" Adam exclaimed, in delight of my continuing small talk to cover the tension in his domestic setting. "You can memorize phrases, but until you get at the deep structural level, you'll never get it. You'll never really see how the language holds together. Everything will seem random."

I bent it back towards the philosophical, "I guess the deep grammar structure is like life. You have to find the patterns in it. The grammar of buildings, economics, roles that bind you."

"Homes after homes after homes are what people want around the world. That is the real structure. Homes are the real thing." I emphasized this last point to be reassuring; Still, I think Adam even took the insight as potentially demeaning. Aya smiled and I continued.

"After I check out of my little space module capsule hotel box, I'll return to my home. Some day I hope to have a home as nice as yours."

"Aya," I offered, making a move to take her out the stupor Adams grammar rap seemed to have put her in, "I'm really impressed with your English."

"Thank you again." She replied automatically, as Aki and Carrie found a girl from Chicago that didn't know anyone at the school.

"Adam tells me you work in a library. How do you like it?"

"It is good."

"I love libraries." I enthused, "I really love books. Do you get to read there?"

"Not enough." She said, with a slightly dour countenance.

"I spent one month researching in the Washington D.C. library." I told her. "Actually it was about the World War II Army language program. There was a neat community of nerds in that library working on their projects.

"It's interesting to see what people investigate."

"It is." Aya agreed. "Right now I'm little frustrated at my work because I get the pay less than the men."

"Really!" I chirped incredulously. "Is this a government library? Can the government do that?"

"It isn't government, but it is largest private university in Japan. So I'm little unhappy about it." Aya relayed, with her head bobbing.

"Wow. Is the fact that you're getting paid less because you're a woman in writing?" I needed to confer, still not believing.

"In Japan women get paid less than men. It is law." Aya affirmed with a bow of submission.

"In the States you wouldn't even think of putting that in writing. Your butt would be sued. If there were documentation, you'd lose the case in a second. Women would set the place on fire." This assessment agreed with her. But it wouldn't make her feel any happier about her life.

Trying to put a happy face on Japan and make her feel better I added that, "But the different pay would never fly in America because the family in America is in terrible disintegration. Women cannot rely on men to be there anymore. Women must get equal pay if they are to raise the family without the man. So she demands equal pay. Our families being so messed up means that we can't pay women less."

Adam picked up on the dangerous implications of this argument, "Perhaps it was the equal pay movement that led to the break down of the family."

I was ready to go half-way down that sober, but dangerous street. "Well, in fact, in something like forty percent of American homes, women make more than men." It does make women independent from men. And people have argued that men are now becoming second-class citizens in the world; not the bread-winner, not the Dad, not respected.

And for fun, I put on a black accent, "Ya baby, that's why here in Japan we likes our womens po' wit lower pay. Let 'em know whose da man. Give us the money. Sheeeet, that's why they needs us."

I thought Adam would join me in the fun, but his lips grew thin and it looked like all the blood had drained from his face as he used his eyes to take me back to Aya.

Adam added, "In Japan the wage system is based on the idea that the man will support the family and so needs a bigger salary. If the woman works, the income is just to supplement the man's.

"Our system is based on the idea that all we are all isolated individuals with rights. America doesn't take social arrangements, like the family, into account."

Aya concluded, "We have an expression, it means something you can't do anything about. So why mention it. That is how my feel about it."

Aya was a master of silence. It was both cultural and personal.

"You could of course," I retorted, "You could pull busses into an intersection and refuse to go...." She thought I was being uproarious again and didn't seem appreciative, so I explained. "We saw a protest today where people did that."

"Really?" Aya lacked belief.

"Yep" Adam confirmed.

A song was playing about needing a rest on weekends after getting-up early the rest of the week.

"That's why Saturdays and Sundays are the days I love the best." They sang.

Feeling like I made up the bus thing and was generally "takin a piss out of life" as the English say, Aya tried to pin me to real feelings and answers with a bit of aggression. Her attempted break-in to the real me started with asking me about my family.

To seem real, I related my dilemma to her as the last Cohan Jew in my family line. I knew not being carefree about my relations would assuage her negative reaction to me. I told her that I really did have trouble relating to the existence of what was supposed to be "my culture."

"I'm not sure if Judaism is a real thing that I could ever take to heart. I don't like tribalism and groupings and stuff like that. I like individuals. I am not even sure if the Jewish culture is real."

"My culture," Aya offered in contrast, "is so real I cannot escape. I'm outside at the work because I don't go to the same university as the other peoples. They treat me as person outside. Life around here can be hard, depending from which group you are. We not just individual who is free."

I wanted to learn from her as I had from Adam, "Adam and I have spoken about how controlling the Japanese culture is. It's the opposite extreme, eh side, of our culture. Our American culture is really alienating. That is because everything is centered on the individual. No one has any place in it."

I thought about how Adam had said that Hebrew has an assumed warmth that doesn't exist in English. But I didn't say anything about that because I didn't want to emphasize the wedge that language put between him and Aya.

When Aaya didn't reply I rounded off my statement. "We Americans have too little sense of culture. I guess that's why I can really appreciate this nice home you've made where you and Adam can belong."

Aya reversed my placating move, "For me it is opposite. I like having home as place where I don't have to belong. I can just with myself at the home."

Her statement expressed what I could have guessed was probably the case for her. Being herself seemed to just mean resting from the wearying battles of life -- the slings and arrows.

"Oh, John, I really like this song. Listen to this one." Aya interjected.

It's Saturday. Kari goes over to Aki's house. Aki is lonely. Her parents are away and she hasn't spoken with anyone all day. You could hear the umbrella being put away as Carrie came inside.

"I miss Japan." Aki declared. "Whenever it rains I think about Japan. I miss it. On rainy days my grandma used to always make tea for me."

"When I'm sad I call a friend or think of some good times. Remember when we got the same sweaters?" Carrie asked.

"Of course." You could hear the smile in Aki's reply.

"Remember. Whenever you feel sad, always give me a call." Carrie said tenderly.

The chorus was about clouds. They served as an allegory for moods. Some were white, some black, some grey. And sometimes they just won't go away.

"Again, Adam, it's kind of creepy in that you seem to have all human experience there. It's like a complete representation of all life."

"Ya think?" Adam squished his face in a way I hadn't seen before.

"Yeah. Sadness, hunger, friendship, the trials of work and fear. They're all in there.

"I think if you told non-English speakers they could only use words and phrases from this CD, there wouldn't be anything in their experiences that they wouldn't be able to talk about."

Adam pulled out his trump card on me again, "Space, pronouns, degrees of disrespect. There are a lot of Japanese things that they couldn't express. A lot of Japanese ideas can't be expressed in English."

I felt chastised, like I hadn't remembered anything.

"John. Tell Aya your big formulation." Adam insisted enthusiastically.

"Well, I can try." I said groggily. "Those without God have only history upon which to build their identity. Those without history have only culture. Those without a culture only have their stories, those without their stories, use media stories, those without media stories use . . . family."

"You forgot language." Adam added. I felt chastised again. When would I learn!

"Oh, yeah. No. Yeah. Now I see that is why this formulation isn't universal. In Japan language gives you a sense of belonging. Ours language doesn't situate you in place or hierarchy."

"Oh he's getting it now!" Adam said proud of himself in front of his wife.

"Not bad for two tired guys that did the drugs." Aya surmised somewhat uncomplimentary, but not incorrectly. "Well, I hope you having home with your Korean girlfriend. You have been together for a long time."

"Within two oceans of each other." I barbed. This home scene was making me see the value in being nothing, in belonging to nothing. Honestly, I was feeling a little claustrophobic. And, I did not wish to go over my relationship conundrum. I was thinking the answer was already coming to me.

"You don't want any more?" Aya asked, combining kindness and insistence.

"No. It was delicious thank you. Thank you so much. I really enjoyed it."

Again she thanked me for thanking her. And, I told her there was no need and thanked her again. Adam had a big compassionate smile over this escalating bidding war of appreciation, and kindly, reassuringly stroked her arm.

"Well," I ventured, "I think it's time for me to say good-bye."

"Well, listen to the last song first." Adam insisted.

The song "Goodbye my good friend" seemed like it was the voice of the songs themselves finally declaring their independence and going away from being part a language CD to being personal songs included in a language CD. That is, this song seemed to be a personal song that Adam had put in the language CD.

When asked Adam confirmed, "It is a personal song, for sure. I wrote it for a friend named Annie. But it is also all about the past perfect. "Had danced" "Had been" "Had ridden," are all in there." Genius.

Aya had started cleaning during the last song and continued to do so as I said my good-byes to her. Adam would walk me back to the train station. As Adam and I left, he handed me an umbrella just in case of storm.

Twenty feet from their house, I exclaimed "O shit! I almost forgot. I want a copy of your CD and book." He went back in and got me one. I felt badly, like I was cheapening our friendship, as I asked him how much it cost. He said it was a gift. The whole evening had been a gift.

Walking to the subway he thanked me profusely, in a relieved and guilty way, for thanking Aya. "Your repeating how good the food was made it all worth while to her. She loves to be acknowledged and thanked for doing housework."

"Well it was true." I jovially offered, "The food was great. And after all of this talking and talking and walking and walking, a nice place to rest and a nice meal really hit the spot."

"What do you think of our place?" He asked directly.

"Its nice. I felt really welcome and like it was a home."

"Do you think she was attractive? Is she the type of girl that you'd be attracted to?" He pushed.

"Well. She isn't exactly my type. But you know I think sex is more about love than bodily rubbing . . . and she loves you, Adam, she does. She'd be there for you, as Soo Hee would always be there for me. That my friend, to me, is the ultimate in sexy."

"Yeah. It's just hard to know what to do, if I should stay. " Adam continued with his second-guessing of his life.

"Yeah. Love and decisions are as much about limiting your horizons as they are about choosing something." I offered.

"And, that is not so easy a trade-off for me, John," Adam beamed suddenly, "because you knoooow I love the ladies."

"I know you do, my friend." My eyes laughed with this reply. Even including his base values, I would miss him, his humor and intellect.

Adam walked me to the subway station. When I was twenty feet past the turnstile, I turned around for one last wave good-bye. He shouted, "Call me tomorrow if you feel like it."

I wasn't sure if he was being polite or what. I never trust kindness. Maybe that is a reason I have so few friends. We had spent a lot of time together. Our good-bye meant something. Affection isn't always a lie, a manipulation or act of distance management. But, I doubted that he really wanted to see me the next day.

A minute later as I was standing, confused, on the other side of the ticket gate, about to look for a bathroom and not sure which track I was to get, Adam's shouting "JOHN!" scared me.

I thought he had come back for his umbrella and gestured at handing it back to him.

"No! That's yours. Keep that. Track two!" He yelled. "Get on track two. Oh, and if I don't see you tomorrow well talk on the phone, eh? Or maybe just see ya' in cyberspace."

Those were the last words Adam ever said to me in person.

As I left the card kiosk and ran up the stairs, I appreciated the small irony of my just seeing the last corner of my subway car speeding away at the very moment I arrived. I had just missed my ride back to my home, my capsule hotel. But, I would get home when I got home and journey until then.

Moments later I realized that I had had almost made a huge error. I hadn't given Adam and Aya one of Michael "Friar Moose's" hearts-of-loving-kindness medallions! These were the little metal hearts that my homeless friar friend had made and asked me to spread around Asia.

I wanted them to have something to remember me by. I decided to turn back around and deliver the hearts.

It was a struggle. But I somehow explained to the station manager that I hadn't used my ticket yet and I'd be right back in just a short while to use it again.

Unfortunately, I didn't remember the way back to his house. I went down a lot of roads before anything looked familiar. Even then I didn't know which road was his.

Finally, clue-by-clue and trial-and-error by trial-and-error, I found my way back to their home.

I remember that the last clue of the series that got me to their home was the address on the letter that had reminded me of Soo Hee's writing, the five. My eager anticipation turned to excitement as I recognized mailbox. The search was over. This was Aya and Adam's home for sure.

Aya was really stunned to see me. I explained that I had to give her a good friend of mine's hearts-of-loving-kindness medallion. Friar Moose gives them to women. It is his way of continuing to flirt, despite his age and quasi-homeless status. The hearts also have a corny messianic love message for my Friar friend. But I just told Aya that it was a token of love from my friend and from me to her and Adam.

"I would really have messed up if I didn't give these hearts to such a loving and kind home as yours. You really have a beautiful home. Friar Moose would be really tickled to know that this heart resides in such a lovely place with such quality friends and family."

Aya looked confused, but really happy to see me. She didn't quite understand my presence there. "Adam can't talk now, He is in the shower." I could hear his showering through their paper-thin walls. "But that is nice of you, John. I thought actually you were going to spend the night with us in our home."

"No. I'm going to go write and see about a ticket to Osaka. But thanks so much." I replied.

"You're welcome. Thank you for coming and being so kind friend to Adam. And come back and stay with us any time."

"Thank you. I'd love to. You have a lovely home."

"Thank you." She smiled.

Though Aya couldn't know about it, I also later gave a heart to each of the massage girls. I found them still working their corner near my capsule hotel back in Rappongi.

This didn't cheapen the sentiment of having one in Adam's nice home. The girls were doing all they could for dignity in a hard world. But, the idea of the massage girls getting the same heart medallion I had given her, would have probably tarnished their sentimental value in Aya's mind.

The massage girls seemed to love them.

I made my way back to the subway. The station manager didn't recognize me until I showed him the ticket again by nearly rubbing it in his face. "How many white guys have come by here in the last 20 minutes?" I wondered. "What is this weird gap in your recognition function about Mr. Station Manager?"

I boarded the train bound for my capsule hotel.

The rest of my weekend in Japan was spent in silent picture taking.

From: "john press" <pressjohn@hotmail.com>
To: pressjohn@hotmail.com
Subject: Re: capsule
Date: Sun, 24 Aug 1925 17:42:08 +0000

Thomby,

And so you have the product of 18 or so hours of engrossed work inside an internet cafe!

After leaving Adam and Aya's home, I tried to go to Osaka, but they did not have an overnight bus. So I got drugs from the same guy that Adam and I got them from before and headed to this cyber café. I complained at first. But hours later, I must say, I am really glad that there was no bus.

It's getting late. Every time I stretch, I see less and less freaks like me still here. A lot of people are just sleeping here. I guess as long as they're paying hourly the management won't wake them.

Some typists are still clicking away too. The guy in the next compartment has been working as long as I have. I wonder what he's writing about?

Love over the wires,

Johnny P.

NEW NUMBER: 646-522-4691
www.pressjohn.com